I0542469

AS

WOULD HAVE IT

AS **Luck**
WOULD HAVE IT

THE
ELK VALLEY
SERIES

CHRISTINE SOREN

SEAHAVEN MEDIA
Prescott, Arizona

ISBN 978-0-578-66605-1

Library of Congress Control Number: 2020910747

Book cover designed by Mariah Sinclair & Associates
www.MariahSinclair.com

Edited by Jen Graybeal
www.JenGraybeal.com

Book interior formatted by Longworth Creative, LLC
www.LongworthCreative.com

First Edition
Printed in the United States of America
Published by SEAHAVEN MEDIA

Visit www.ChristineSoren.com to learn more.

This book is dedicated to Sandi Howerton.
Thank you for your encouragement, I wish you were here
to see this book finished. We all miss you.

Acknowledgements

A big thank you to my critique friends, Colette, Paula, Tina, Randi, Susan, Denise and my sister, Sally.
A special thank you to my wonderful husband and my son and daughter for cheering me on. I couldn't have done this without you.

Chapter 1

*C*het, I want Rambo back!" Willow James yelled into her cell as her open hand came down hard on the table, causing her iPad to do a slight jitterbug. She cringed, hating the angry tone in her voice. Normally even tempered, her soon-to-be-ex-husband knew which buttons to push to get her riled up.

The lying, cheating bastard was over the moon that she was upset. She'd had Rambo since before Chet came along, and now he wanted to keep her dog just to get back at her for divorcing him for something so minor, as he put it. As if sleeping with his secretary was minor.

Fool.

With her elbow on the table and her head in her hand, she half listened as Chet continued spewing bullshit in her ear. She heaved a sigh. He'll never change. He simply loves the sound of his own voice.

Not her problem anymore.

Remembering where she was, Willow quickly surveyed her surroundings. The barista turned back to the espresso machine in an effort to look busy while a man at the table behind her gathered up his newspaper and coffee before heading out the door.

She held her iPhone to her chest and watched his broad back move toward the outside tables. Pulling a chair out with his cowboy boot clad right foot, he set his cup on the table then sat, making himself comfortable before opening his paper.

Great, she was scaring people away.

She'd only lived in Elk Valley, Wyoming, a few months and this wasn't how she wanted to start over. Setting her cell on the table she took the clip out of the bun at the back of her head and shook out her long, golden hair. She'd done nothing wrong except say, "I do" to Chester Cromwell who was still talking "at" her. With a brief touch to end the call, silence reigned again.

Who names a baby Chet anyway? She stared down at her smart phone, hoping for some wisdom and laughed. Her divorce would be final by the end of next week. Thank God, she hadn't changed her last name before things went all wrong with her seven-month marriage.

Willow Cromwell.

She never did like the sound of it but didn't marry the man for his name. She was embarrassed to admit she'd fallen for his movie-star-handsome face. Her scalp felt prickly recalling their wedding reception. She'd overheard Chet's best man telling a groomsman, "The bride is almost as pretty as the groom," and they both laughed. It was all downhill after that.

Running her fingers through her hair, she twisted it back up into a bun and put the clip in place. She stuffed her iPad into the faded black nylon backpack, still thinking about her stupid almost-ex. She wasn't too smart for marrying him in the first place. It'd all happened so fast.

"Why didn't I insist on a long engagement?" she muttered. If they'd waited, she'd probably have seen him for what he really was. "Let's get married right away before something goes wrong," she mocked. "What was I thinking?" Her shoulders drooped with her exhale.

Never again. Next time, if there's a next time, I'll be smarter.

She did miss a warm body in her bed, someone to snuggle up to in the middle of the night. Chet was good for that at least. Though she couldn't help wondering how many other women he was boinking besides his secretary. She gazed up, her attention automatically going to the beautiful mountain scenery.

Elk Valley Roasting Company was such a good find. It had some of the same elements as her favorite coffee bar in California, except her best friends. The small former house sat alone on a side road off Main Street on the edge of a meadow often frequented by deer and other small wildlife. Tables sat all the way around the deck taking advantage of the sun as it moved across the sky. Four steps down led to a few more tables set on pea gravel, which is where she preferred to sit since it always seemed to be in the sun.

The cowboy who'd gone outside because of her

outburst caught her attention; gray cowboy hat, gray boots and gray leather jacket covering up what appeared to be a muscular set of shoulders and arms. The newspaper covered his face, so no telling what he looked like or how old he might be. Tall, she thought, eyeing his long legs stretched out in front of him. If her best friend, Norma, was here they'd be playing the "guess his occupation" game.

Willow continued to study him. His clothes were certainly nice. Gentleman rancher or maybe a celebrity who moved here to get away from prying eyes. She craned her neck hoping to get a look at his face and felt silly. This would be much more fun if Norma was here.

She didn't want him to think she was a lunatic in case they ran into each other again, here or at the supermarket. Willow wanted to be able to say hello and not feel like she had to hide under a big hat and dark glasses or behind a stack of Diet Pepsi because of Chet.

Buttoning her jacket, she looped the scarf around her neck before stepping out into the cool, late spring morning, setting her things on a table near the cowboy who seemed to be devouring his paper. She felt pretty certain he knew she was there but didn't want to acknowledge her.

"Excuse me." She took a step closer. "Sorry to interrupt you."

Gray Cowboy folded the corner of his newspaper forward.

"Hi, I'm Willow James and I've only just moved here, well, a couple of months ago actually."

He gazed up at her as she stood in the spotlight of the rising sun.

"Oh," she said just above a whisper, feeling a rush travel through her. She stared into the real-life face of the imaginary hero from her book. Willow's description of him had been a shopping list of her idea of the perfect man; dark blue eyes, dark hair, strong jaw and dreamy. She fought the urge to run the back of her fingers across his smooth complexion. Even the dark outline of his recently shaven jaw was sleek. She couldn't help wondering where he got that great tan this time of year?

Noticing his raised eyebrows, she shook her head lightly and blinked. "Um, sorry to make such a spectacle of myself on the phone." She motioned with her head toward the coffee shop, adding a gesture with her thumb for emphasis. "Inside, I mean."

Cowboy lowered his newspaper to give her his full attention. "No harm done," he said with a smile. "But I'm glad I wasn't the one on the other end of the line."

Heat crawled over Willow's face, which she imagined had now turned an unattractive shade of red. *Smart ass.*

"Yes, well, I just wanted to apologize. I don't usually scream into my phone in public, but my husband... ex-husband...well..."

He shrugged those broad shoulders. "No worries, ma'am."

Ma'am? Willow obviously wasn't doing well here, but she let it go. "Do you come here often? To the Roasting Company?"

I am such a dork.

"This is my first time, but probably won't be my last. Coffee's not bad and the pastries looked good."

Willow detected a slight accent but moved on so as not to appear any more stupid than she already had. She reached for her backpack.

"Sounds like you're a newcomer here as well."

"Yes, just two months." Like I said. Hmm, not a good listener. "How about you?"

"Just got here last night," he said, this time there was definitely a bit of a drawl.

"Oh, well, you look like you belong here. I, on the other hand, stick out like a sore thumb." Her city clothes consisted of gray wool slacks, light blue, long-sleeve shirt topped with a navy blazer and blue and yellow plaid scarf. Clearly, she'd dressed as though she were going to work at the newspaper this morning.

Terry's gaze roamed over her in a head-to-toe body scan, not missing a thing.

Willow's face heated again. She wasn't sure if she wanted to slap him or kiss him. She couldn't remember the last time a man had so obviously admired her.

"Maybe you should get yourself some Wrangler's and a pair of boots." His eyes finally landed at her tan loafers. "And maybe a cowboy hat. If you want to blend in, that is."

She was thoughtful a moment and unconsciously looked down the length of her body. She already owned a dozen pair of jeans, but cowboy boots might help her feel more like a local. "Yes, well, thanks. You might be right." Maybe it is time for one more change in my life. "Enjoy your day."

She swung the backpack over her shoulder and walked toward her SUV, knowing Gray Cowboy watched her every move, which made her smile. Something she needed to do more often.

Willow headed home to her empty house, empty except for her two kittens, Stormy and Midnight. They were probably napping after having free run of the house. She'd intended to stay in town and write until noon then run errands and wondered why she'd left the coffee shop. The cowboy threw her off. What kind of reporter am I that I didn't even get his name? Not a reporter anymore. A novelist. Odd, she thought, he didn't offer it either. At least she could make up her own story about what his name might be, and no one would call her on it.

Pulling onto the circular gravel driveway, Willow parked, then stepped out and admired her farmhouse. It was the center piece of the three acres it sat on. She did love it all painted white with dark green shutters and front door with shiny brass hardware. The porch wrapped around the house, which was one of the reasons she'd fallen in love with it. The view of the mountains added to its appeal.

Contrary to her original plans, working at home would be good for her today. She went inside, turned on the Native American flute music of R. Carlos Nakai, opened a window in the living room a couple inches then checked on the kittens. They were indeed cuddled up together fast asleep.

Stepping back out on the deck, she sat cross legged on the wicker sofa with its pretty floral cushions. With her iPad on the coffee table and wireless keyboard in her lap, she was ready to write until hunger set in. The music played just loud enough for her to fight the loneliness, but not totally distract her as she completed another chapter of her novel.

Rotating her shoulders to ease the tightness, Willow realized she'd been seeing Gray Cowboy's face and hearing his voice while writing the last several paragraphs. This time it wasn't just her face that heated. Her body tingled from the warm glow running through her. Leaning against the back of the sofa, she looked out at the horizon.

Did she want to know his real name? What if it was something dorky? Gray Cowboy sounded like a character from an early Clint Eastwood movie; rugged and slightly dangerous. She smiled and exhaled a sigh that felt like longing.

~

Every time he tried to focus on his newspaper, Terry Du Champs' mind wandered back to the beautiful woman named Willow. She'd brought a smile to his face, but he had other things to think about and a nutty woman, no matter how beautiful, wasn't one of them. He didn't want to go back to the motel, but a drive around Elk Valley might be what he needed. Familiarize himself with the area again.

He dropped his paper cup in the recycle bin and took the paper back inside. Someone else might want to read it, he thought, then headed to his rental car.

His tall, muscular frame overpowered the compact car. He carefully positioned his right leg before sitting so it wouldn't hit the steering wheel. Bending his left leg, he grabbed just below his knee, easing it inside the car. Pulling the seatbelt around him, he was finally able to close the door, hitting his left knee in the process. Grumbling an expletive, he turned the key and the engine purred as Roy Rogers began a rendition of "Don't Fence Me In." Terry chuckled, "I hear ya, Roy."

I should go buy a truck, he thought. Definitely four-wheel drive.

Terry was feeling better about being back in Elk Valley as he drove through town, taking everything in. So much had changed since he'd left thirteen years ago, though a few things remained the same. Like the Red Kettle Café. Just a brighter red than he remembered. The big box store was new, and the feed store had become an antique mall.

He wasn't ready to see the house he'd grown up in, so Terry drove out to Pine Lake and was pleasantly surprised that the area hadn't changed much at all. He and his dad had fished the lake since he was five, had some of their best conversations while waiting for a tug on their line.

The sun warmed his left arm resting on the open window. Turning off the ignition he got out and leaned against the closed door. He tilted his head toward the sun, eyes closed. Air still smells the same; fresh and clean with the scent of pine. His breath caught at the gentle stirring of pine trees in the breeze. The welcoming sound embraced him. He didn't realize how much he'd missed hearing it. Pushing himself away from the car, Terry walked along the lake toward the empty boat slip where they used to sit and fish. He made a mental note to buy a fishing rod and reel. Probably have them at that big box store.

His throat tightened as he took in the small grocery store and tackle shop. He hoped to have children of his own to bring here to swim and fish, but most of all to pass on the values his parents taught him.

He inhaled deeply then let out the breath slowly, rubbing his chin, grateful for good memories of happy times with his father, shoving the senseless loss from his mind as best he could.

A rustic restaurant had been added with a small deck overlooking the lake. The sign on the window said it would open the first of May. He walked out onto the dock and sat, pulling his knees up. If it wasn't so much trouble, he'd take his boots off and stick his feet in the water.

Hell, how much trouble could it possibly be? he mumbled to himself then tugged his boots and socks off and pulled his jeans up a bit before sticking his feet in the water. He cringed then reminded himself, it was only April. Bound to be cold.

Terry watched a pair of mallards riding the ripples on the lake as a breeze kicked up and thoughts of his father continued. How lucky he was to grow up here. So many people to help him along the way.

The folks of Elk Valley, many of them faceless now, had been there for him, wanting him to lean on them to lessen his sorrow and anger. His desire to get away from all of them pulsed with the memory of the fire, then the trial. It'd been too much, especially for a seventeen-year-old. He'd wanted to go where no one knew what he'd been through, get away from all the sad faces he saw on a daily basis.

Friends and neighbors had tried to console and reassure him that everything would be better in time, but he didn't believe a word of it. They meant well, but they were a reminder of what had happened and, hard as they tried, no one could take the place of his family.

He leaned forward and peered into the water until he could see his reflection hoping to catch a glimpse of the teenage boy he'd been the day he left Elk Valley.

Terry had driven to the house in his dad's old blue truck, found his passport and his camping backpack, filled it with most of his clothes and a few things he couldn't bring himself to leave behind. Like the photo of him holding a 4-H trophy he'd won, his parents smiling, standing on either side of him. The rest of it, anything important, like his shotgun, stowed easily in the attic. He gave no thought to how long he'd be gone. After the trial, he'd been able to add his name to his parents' savings account. The balance of that was in his pocket, it wasn't much but it was more than enough to get him far from here. He was supposed to graduate high school in three months, but he'd be long gone by then. The sheriff would search for him, of course, but he'd do his best to end the trail in Greybull.

He pulled into a supermarket parking lot, dropped the keys on the floor mat, and walked east for about a mile to the state road heading south. Carrying the heavy pack, he hitched a ride with a ranch hand who took him fifty miles farther.

He made Casper by late afternoon where he had dinner at a truck stop. He struck up a conversation with a trucker who offered to take him as far as Cheyenne where he'd get a room for the night then continue south the next day.

It took him four days, but Terry finally arrived in Galveston, Texas and made his way to the port. He found a listing for a freighter that was leaving at midnight heading to Melbourne, Australia.

The name of the freighter matched his mother's, *Marianne*. "Awesome," he said, smiling for the first time in weeks.

The whisper of rustling brush startled Terry back to reality. He smiled as four mule deer emerged on their quest for food, then realized his toes were numb from the cold water. Yanking his feet out of the water, he began rubbing them to get some circulation flowing.

"Lucky. I'm a lucky guy."

Terry pulled his socks and boots back on then hoisted himself up, exploring his way around the lake before glancing at his phone out of habit. It'd gotten late. His stomach was usually his mealtime alarm clock, but not today. Too many things to distract him.

He headed to his car and took one more look around, inhaling a deep breath then slowly letting it out, thinking, it's all good. Really good. He tugged on the brim of his cowboy hat then pulled it off, setting it on the passenger seat before he got into the car.

Driving into town, he stopped to have lunch at the Red Kettle.

~

Feeling hungry, Willow drove back to town to grab a quick bite before going to the grocery store. Pulling into the Red Kettle parking lot she spotted the Gray Cowboy. Quickly grabbing her cell, she pretended it'd been ringing to avoid an awkward moment if he invited her to sit with him. But, why would he? They didn't know each other. They'd only had a brief, casual conversation and she hadn't been very eloquent. Funny, she thought, since I earn my living putting words together on paper. He walked toward the entrance, glancing at her with a nod. She raised her left hand in response but continued to cover her ear with the silent cell.

She sat a moment, wondering if she should leave, but felt silly just thinking about it. They weren't in high school they just happen to be at the same place for lunch. She got out of the car and went into the restaurant, not looking around, but taking a booth by the window.

"Howdy. Our special today is chili verde," the waitress said as she handed Willow a menu. "What can I get you to drink?"

"Um, iced tea, please."

Returning with her drink, the waitress took her order. As so often happened when Willow wasn't focused on anything in particular, thoughts worth noting moved across her mind like a ticker tape on Wall Street. She reached for her iPad to jot them down and was lost in thought when her salad arrived, causing her to start.

The waitress didn't notice. "Is there anything else I can get you?"

"No, this looks great. Thank you." She ate, making notes for several minutes. Coming up for air she asked the waitress for her check and was surprised to hear her say, "The guy who was sitting in the corner paid your bill."

"Well, why would he do that?" she asked glancing over at the booth in the corner, now empty. She jerked her head around just in time to see the Gray Cowboy get into a small blue car. Feeling almost giddy and unable to hide the smile lighting up her face, Willow felt pretty sure she'd made her first friend in Elk Valley.

Chapter 2

Three days later, Willow lay in her comfortable bed a few minutes longer, feeling very pleased with her progress. The book was coming together.

Sun flooded her bedroom, so she threw back her comforter and headed for the bathroom, hurrying through her shower as if on a mission. She'd shave her legs tomorrow. It's not as if anyone will see them but me, she thought with a sigh. After a quick blow-dry and doing her hair in a French braid, she reminded herself she was only going for coffee then writing for a few hours. She couldn't wait to get busy.

Was she hoping to see the Gray Cowboy there today? She shrugged. Maybe. After giving the kittens a cuddle, Willow headed into town, leaving her warm cozy home bundled up against the morning chill. On the ten-minute drive to Elk Valley Roasting Company she wondered why she didn't stay home to have coffee. She had her favorite coffee in the cupboard and freshly made muffins with wheat-free flour. After pulling into a parking space, she carried her backpack inside.

This is why, she thought stepping into the warm coffee shop with its fresh brewed aroma. A few people sat at the half dozen tables and a young couple snuggled on the leather sofa in front of the potbelly stove, absorbing the warmth.

Willow paused as the door closed. The room vibrated with a low buzz of chatter, the whoosh of the cappuccino machine adding steam to a large cup and the occasional rustle of newspaper.

She laid her backpack on an empty table before heading for the counter to place her order. Pumpkin spice latte sounded perfect. Probably the last one until next fall. Turning back to set up her iPad, she decided to brave the cool air to sit outside. Hearing her name, she retrieved the hot cup of steamy winter coffee. Taking the first sip, she looked around the room again and felt lonely, yet comfortable at the same time. Willow thought about her family in California living without her in the house she'd grown up in. She lifted her chin slightly, feeling good about being in this room with strangers, some of whom she might become friends with in time.

Outside she chose a table with full sun, then settled into the chair to admire the beautiful view once again. She'd had to get away from the safety net of her family and longtime friends. But most of all she'd had to distance herself from Chet, his other women, and from the gossip.

So, here she was living in Wyoming, the location her first novel took place. Alone.

The scrape of a chair brought her back to the moment. Willow turned to see The Gray Cowboy setting his coffee and newspaper on the table next to hers.

"Good morning."

Squinting, she shielded her eyes to look up at him and smiled. "Another beautiful day, isn't it?"

"It is that." He moved his chair to face her. "Do you always travel with that backpack?"

"Yes, mostly." She enjoyed the sound of his voice, deep and pleasant. "Are you settling in here?"

"I'm trying." He nodded, "Still looking for a place to live. Harder than I imagined it'd be."

A man of few words, but he revealed more than she thought he would. "What brought you here? Do you have family, or do you work here?" Now she was getting to the nitty gritty, she almost wanted to rub her hands together. Next she'd go for the jugular, his name. She hid her smile in the latte.

He took a long sip of coffee, eyeing her over the top of his cup then took his time setting it down. "I spent some time here several years back. This scenery has a strong pull."

"Well put," she said, making a mental note to save that line for future use. "Are you a writer by any chance?"

"No, a reader," he said lightheartedly, crossing his leg. "Are you a writer by any chance?"

She chuckled and, with a bit of smugness, said, "Why, yes, as a matter of fact I am."

His eyes narrowed and he didn't respond. Apparently, she'd

hit a nerve. Why does me being a writer make him nervous?

Just when Willow thought he wouldn't say anything more, he asked, "What sort of writing do you do?"

"Contemporary romance novels. I'm working on book number three."

"Oh," he said, seemingly relieved. "That must be interesting."

His expression didn't indicate that he really thought so.

"You don't strike me as someone who might read romance novels, but believe me there are dozens of authors who continue to hit the bestsellers list. I hope to be one of them soon."

"So, who does read romance novels?" he asked. His brow furrowed. "Teenagers?"

"Nine out of ten are women of all ages, but the largest age group is thirty to forty-four." She leaned forward a bit with her left arm resting on the table. "We women love romance. We love to be romanced. We want flowers, dinner in a nice restaurant, and we love being complimented. But most of all we love the attention and effort a guy puts into a date." At least I do. Willow smiled at giving him fair warning.

He cleared his throat, "You seem kinda young to be a published author."

Is this his way of asking how old I am? "I was a newspaper reporter for four years until I decided to focus on fiction for a while. Age isn't a factor in being a writer. I follow a bestselling romance author on Instagram who is seventy years old. I'll be twenty-eight in a few months."

"I would've thought twenty-one or twenty-two."

Willow's eyes narrowed. "I don't think I'd want to be twenty-two again, but I guess I should say thanks." She shrugged. She wasn't exactly over the hill.

"My birthday's coming up too. It's a big one."

"Thirty?"

He gave her a slight nod. "Yeah, thirty. Where did your name come from, Willow?"

Interesting segue. Willow tilted her head to feel the warmth of the sun on her face a moment before responding. "My parents were flower children, free spirits, and they belonged to a commune before they got married. Since I was long and thin when I was born my grandmother said I was willowy." She flipped her braid back over her shoulder. "My mother is a strong woman and she wanted me to be as well. She would tell me, 'Willow trees bend with the wind, but they don't break.'"

"I like that." He said with a warm smile. "Nice story."

They both reached for their coffee and took a sip. He's even more handsome when he smiles, she thought.

Cowboy set his cup down first. "You said you recently moved here. Where did you move from?"

"I lived in Santa Barbara my whole life." There were times in the past few weeks she'd longed to be back there with her family and friends. She'd left everything that was familiar but now she shrugged off that feeling of homesickness.

"I've never been there, but I know it's on the ocean. Why did you leave? What brought you to Wyoming?"

"My writing," she said, setting her cup back on the table.

"I don't understand. Why would you need to come all the way up here just to write?"

"My first three novels are set in Wyoming and my publisher thought I should come here to write so my stories would be more authentic."

He was still puzzled. "But why Wyoming? I am sure Santa Barbara is beautiful. Why not write about life there?"

She tipped her head and thought a moment. "There's something romantic about cowboys and life in the west that readers love. They just can't get enough."

Cowboy's brows furrowed again, "Huh," was his only response.

"I'm sure I'll write a novel set in Southern California at some point. Authors write about what they know, and we usually don't know anyone better than ourselves."

"Is that the only reason you came here?"

"It's the primary reason," she replied, reaching for her coffee again. She thought his curiosity was a good trait. "There are more personal reasons, but my writing is the most important thing to me right now."

I haven't spent this much time talking to anyone since moving here. She'd had a busy social life in California but hadn't taken time out from getting settled into her house and reaching her writing goals to seek out ways to meet people. Coming to the roasting company was a good first step.

Cowboy mulled over her response, but obviously wasn't totally convinced. "And what about the guy on the phone last week? Is he here or is he in Santa Barbara?"

She had moved here to get away from questions about her marriage and why she divorced Chet. Willow thought it was too nice a day to share that part of her life with this man right now. She was enjoying his company and didn't want to spoil it.

"Why do you ask?"

"Just wondering. You sounded mad at him and I wouldn't want to think he'd show up without your knowing it."

She sat forward, "Really?" She was amazed he'd even think that, but how nice that he did. Where was he before Chet sauntered into her life? "I doubt my ex has any idea where Wyoming is, and he doesn't want me. He just wants to make my life miserable and the fact he won't give my dog back, well, it hurts, that's all."

She glanced down at her naked ring finger and continued. "I asked Chet to keep Rambo for a while when I was up here house hunting. He obliged, but when I got back, he said Rambo had run off and he couldn't find him. He said my dog must have thought I'd abandoned him and went searching for me. As if I'd abandon my dog!"

Her stomach churned at the thought. "The local animal shelter proved to be a disappointment, so I ran an ad in the paper. Nothing happened. The next thing I knew one of his friends told me how nice it was of me to give Rambo to Chet."

She couldn't imagine him doing such a cruel thing to her. Unfortunately, Willow hadn't seen this sadistic side of him. She could still feel the anger and sadness as though it had just happened. She turned away, fighting back tears.

"Is that why you were yelling at him on the phone?" he asked, his tone subdued. "Because he wouldn't give you your dog?"

"Yes," she said, defeated. "It's been over three months since I last saw my dog and I wonder if I should even pursue getting him back." Her voice faltered. "He's a black lab and twelve years old. Chet was always so good with him, maybe I should just leave him be."

"That's a tough decision, for sure. I had to leave my dog behind when I came here."

"And why did you come back here?"

"Unfinished business." He checked his cell then prepared to leave. "I have a few things to take care of," he said as he stood. "Nice talking to you."

With a nod and a tug on his gray hat, he walked off.

Brows arched, she nodded, pretty sure he left abruptly to avoid answering her next question; what's your name and why are you so secretive about who you are? There's something refreshing about his attitude though, different than California guys who seemed to be on all the time.

She watched him drive away thinking he looked silly in that disco blue Chevy Cobalt.

Out on her porch that afternoon, Willow closed her eyes and leaned against the sofa cushion. She struggled to stay focused, feeling tired and out of sorts. Might be time for an iced mocha, she thought and continued to sit, enjoying the feeling of being idle. She'd worked on her book every day for the past six weeks. Was she overdoing it? Moments later, Willow jolted at the sound of a horn honking.

As the car approached, she recognized the black Mercedes with its darkened windows, black wheels and

California license plate. It was Norma's car, all right, but what the hell was it doing in her driveway?

Launching herself off the sofa, Willow nearly dumped her iPad, her feet barely touching the porch steps, arms waving wildly as Norma came to a stop.

Yanking the door open, she waited while her friend eased herself out of the car. Willow gathered her into a hug, both squealing with delight.

"I can't believe you're here! What a wonderful surprise. Why didn't you let me know you were coming?"

"I guess I wanted to see the look on your face." Norma said then dabbed at tears pooling in the corner of her eyes before she stretched and attempted to rub her lower back. "Can I stay for a few days?"

"Are you kidding? You can stay as long as you want." She couldn't remember seeing her friend looking so exhausted and haggard. But then she had just driven 1,200 miles on her own.

"Are you okay?" she asked, searching her face.

"Yeah," she said lowering her head. "My back has been aching the last five hundred miles. I'm just not used to driving long distances."

"Well, you're here, and I'm thrilled you drove all that way to see me." She knew the drive was out of Norma's comfort zone. Maybe that's why she seemed nervous.

They unloaded an over-stuffed garment bag and two large suitcases from the trunk, plus two smaller bags from the back seat, then wrestled them down the hall to the guest room.

"This is a lovely room," Norma said. "I may never want to leave."

She noticed Norma's eyes glistening before turning away to set her handbag on the bed. We've been friends since sixth grade and cried on each other's shoulders far too long to hide our feelings now, Willow thought.

"How about a cup of tea? We can break out the champagne later," Willow said then put her arm around Norma, who could only nod.

"Okay then. We'll put sheets on the bed later, take your time getting settled. There's a small walk-in closet," she said pointing to the door on the left, then motioned toward the open door, "And, that's the bathroom."

She hugged her friend again before quietly closing the door.

Walking toward the kitchen, she sensed something was definitely wrong. It looked as if she'd run away from home with every piece of clothing she owned. She knew Norma would tell her in time but felt uneasy for her.

Willow was pouring hot water over Pomegranate Green Tea bags in two large mugs, the same two she used in California, when Norm stepped up beside her.

She'd changed into black sweats instead of the gray pair that looked like she'd lived in for days. Strange, since she was always meticulously dressed.

"I made our favorite chocolate chip cookies this morning, and I was thinking about you the whole time, and here you are!"

"Just once, couldn't you make cinnamon rolls or bear claws? Or, better yet, cream puffs," she added wide eyed.

Willow laughed knowing she was only half serious. "I'm so glad you're here. I've missed our juicy chats." She picked up the tray of mugs and plate of cookies then headed toward the door. "Let's sit outside and enjoy the last bit of sun."

Norma held the screen door while Willow stepped out onto the deck setting the tray on the wicker coffee table, gesturing for her to sit on the sofa while she sat on one of the chairs facing her.

She began talking about the things they would do while Norma was visiting until Willow realized her friend was softly crying.

"Sweetie, you're scaring me. What's wrong?" She stepped around the table and sat by her friend putting her arm around her. "What has you so upset?"

Norma pulled a tissue from her pocket and blew her nose. "I'll start with the good news."

Willow nodded and sat back.

Chapter 3

I went to the house where Chet's been living," Norma said, her voice cracking. "I opened the gate to the yard and saw Rambo. He wagged his tail when I walked toward him. The poor guy was tied to a rope, can you believe that?" She exhaled, "I unhooked it from his collar and led him through the gate and into the back of my car. Then I took him to your Mom and Dad's. No one was home, of course."

Willow pulled in a sharp inhale, "It was you! Thank you so much for doing that. Mom called and said Rambo was in their yard, but didn't know how he'd gotten there. She figured Chet was tired of him and brought him over." She sat back, "Well, I'm glad you didn't have to see Chet."

"It wouldn't have mattered. I'd have still taken him. I'm just sorry I couldn't bring him with me, but you saw how loaded my car was. And you know I'm not a dog person, even though I love Rambo."

Willow nodded, knowing rescuing Rambo was a major stretch for Norma. She'd never had a pet while growing up.

"So, what's the bad news?"

Norma shook her head. "There's no easy way to say this..."

Willow's heart began to beat wildly, afraid for what she was about to hear. Norma was her rock, always practical and honest with her feelings.

"I'm pregnant," she confessed in a soft whisper, a huge weight lifted off her, but that was only the beginning.

Did Norma Wasserman just say she was pregnant? "Did I hear you right?" she asked, eyes wide and every nerve in her body tingling.

She looked Willow in the eye and repeated, "I'm pregnant. Ten weeks to be exact."

Willow shrieked with delight, hugging her friend. "I can't believe you're going to have a baby!" then added, "And, you drove all that way just to tell me in person." She was already thinking about a baby shower and hoping Norma would want her to be the baby's Godmother.

Norma began crying again. Willow thought her hormones must be raging. But, knew there was something else going on, and getting it out in the open was becoming awkward. So unlike Norma, she thought.

"Who's the baby's father," she asked tentatively. Norma sobbed. "Okay, so it's not someone you would want to marry."

Norma pursed her lips, and lightly shook her head.

"Is it someone I know?"

She nodded, and Willow's brain began searching for a face or name of someone they both knew, someone Norma might want to get into bed with, but not marry.

"It's..." she gulped.

Willow bent her head in an effort to look into her friend's face now buried in her hands. "It's who?" bracing herself for her response.

"Chet."

Willow waited for Norma to say his last name; certainly, she hadn't been married to the only man named Chet. She watched her friend's body stiffen, knowing their eighteen-year friendship was at stake.

The only sound came from a late afternoon breeze rustling leaves on the cottonwoods.

It felt like an eternity before she realized her friend wasn't going to add anything more. Willow began shaking her head in disbelief then the rest of her body followed. "Did you just say Chet? My ex-husband?" She wasn't even aware she was screaming, but didn't know whether to laugh or wrap her hands around Norma's throat.

The operative word here is friend, she reminded herself.

Again, she nodded and continued to cry.

Willow leapt up and began pacing the length of the deck and back, stopping in front of Norma.

"Are you telling me you had sex with Chester Cromwell, the man you said wasn't good enough for me?" She slumped down in the chair and tried to sound calm. "How did this happen?" then leaned forward shaking her index finger, "And don't say the usual way!"

Knowing that was on the tip of Norma's tongue. "How could this have happened?" her voice now full of anger, arms flying around.

"I don't know. I *don't* know!" she said, looking completely wrung out. "I'm so sorry. You can't imagine how horrible this has been for me, knowing I would have to tell you this."

After a big exhale, she said, "Okay, tell me what happened."

Norma proceeded to explain that she and a business client had dinner the day Willow left California for Wyoming. Later, they'd gone into the bar for a glass of wine when Chet walked in and sat down with them, uninvited. He insisted on buying another round and went to the bar to pick up their order, bringing his beer and her friend's white wine. He went back to the bar for Norma's red wine and seemed to take some time doing it.

"Chet offered a toast to you," she said pointing to Willow, "wishing you good luck in your new home and career. I don't remember anything after that," Norma said. "Until I woke up the next morning in my bed with no clothes on. I thought I heard my front door close," she continued, "So I made my way into the living room and locked it feeling disoriented and unsteady. I went to the window to see Chet crossing the street."

Willow was vibrating, her heart pounding in her ears. A thousand thoughts bombarded her while processing this disgusting revelation, all wanting to take center stage at once. She was beside herself with anger and guilt at allowing this despicable person into her life and the lives of her family and friends.

Apparently, she didn't move far enough away. The ugliness of her ex followed her here even if he didn't. Could it get any worse? Could she feel any more ashamed? Willow was a wreck, filled with emotions she wasn't used to feeling.

When they ran out of words, Willow fixed them a lite supper of chicken salad, before making up Norma's bed, and calling it a night.

Willow lay in her bed staring at the ceiling, thinking how little she knew about date rape. She'd never known anyone who'd been assaulted that way, until now. At least that was what it felt like though she remembered hearing gossip during her college days, but it was never about anyone she knew personally. A few stories came across the newswire at the paper using the term 'club drugs.'

Tomorrow she'd start doing some research. But right now, she knew crying herself to sleep was the only option to shut off all those horrible thoughts.

The nagging sound of her ringing cell was relief from the nightmare Willow was suffering through over and over again as though on a loop. Fumbling for her phone, she gave a gravely hello. Norma's barely audible voice pleaded for help. Willow bounded out of bed, phone in hand, and sprinted down the hall, nearly taking the guest room door off its hinges as she barged in. Norma was curled into a ball, obviously in pain.

Within minutes they were on their way to Elk Valley Medical Clinic where Willow pulled up in front of the Emergency Room door. Once inside, Willow told the nurse on duty Norma was pregnant and in pain. The nurse brought a wheel chair for Norma, and Willow followed as they went through double doors to an examination room where the nurse helped Norma to the bed and out of her sweats and into a hospital gown. The ER team quickly decided they needed an obstetrician and said one would be down shortly for a consultation.

Willow held Norma's hand when she curled into a ball again. "Everything's going to be okay," she said.

Several minutes later, a doctor in pale green scrubs stepped around the curtain. "Miss Wasserman, I'm Dr. Frederickson and I'll be looking after you." He glanced at Willow, "Did you bring her in?"

"Yes, I'm Willow James. Norma and I have been friends for a long time. She's staying with me."

"Tell me what's going on. I understand you're pregnant. Is that right?"

"Yes, ten weeks."

"You've been to an OB?"

"In California."

He nodded grimly. "You're in labor which is why you've had lower back pain the past several hours, and you're most likely having a miscarriage. I'll order something for pain, but I recommend a D & C. The nurse will be back with a consent form for you to sign, then we'll get you up to the operating room."

Norma began to cry, and Willow reached for her hand again, not sure if Norma was relieved or genuinely upset to lose the baby.

"I'm sorry to sound so matter of fact, Miss Wasserman," the doctor said in a gentle, sympathetic voice.

She nodded, sniffling and the doctor handed her a tissue, then said he'd see her upstairs.

Norma added her signature to the form the nurse brought in and handed Willow a plastic bag with Norma's clothes and slippers. "You'll want to keep these with you."

The nurse raised the rails on the bed then pushed it down the hall toward the elevator, Willow following behind. When the door opened on the second floor, the nurse indicated the room on the left. "You can wait in there; someone will let you know when Norma's in recovery. You'll be able to see her then."

Willow stepped closer to Norma, smoothing her curly mane from her face. "You're going to be okay. It's all going to be okay. I'll see you in a little while." Tears flooded Willow's eyes as she squeezed her friend's hand, then stepped back as the nurse gave her a reassuring nod.

"We'll take good care of her."

"Thank you for everything," she said, then watched them disappear behind the double doors. Willow sighed heavily, feeling as though she were in a thick gray fog. She was all by herself in the pasty green waiting room feeling cold and lonely, but this wasn't about her comfort.

She checked her cell: three-thirty. "No wonder I'm exhausted." She curled up as best she could in the most comfortable looking chair and dozed.

Dr. Frederickson came in at four forty-five startling her awake. "Miss James, Norma is in recovery, everything went well, and she's doing fine."

"Oh, that's wonderful. I'm so glad, thank you," she said. "Can I see her?"

"Of course, I'll take you to recovery. She'll be groggy for a while and will most likely sleep, which is what we want her to do. If all goes as expected, she should be able to leave today around eleven o'clock."

Willow nodded and followed Dr. Fredrickson to Norma's room. "Thank you again," she added when he held the door for her. Stepping up beside the bed, she appreciated the peacefulness of Norma's face, a much different person from a few hours earlier when she was scared and in pain.

Norma opened her eyes, "Oh, hi. I'm so glad to see you." She slurred her words a bit, but Willow thought her face had more color.

"I'm relieved you're ok."

"Um huh," she murmured, eyes closed.

"I'm going to go find some coffee and run home to shower. Dr. Frederickson said I can take you home in a few hours."

She smiled, "Thank you for taking care of me."

"Of course. We're always there for each other." Willow said, knowing Norma would have done the same for her.

On the way out, she stopped at the nurse's station and left her cell number in case she was needed. "Otherwise, I'll be back before eleven."

The sun was beginning to peek over the horizon when she drove out of the hospital parking lot at five-thirty. She exhaled a deep sigh thankful for the care Norma had received. If she didn't stop thinking about the last eighteen hours, she'd start to cry again. "I need some coffee and a nap," she said. Deciding against the Roasting Company, for reasons she couldn't explain, she headed for the Red Kettle.

Ten minutes later, she turned into the nearly full parking lot, but managed to get a spot up close as someone was driving out. Stepping inside, she noticed a few regulars and appreciated the bright cheerful atmosphere. Much needed relief from the seriousness of the sterile white hospital.

Willow placed her to-go order, thinking what she really needed was a hug and someone to comfort her. The last time she'd had a hug, beside the hugs from Norma, was from her parents the day she left California. She didn't realize how much she missed that physical contact; a hug, someone holding her hand, or a simple pat on the back. She was alone, then decided, small price to pay for what Norma went through.

Willow paid for her coffee, thanked the waitress, and stepped back out into the cold morning, nearly colliding with the Gray Cowboy. Hot coffee sloshed onto her hand.

"I'm sorry," he said with a startled expression. "I didn't realize you were coming out."

She passed the cup from one hand while she shook the spilled coffee from the other. Lifting the offended hand, she put her mouth on the web between her index finger and thumb in an effort to soothe the sting.

"Are you okay? Here," he reached for the paper cup. "Let me take that while you wipe your hand."

She watched him as he offered to help her, appreciating his concern. It's was nice to be the center of his attention right now. She never really was with Chet. He was always looking over her shoulder not wanting to miss whoever might be nearby. But this guy made her feel like she was worth his concern.

"I'm okay, no harm done," she said pulling back. Her voice sounding as tired as she felt. The back of her right hand covered the yawn she tried to stifle.

"You sure you're okay?" Her trench coat not quite covering pink polka-dot pajamas tucked into Uggs made him smile.

"Yes, thanks. I'll be even better after some sleep and a shower." She wanted to throw her arms around him, tell him about her night and demand a sympathy hug.

"Are you up early or…"

"Or, what? Up late?" She gave him an exhausted smile. "A little of both really."

"Well, looks like you left home in a hurry. Just checking to make sure you're okay."

There he goes again thinking about my welfare, she mused. "Hey, I'm the investigative reporter here. You think you're the curfew police or something?" She was enjoying this exchange as much as he seemed to, but she was cold and bone weary.

He chuckled as she stepped forward.

Willow turned back. "Speaking of getting up early, looks like you're off to work." What's wrong with me? He needs his breakfast and I need some sleep.

"No, I am on my way to buy a truck. Thought I'd get an early start."

"Well, happy truck shopping," she said, then turned to leave.

"Ah…" he got her attention, "I just happened to think of a dilemma. If I buy a truck, I'll have the rental car to bring back. And it might be fun to continue this conversation on the drive over."

Was he really asking her to go with him? Under other circumstances she might've considered it, but at this point she wasn't amused or interested and yawned. But wouldn't it be lovely to spend the day with him? To run away from all the ugly thoughts that filled her mind right now. I have a feeling he'd be a really good distraction.

"Some other time, maybe. Besides, I'm sure the dealership will help you with the rental car." She sighed again. "I need a shower. See you later."

She could feel his eyes on her as she walked away. It was all she could do to keep from running back for that hug she needed. The voice in her head reminded her, don't wait too long, there might be another damsel in distress needing a hug.

~

Terry's eyes were glued to Willow as she walked to her car. Just above a whisper, he said, "Want some company? I'd be happy to wash your back. I could tuck you in." His tone became sober, "I could hold you and make your troubles go away."

He continued to watch as she backed out of the parking space and headed for the driveway, pausing to check for traffic while he fantasized about being in the shower with her.

Chapter 4

Willow didn't have the energy to walk down the hall to her bed, so she laid on the couch in the living room for two hours then showered and made herself a quick breakfast of scrambled eggs before driving back to the hospital.

Dr. Frederickson was with Norma when Willow stepped around the curtain, pleased to see her friend sitting up in bed in her sweats.

"I'm sorry you lost your baby, but I see no reason why you can't carry a baby to term in the future," the doctor offered after reading notes the nurse had written down.

"Thank you. I know it was for the best."

"That's an excellent attitude. Our body knows what's best." He nodded to Willow, then said, "Take it easy for a few days, and if you have any problems, you let us know."

Willow was sure Norma appreciated the doctor's encouraging words, but she also knew her friend was probably a little tired of being the center of attention and was eager to leave.

Norma spent the next few days napping on the wicker sofa out on the deck. She was starting to look like her old self again.

Willow used that time to search the internet for anything she could find on date rape and the drugs used to facilitate sexual assault. Fortunately, there was plenty of information. She settled on the *U.S. Department of Health* site, which seemed to cover every aspect of date rape.

After reading a few paragraphs, Willow understood why Norma wouldn't remember spending the night with Chet. He may have slipped a liquid form of Ketamine into her wine and Norma never would have known it.

Any more than she did. She wanted to scream at the image of sitting in her living room having wine with Chet, then feeling very hung over the next morning. Everything in-between was missing. How could I have married such a monster?

Willow hadn't told anyone but knew she'd share that incident with Norma. It was incomprehensible, but she couldn't deny the possibility that it had happened. Especially after hearing Norma's story. But why would Chet drug me when I would willingly have had sex with him?

Maybe I was the guinea pig! Her hand covered her mouth. What a sickening thought. If it worked on me, he could try it on other women. But why?

Willow dropped her head in her hands forcing the breath from her lungs as her shoulders drooped. There's no taste, no smell and it's very fast acting, according to the article.

Dammit! How can we women safeguard ourselves against this kind of hideous assault?

She continued to read then got to the part about 'How to protect yourself when out in a social setting.' Top of the list, 'Don't accept drinks from other people.' Willow knew Norma wouldn't have had any reason not to trust Chet. She may have thought he was a jerk but would never have expected this kind of behavior from him.

When Willow had been club hopping with friends, she recalled seeing a few women take their drink into the restroom with them and knew that was the reason. Also, on the list, "Open containers yourself," along with several other recommendations for staying safe.

It had never occurred to Norma to go to the emergency room where doctors could run test to determine if she'd been drugged or raped. She'd been disoriented and felt hung over when she woke up, she'd told Willow. In fact, she couldn't swear under oath it was Chet she saw leaving the apartment. She'd showered and put her clothes in the washing machine to wash away the ugliness of the situation. Two things that destroy evidence according to the website.

This might not be as easy to pin on Chet as Willow thought, even though she felt certain it'd been him.

What was his motive? she wondered, then remembered Norma making some snide remarks about Chet at their engagement party, all true now of course, in a tone just loud enough for him to hear. She wasn't surprised Norma had been his target. "He's going to get away with this. That dirty, rotten son-of-a-bitch."

Willow shoved herself out of the chair and went to the railing, gripping it for support. Normally, she loved this time of day with birds chirping, flitting from one tree to the next and a crowd scratching at the ground for bugs and worms. But today she wanted to scream at them to go away. She had an eerie sensation of being on the edge of a cliff with no choice but to go ahead and jump. For a brief moment, she didn't think she'd ever be happy again.

Looking out across the prairie grass, she thought about the Gray Cowboy for the first time in days. The corners of her mouth began to form a smile, and the despair she felt faded a bit. She wondered if he was still going to the coffee shop. It seemed like months since she'd enjoyed his company.

Willow knew she should be consoling her friend, not feeling sorry for herself. None of this was her fault any more than it was Norma's. Willow turned and saw her friend watching her. Stepping forward, she slumped down in the chair like a deflating blow up doll.

Words weren't necessary.

"We were victims." Norma broke the silence, "but we weren't traumatized. He didn't hold a gun to our head. He isn't that brave. Chet's a coward. He's afraid of rejection so he has to drug his so-called conquests. I didn't complain because I wasn't sure what or who to complain about. In his eyes, I must have been okay with it and with him. That way he could feel good about himself."

Tears rolled down her face as Willow nodded. "Norma, we'll get him for this. I'm calling Sheriff Mac and telling him our suspicions. I want to know if he's had any complaints. Otherwise, Chet is free to do this to someone else."

"No Willow," Norma pleaded, sitting forward on the sofa. "You can't tell him it was me or that I was pregnant." She wrung her hands. "I don't want anyone to know about this."

Her response surprised Willow. She was sure Norma would be all over stopping Chet in his tracks, but she also knew Norma would have to live with her mother's reaction to this mess the rest of her life.

"Normie, I promise I won't give him any names until we have something concrete to pin on Chet. Even then, I won't mention your name. You have my word on that."

It was dark now and had turned cold when Willow lit the two lanterns on the wicker coffee table. She stepped inside to get jackets and a lap blanket along with two shot glasses and the bottle of Jack Daniels. They toasted their friendship and promised no more tears.

"You know what this house needs?" Norma said, after slugging back her second shot.

"You aren't going to say a man, are you?"

"Well, sure that too, but I was thinking of a hot tub. Until that man comes along."

Willow's face lit up. "Remember those nights in high school, we'd sit in my parents' hot tub eating popcorn and drinking ginger ale from a champagne glass." She laughed, "We couldn't wait to grow up." Suddenly feeling melancholy, she added, "And here we are all grown up and still sitting alone in the dark." She shrugged her shoulders, "And we don't even have that hot tub."

"Well, we can take care of that tomorrow, but you're on your own as far as the guy goes."

They continued to talk late into the evening. After Willow expressed concern, Norma assured her she was not going to let this episode smother her from returning to the person she was.

"I drove down to UCLA to talk with one of my psych professors," Norma said.

"What did she say?"

"She told me I needed to not blame myself, that I was simply in the wrong place at the worst possible time." Norma reached over and squeezed Willow's hand. "I had three days to think about that on my way here. I yelled, I cried, and decided she was right. I did nothing wrong. I just want to move forward, now."

Willow wasn't sure how to move forward if Chet was still out there able to drug someone else. But this wasn't the time for that battle. Tonight, she needed to support her friend.

"So, what size hot tub do you think I should get?"

~

Terry expected to see Willow at the roasting company the following few days, always taking his usual outside table.

His disappointment at not seeing her was making him cranky. He had no way to contact her. He hoped she was all right. Shifting in his chair, he wondered if she went out of town. But none of that satisfied his curiosity for her absence. Then it dawned on him, he missed her. He missed seeing her beautiful face, those long legs and everything in between. But mostly he missed hearing her voice.

However, he didn't have time to worry about where Willow might be. He made to stand then slumped back down in the chair. Pulling his hat off and dropping it on the table, he raked both hands through his hair reminding himself he had to buy property, livestock and hire hands. Hell, he probably needed to buy a tractor. If his father were here, he'd say he had spring fever.

Anyway, first on his agenda was finding a place to stay until he could buy property and build a house. There wasn't much in the 'For Rent' section of the local paper unless he wanted to live in a boarding house. No, he wanted time to be by himself after living out on the cattle station with all his mates. He thought the world of those guys but was hardly ever alone unless he was riding the fence line.

Out on that outback station he grew into the man he'd become, the blokes teaching him everything he needed to know about being an Australian cowboy.

And then there was Harley.

A chill swept through him as the hair on the back of his neck prickled. He looked over his shoulder feeling uneasy. Man, she really did a number on me. He felt foolish since she was thousands of miles away. Then couldn't help wondering if she was pissed when she found out he wasn't coming back. It was a relief not to think about that crazy Amazon woman again. She's probably already sleeping with one of my single mates' anyway and hasn't given me a thought.

At noon, he drove to the Red Kettle Café to meet up with his childhood buddy, Sheriff Tommy Logan who had just returned from a week's vacation. They hadn't seen each other in thirteen years but had talked on the phone a couple times a year while Terry was out of the country.

He decided to wait in his rental car until the Sheriff's cruiser pulled in. When Tommy arrived, Terry gave him a bear hug, and they slapped each other on the back.

"Man, it's great to see you," He said, blown away that Terry was finally back home.

"Yeah, hard to believe it's been thirteen years." He stepped back to assess his friend. "The uniform suits you." He thought Tommy looked fit and had an air of confidence. "I'm sorry you weren't able to make it over to Oz. I'd have enjoyed showing you around." Tommy's brows furrowed, and Terry added, "Slang for Australia."

"When I traded my Army uniform for Deputy duds, then this sheriff's getup, it didn't leave much time for traveling," he said as they headed to the door.

Brenda, a waitress at Red Kettle since high school, nearly dropped the plates lined up her arm when the guys walked in. "I heard you were back," she said with a big grin before setting the food in front of her table of customers, then turned to greet Terry.

"Brenda, nice to see you," he said when she gave him a hug.

"You don't look much different," she said, face flushing. "Nice tan though."

He chuckled. "Well, it's good to be home."

Tommy lead the way to his table in the back corner of the restaurant where they ordered while Brenda jotted it down.

"Kinda feels like old times," Terry said, "The three of us together in the Red Kettle."

He noticed Brenda's face flush again.

"So, where are you staying?" Tommy asked, after Brenda left to place their order and bring coffee.

"OK Corral Motel on the edge of town."

"You know, you're welcome to stay at my place. I have a spare bedroom. It's full of my brother's stuff though."

Terry nodded, not sure he wanted to move into a room full of Joey's things. "I knew you'd ask, and I appreciate it. But I need to be on my own right now."

"Afraid you'll get too comfortable?"

"Yup. Something will come up. It has to, I've got to get out of that musty, noisy motel."

"Well, let me know if you change your mind."

Brenda set a creamer on the table and poured coffee.

"So, last time we talked you mentioned a woman, Harley I think you said. Didn't she want to come back with you?"

"She wasn't invited." He sipped the hot coffee then set it down. "I woke up early one morning not long ago to find my wrist tied to the bed post."

Tommy chuckled, "I didn't know you went for that kinky stuff."

Terry gave him a you've-gotta-be-shittin'-me glare. "That would be funny if she hadn't pulled her hunting knife on me when I reached up to grab her arm." He'd laughed to mellow things out but was fed up with her needing to be with him every minute of every day. He knew she wanted to make a point about being able to control him. Leaving the cattle station and moving back to the States was the only way he'd be able to get away from her.

"Whoa, makes it hard to get a good night's rest."

"Yeah, pretty much. I felt I had to sleep with one eye open." He exhaled remembering those nights when he'd lay awake and Harley would roll over. Would this be the night she'd stab him? He was never sure what she was capable of doing. "She was very competitive, needed to be better at everything I did. Like she had something to prove. I'm guessing she was abused at some point in her life. But I treated her with respect. I don't know why she was punishing me."

"Maybe she'd learned not to trust men who were... um respectful or gentlemanly."

Terry shrugged, "Maybe, but I knew it was time to go, so I packed up a few things, those boxes I sent you, and told my partner I was going back to the states in six weeks. He and I had talked a few months earlier about my leaving, said he'd keep Harley busy the day I left so there wouldn't be any drama." That part of his life was over and he wanted it to stay buried.

The restaurant grew quiet as though patrons waited to hear the rest of the story. But, the two guys were deep in thought. The sizzle of bacon on the grill prompted conversation at a couple of tables.

Terry drained his coffee cup, "I was sure you'd be married by now."

"Haven't found the woman who'd put up with me and my job." Tommy sat back then added, "I'm sorry I wasn't here when you pulled into town."

He shook his head, "It took me longer to get my bearings than I expected. I ended up staying in Hawaii five days instead of two."

"What'd you do in Hawaii for five days?"

"I let a flight attendant pick me up. She was the perfect distraction, knockout blond from Southern California. We had dinner and drinks in the hotel bar, but when a couple of guys stopped at our table to say hello to her, I knew it was time to say goodnight. I did sleep peacefully for the first time in months though."

He chuckled, "What made you take up with Harley in the first place?"

"I didn't choose her, she chose me. She showed up about a year ago and moved into my place. She wasn't..." he shrugged, "beautiful but she was striking. I know this sounds crazy, but it almost felt like she had a hypnotic effect on me. At first it was okay, but when I tried to break it off, I found a dead animal at my door."

Tommy gave him a startled expression. "I can see why you'd want to get away from her. So, where'd you go from Hawaii?"

"I flew into Vegas but couldn't bring myself to get on that plane to Denver. I needed more time to adjust, so I stayed there a few days before driving out here."

"You drove?"

"Yeah, I took my time, did some sightseeing; Grand Canyon, and most of Utah's national parks." And, littered the highway with memories of Harley.

"I wondered why it took you so long to get here. I was hoping you'd join me on my fishing trip."

Terry nodded, "Next time."

When their breakfast arrived, they polished it off like the hungry men they were.

Chapter 5

At seven-thirty the next morning, Willow woke with a dull headache and a chalky dry throat. Norma hadn't fared much better and agreed they both looked like hell.

Willow was excited to take her friend for coffee at Elk Valley Roasting Company. She wanted to share the experience with her, and okay, maybe hoping the Gray Cowboy would be there too. She wanted them to meet and couldn't help smiling at how important it seemed to her. For approval, maybe?

They took Norma's car and sang along with the music blasting from the car stereo when they pulled into the parking lot at the coffee bar.

"This place is cute," Norma said as they walked up the steps. Inside, they were greeted by that familiar coffee scent and the wood burning stove going full bore.

Once they were seated outside at Willow's favorite table, Norma said, "I can see why you love coming here, the views are beautiful."

She nodded, enjoying the scenery through her friend's eyes.

"So, have you met many people here?" Norma asked before taking a sip of her hot coffee.

"Only one so far. I hope he's here today. I'd like you to meet him."

Norma nearly choked on her coffee. "Him? You know a 'him' and you haven't told me?"

She shrugged. "He's new here like me, so I guess we gravitated to each other. That and the fact I made a fool of myself his first day in town. I'm sure he thinks I'm a brainless twit." Willow told the story of their first meeting.

Norma laughed, shaking her head in disbelief when her gaze drew distant. "If there's a God in Heaven, I hope this is the 'him.'"

Willow gave her a quizzical look then saw the Gray Cowboy walk toward them, placing his coffee and newspaper on the table next to theirs. He turned to look at Willow and smiled. "Good morning, ladies," he said with a tug on his hat brim.

Norma's mouth went agape as Willow returned the greeting. "Cowboy, this is my dearest friend Norma Wasserman."

"Nice to meet you, Cowboy," she said with a flirtatious smile.

"My pleasure." Gray Cowboy's eyebrows knitted together as he turned toward Willow. "Why do you call me Cowboy?"

Leaning forward in her chair, she asked, "What would you like me to call you?" And yes, she was flirting with him.

He exhaled. "Terry, please, call me Terry." He chuckled.

"Okay, Terry." Willow knew, at some point, he'd tell her why he'd been so secretive about himself.

He turned to Norma. "Are you a writer too?"

"No, I'm a life coach and business consultant."

"Interesting," he said, seemingly mulling it over.

"Do you live nearby?" Norma asked.

"I'm staying at a motel in town, but looking for someplace temporary until I find a piece of property that interests me." He turned to Willow. "How's your writing coming?" He shifted his weight in the chair then crossed his leg.

She could see he was feeling uncomfortable. "Great, thanks for asking. I'm coming down to the last quarter of my story."

"I think it's her best work so far," Norma added, having been given editing rights while recuperating.

The next hour passed quickly while the three of them chatted easily about nothing more serious than the weather or the latest in technology. Norma was a whiz at what was current and what to stay away from.

"I'm in need of a computer," Terry said, "I want something that I can run my business from, but it has to be nearly indestructible, too. I'll most likely be using the barn as my office for a while."

"Call me if you have any questions," Norma said as she pulled one of her business cards from her cardholder and held it out for him. "I'd be more than happy to steer you in the right direction."

"Thanks, that's nice of you." He stood and took the card from her. "I just might give you a call."

"No problem," she replied.

Terry checked the time on his cell. "You ladies have a good day," he said, gathering his empty cup and newspaper. Turning toward Norma, he offered, "enjoy the rest of your stay." With a smile and that familiar tug on the brim of his gray cowboy hat, he gazed down at Willow a moment before leaving.

"That man is some kind of gorgeous. Do not let him get away," Norma scolded then turned in her chair to watch him walk toward the parking lot.

"He does look like a young George Clooney, doesn't he?" Willow said with a sense of excitement. "But I don't think he knows it. I'm anxious to learn the full story he keeps so closely guarded."

"Terry likes what he sees in you, too. Just be careful not to pry. He seems to be a private person and you need to earn his trust before he reveals his past."

They gathered up their things and headed for the car. Norma had an appointment with the doctor who had taken care of her in ER. He'd given her his card, encouraging her to come see him in a week, to follow up on her recovery.

Willow was checking email when Norma got back in the car, her eyes sparkling.

"So, what did he say?"

"He checked my vitals and asked how I was doing." She exhaled, "He's very nice and kind of cute in a nerdy sort of way. And very tall," she added, glancing over at Willow, handing her a birth control brochure with the doctor's card tucked into a slot on the cover.

Willow agreed, remembering she'd had to look up at him when they met in ER. "What's this for," she asked suspiciously, waving the brochure at Norma.

"I'm pretty sure you'll need his card before I will."

She shot her a you've-got-to-be-kidding expression before slipping the card into her handbag.

"You know what?" Willow asked as they continued into town.

"You're falling for Cowboy?" Norma said with a sideways glance.

"No, that's not what I was going to say," she defended with a smile she couldn't hide. "He's very nice and has been a gentleman the few times I've seen him." But then so was Chet when she first met him. Her body gave an involuntary shudder.

"Yoo-hoo," she said, bringing Willow around. "You don't have to decide right this minute if you want to marry the guy. He seems like a good catch though. Oh, but wait, he hasn't even asked for your hand yet."

"Very funny," she replied with her nose in the air. "I was just thinking how charming Chet was when I first met him."

Norma bristled at the sound of his name. "Yeah, that he was." Looking out the window, she took a deep breath. "But he became a jerk very fast. Just took you longer to see it."

Willow hunched her shoulders, feeling a bit deflated. "I know. Normie, I don't want to repeat the same mistake. I just don't trust myself right now to make the best choice for me."

She put her hand on Willow's arm. "Don't be in such a hurry. You have some time yet before you turn into an old hag."

"I can always count on you to bring me back to earth."

"As a wanna-be psychologist, it's part of my service." Norma braked for a red light then turned toward Willow. "You know what you need?"

"I refuse to pay for sex."

They both laughed, lightening the mood.

"Oh, I don't know. I bet if you let Terry know you had an itch that needed scratching, he'd offer himself up." Norma turned, leaning toward Willow. "Free of charge."

"You're wicked," She retorted, laughing at the imagined scene.

"I think you're just lonely, Willow. You're a people person who's hardly been alone since the day you were born. And here you are living by yourself in this quiet little town with all this open space."

"Thanks for reminding me," she replied with mock sarcasm.

"I'm surprised you haven't made more friends or joined some charity or committee."

"I've been busy writing. I'll get out more when this book is finished." That sounded like a good excuse, since it was the only one she had.

"Sometimes I have felt isolated out at my house, but it's only a ten-minute drive to town. Right now, I'm pretty OK living where no one knows my name," she added, but left off the bit about not being ready to share the embarrassment of her short-lived marriage with new faces.

"Well, at least the kittens snuggle up to me at night."

"You sound pathetic. You know that, right?"

"Yeah, I know." She'd resigned herself to her dull lifestyle already.

Arriving at the hot tub store, Willow and Norma checked out most of the display models, giggling at some of the new features; cushioned seat backs and twinkling lights. Willow decided on a sea blue model with four seats. Once the salesman learned the hot tub would be installed on the deck, he said he'd need to inspect it to ensure it would support up to two tons. They set a date for him to drop by in a couple of days.

The following morning, Willow smelled coffee brewing and threw back the comforter, grabbing her jacket, she padded down the hall to the kitchen. Norma had cups set out on a tray and was adding cookies to a plate.

It was a glorious morning, sunny blue sky with those big fluffy clouds hanging around the edge of the universe. It was the sort of day Willow just wanted to sit outside and enjoy whatever came along.

"So, Normie," she ventured after they finished their first cup of coffee on the deck and only crumbs were left on the cookie plate. "What's up next for you?"

"I have appointments with two clients today, if that's all right." As a life coach and business consultant, Facetime allowed Norma to stay connected with her clients no matter where she was.

"Of course," Willow replied. "Make yourself comfortable in the living room."

"And," Norma added, "I have to leave tomorrow."

"So soon?" She didn't try to hide her disappointment. "I was hoping you could stay longer. Like forever."

"Just you, me and the cats, huh?"

"Something like that," she offered meekly.

"That doesn't leave much room for Terry."

Willow gave her an exasperated expression. "We don't know anything about each other. Just superficial stuff," she said, waving her arms around.

"All the more reason to be unencumbered. You need time to get to know each other, just the two of you. I'm serious, Willow," she added. "I think there's more to this guy than he's letting on. From what you've told me, something may have happened to him, he may have been hurt as well. Maybe you both need a friend to share things with before it develops into something deeper and more meaningful."

Willow silently agreed with everything her friend was telling her but couldn't help feeling like a little girl being lectured by a parent.

"The guy gives off positive vibes and I think you could be good for each other."

"Spoken like a psychologist." She gave Norma's hand a squeeze. "Thanks for your insight. You just might be right."

"I want to make sure you don't hole up here on your deck and not get out and see this beautiful country. You need to meet people, make some friends. Your writing will always be there." Norma patted Willow's hand in return.

With pursed lips, she nodded. "Where will you go then? Chicago, to see your cousin Sydney?" She knew they were close, more like sisters than cousins. Sydney was also Willow's editor.

"Yes, until I decide where I want to end up. It'll be a while before I can go back to Santa Barbara," she said with a note of relief and sadness at the same time. Then she shook her head and took a deep breath, "No more tears."

The next morning Norma was up early, loading her bags into the trunk and back seat of her car. Willow tried to hold back tears but wasn't doing a very good job of it.

"Willow, I noticed your garage has a second story," she said, tilting her head toward the garage. "What's up there?"

"It's a small apartment. I went up once with Mom when we made an offer on the house."

"Can we go have a look? I'd like to see it."

"Sure, I'll go get the key." She hurried off, hoping it might be something Norma would like to come back to. Willow led the way up the outside staircase, unlocked the door, and stepped in, Norma behind her.

"Wow, this is nice," she said, taking the room in. There was a kitchenette with microwave, sink, small table and two chairs. The living area held what appeared to be a comfortable sofa, coffee table and cozy chair. A door opened into a small empty bedroom with an adjoining bath. "Didn't Terry say he was looking for a place to live until he found some property?" Norma asked, not waiting for her answer. "This would be perfect for him short term."

"Oh, I doubt he'd want to live above the garage. Besides, I'm not sure I'd want to have a renter." She did like the idea of having a neighbor, though. She'd enjoyed Norma's company the past week and didn't want her to leave.

"Are you sure I can't convince you to come back and stay a while?"

"I'll come for a visit after I get settled in Chicago."

Willow knew Norma had her own life to sort out. We both do.

After locking the door, they headed down the stairs to Norma's waiting car.

"Willow, I don't know how to thank you for taking care of me and helping me get on the other side of this mess."

She gave her a weak smile, tears rolling pretty good now.

"Love you, Willow." They hugged before Norma slid in behind the steering wheel, pulled the seatbelt across her and clicked it in place.

"You call me twice a day," Willow said, wiping away tears with the back of her hand.

Norma smiled up at her blinking back tears of her own. "Promise." She put the car in gear and rolled forward then stuck her arm out the window waving one last time. The black Mercedes headed toward the road, made a right turn, and she was gone.

As she ran up the steps into her now quiet house, Willow cried tears of disappointment at being alone again, but relieved that Norma would put the ordeal with Chet behind her as best she could.

The kittens greeted her with hungry meows, reminding her, she wasn't really alone. Picking them up for a cuddle, she made herself comfortable on the floor and was soon laughing, watching them crawl over her, grabbing at her hand or attacking her toes when she wiggled them.

She got up to pour dry food into their bowls and check to make sure they had enough water. She took pleasure watching them chow down. Naptime was next on their agenda.

After tidying up the kitchen, she made her way down the hall to the guest room, gathering up the sheets Norma had removed from the bed. As she carried them to the laundry room, she had a strong urge to go for coffee, hoping Terry would be there. Praying he'd be there.

Maybe he would be interested in renting the apartment above the garage. It'd only be for a short time, he'd said. She hurried through her shower, dressed carefully, feeling silly about worrying what he might think of what she wore. Pulling on her best fitting jeans she chose a long sleeve T-shirt and her favorite pullover sweater. She still didn't look like a local, time to find a shop that carried western wear, she thought tying her Nikes.

Before leaving, she paused to check on the kittens curled up together in their bed. They're good for a few hours. She hurried out the door, sprinted to the garage, wishing it was attached to the house. Probably mess up the look of the house as well as cut down on the deck area, she decided, but in winter it might be worth it. In a matter of minutes, she was turning right onto the road toward town.

She was excited at the thought of seeing Terry. Norma was right, they needed time to get to know one another. Deep in thought about what she might say to him, she noticed flashing lights in her rearview mirror.

"You've gotta be kidding!" She pulled to the side of the road, rolled her window down and turned the engine off.

A tall, brawny guy in uniform swaggered up to her door. "Good morning, ma'am." He nodded with a tug on the brim of his cowboy hat.

"Hello, Sheriff," she said, smiling up at him.

He removed his shades and studied her face. "Are you visiting or driving through? I thought I knew everyone in town, but you don't look familiar."

"I moved here a couple of months ago."

"May I see your driver's license and registration, please?"

She provided both, and he took them back to his patrol car. A few minutes ticked by before he returned, handing over her documents. "Miss James, this is just a friendly warning to hold your speed down. I clocked you at nine miles over the limit. Not a speed demon by any means, but we want to keep all our citizens safe."

"Thank you, I appreciate it."

Again, he gave his hat brim a tug along with a nod. "Welcome to Elk Valley," he said then headed back to his vehicle.

Willow signaled and made sure to look over her shoulder before carefully pulling back out onto the highway. It was nearly ten-thirty when she arrived at the roasting company and no sign of Terry, or that electric blue rental car. Oh well, might as well get coffee, she decided. He could be running late himself, but she didn't believe that.

Settling in at one of the tables on the back deck, her cell rang. "Hi, Normie."

"Hey girlfriend. What're ya doing?"

"Having more coffee at the roasting company," she

responded in a playful manner, then in her usual voice, "By myself unfortunately."

"No Terry?"

"No, he's most likely been and gone."

"Willow, I called because…"

She could tell by the tone of Norma's voice something significant was coming. "Yes, what is it."

"I want you to go after Chet and I don't care if you use my name or not. The man is sick and needs to be stopped before he does this to one more woman."

"Norma, are you sure?" She prodded, her senses on full alert.

"Yes, no doubts, but I will wait to break the news to my mother when I feel I'm ready."

"Okay. I'm with you the whole way, you know that. I'll call you before I call the sheriff in Santa Barbara."

"Thanks," Norma said then let out a breath. "I feel so much better about everything. I don't want to hide behind this."

"I think you've made the right decision. Drive safely and call me later. Love you."

"Love you too, girl." They disconnected.

Willow pumped air with her fist. "Yes!" She felt good about Norma's decision and would get her thoughts together to present to Santa Barbara's finest, Sheriff Mac McCauley.

Chapter 6

*H*e hadn't planned to turn onto the narrow gravel road leading to the house where he grew up. But Terry's instincts had kicked in as though it was thirteen years ago. He stopped abruptly, tires skidding on the gravel.

"What am I doing?" He wasn't sure he was ready to see the house. He leaned forward arms on the steering wheel, taking everything in. It all looked familiar yet different. The trees had grown, of course, then he spotted the house up ahead. No turning back now, he needed to have a closer look. Hoping no one was home, he continued on.

The house sat alone now looking bare without the barn. He was surprised no one had rebuilt it. The house had been well kept with fresh paint and hardware. He turned the engine off, rolled down the window and sat. It was quiet, no barking dog, and no one at the door to question his arrival.

A prickly sensation crept up his spine and scalp while he chewed on his bottom lip.

Home. No longer home with no one to welcome him back.

After being away, he hadn't expected to feel anxious but his stomach was in a knot. He hauled in a breath, exhaled, then got out of the truck and went up the steps to the door. He knocked but heard nothing and assumed no one was home. Walking along the deck he looked down on the flower garden. It was as pretty as when his mother cared for it, made him feel good. He heard the sound of a car and turned back to see Willow step out of her SUV.

"Willow?"

Then she saw him.

"Hello, Terry," she said, moving to the steps, one hand on the railing and right foot on the bottom step, looking up at his stunned face.

"What are you doing here?" he asked and not in a friendly way. Did she follow him?

"No," she retorted. "What are you doing here?" He seemed to be in a stupor as he stood staring down at her. "This is my house. I live here." She walked up onto the deck and sat on the sofa, "Come and sit," She said, motioning to the wicker chair.

"Why didn't you tell me you lived here?" he asked, sitting down opposite her, sounding more aggressive than needed.

"How would I know I should've told you I lived here?" she said in an effort to lighten things up, but he looked even more confused. "Terry, why did you come to my house?"

"Thought it was time I came back to the house I grew up in," he revealed in a calm, quiet voice.

"I can't believe you grew up in my house." She shook her head in amazement. "That's crazy."

"Well, somebody had to buy it," he said, running a hand through his hair. But, why didn't he want it to be her? He liked Willow, and didn't think she had an ulterior motive. Nothing had developed from the information he'd shared with her so far, unless she's writing a story about the trial. He didn't believe that. She's simply living in the house he grew up in. Period.

"You've been secretive about your past, so this probably isn't easy for you."

He felt like a kid, reluctant to confess, but he had a strong need to unburden himself. Would she want to hear how his once happy life had turned to shit? Would that make them friends? Or, was she fishing for a story? He wasn't a suspicious person by nature, but she did say she'd been an investigative reporter.

Willow leaned forward to lay her hands on tightly clasped fists resting on his knees. Her hands, soft and gentle, put him at ease. He relaxed, reminded himself she'd only shown kindness and interest in the story of his past.

"Do you want to tell me about it?"

He looked at her for several seconds, still unsure. "I don't know where to begin," he said then turned to look over his left shoulder at the flower garden. "My father and mother built this house, and that flower garden was my mother's pride and joy. Dad cultivated that plot for her and this house," he looked up, eyes sweeping the length of it, "was always full of her flowers."

His forearms rested on his knees; his hands relaxed now. He looked at Willow.

"We were a happy family until my mother got sick when I was sixteen. She died within a few months." He sat back in the wicker chair that was one size too small for him. "Everything was arranged for me to go to Australia with the 4-H Exchange Program. But I didn't want to leave my father, he insisted though, said my mother had been excited about my going. She'd be disappointed if I didn't. I was only gone three months, but when I got back everything had changed. A woman named Noreen Purvis had moved in while I was away. It was almost as if she knew I'd be gone and swooped down on my grieving father.

"My name is Thierry Robert Du Champs. I go by Terry though. It was easier for teachers and kids in school. My father was French, Alain Du Champs. My grandfather's name, on Mom's side, was Robert."

Terry hadn't spoken to anyone in Australia about what his life had once been. He appreciated Willow listening to him while he rambled on, wanting to unlock these events and memories in his mind.

He ran a hand down his face, his eyes landing on a spot just under the big picture window, his stomach tightened. "I remembered seeing Noreen at our house having tea with Mom. They met at a shop in town where Noreen worked, and she delivered something Mom had ordered. The woman had a hard look to her as though her life had been rough." He shrugged his shoulders, "Maybe Mom felt sorry for her and invited her to come again. It wasn't long after that my mother became lethargic and had a hard time focusing. Noreen would come over to make tea and visit for a short time, but Mom only got worse. She died two months later, and I left for Australia three months after that."

"That's not the whole story, is it?"

"No," he glanced over at her. "Not by a long shot."

The sound of a Cooper's hawk filled the air. Terry looked up to see the raptor spring from a lodgepole pine across the yard and soar until it was out of sight.

"Would you like a glass of iced tea or I could put a pot of coffee on?"

He stared at her as though she were speaking a foreign language, then blinked a couple of times. "Iced tea sounds great." She seemed to know he needed a break.

"Okay. It'll just take a minute," she offered as Terry stood.

"Maybe I can help."

"Sure, come on in."

Not wanting to sit alone on the porch with his thoughts, Terry was glad to have something else to focus on.

When they stepped inside, the kittens were at their feet, crying for food. "Oh, kitties, I'm sorry. I didn't mean to forget you."

Terry bent down to pick up the black kitten. "Sorry guys, it's my fault."

"Did you have pets when you were growing up?"

"Yes. We always had cats and dogs and a few farm

animals. My mom had kept goats and made cheese from their milk. I do look forward to getting a dog when I have a place to live."

Willow watched him. "That's Midnight and that's his sister Stormy," she said, pointing to the dark gray and white kitten. She went about filling their food bowls while Terry had both kittens in his arms before releasing them to eat.

"When did you get the kittens?"

"Not long after I moved here. They're good company and very entertaining." She took two tall glasses from the cupboard and a lemon from the fridge, cutting two slices. Terry couldn't take his eyes off her. She was graceful, almost floating across the floor, like a swan, he thought.

"Would you like lemon?" Willow asked over her shoulder.

"Yeah, thanks."

She added cookies to a plate, and they went back out on the front deck where they sat sipping tea, eating chocolate chip cookies and enjoying the afternoon sun.

"I went to the coffee bar looking for you today," she confessed.

Terry swallowed some tea, then set his glass down. "You did? I wasn't there." He grinned, "But then you know that."

"Yes, and I was pulled over for speeding in my haste to get there."

"Sheriff Logan pulled you over?" he asked. "Shame on him."

"You know the sheriff, then?"

"We went through school together. What made you come looking for me?"

"It was Norma's suggestion." She'd blame it on her friend. "She thought since you were looking for temporary housing you might be interested in renting the apartment above the garage. And I thought it might be a good idea too," she hastened to add.

Couldn't all be Norma's idea.

His eyebrows furrowed as he stood then walked to the side of the house. "I didn't notice that. It must be a new addition, new since I lived here anyway."

"I don't know when it was built, but I think it's fairly new."

"I'd like to see it. I hate the thought of going back to that motel." He'd checked out of the motel every day hoping to find other accommodations, only to go back and check in for one more night.

Willow was already on her feet. "Absolutely. I'll get the key."

"This is nice," he said after stepping inside, looking around. It was bright and clean, like it'd never been lived in.

"Let's check the kitchen cupboards to see what's there. I haven't been curious enough to look before now."

Sure enough, there were plates, glasses and silverware in a drawer along with just about everything he'd need to prepare a meal.

"The only thing missing is a bed in this bedroom," she said, as he followed her into the room. "Needs towels and bathmat too," she added after surveying the bathroom.

"That's easy. How much do you want for it and how soon can I move in?"

"I don't know, um, way less than California standards, I'm sure. What would you expect to pay?"

"How about four hundred a month?"

"That seems high, but if you're comfortable with that, I'm okay with it. I'll even buy the bed and linens. We could probably go get everything right now and you can move in any time."

"That's too good to be true," he said, just as eager as she sounded. "I'll take it."

At the bottom of the steps, Terry paused to look back up at the apartment. He couldn't believe his luck. Willow saw a smile form at the corner of his mouth. His smile broadened when he turned to see her watching him.

~

Walking back to the house, Willow's mind was on overload. What had caused the death of Terry's mother. Had she been ill before this Noreen person showed up? Was it possible she wanted Terry's mother out of the way and was slipping something into her tea? She blinked back tears recalling the sadness in his voice.

Willow stepped into the kitchen for her purse before they headed to town in Terry's new truck. She liked the idea of them becoming friends, but now she'd be his landlady. And that's fine. Right now, she couldn't handle anything more serious and suspected he couldn't either.

But they weren't just spending the day together; they were buying a bed and linens. Yikes! She huffed out a breath as heat crawled up her neck, and hoped she wasn't blushing.

He opened the truck door and once she was seated, their hands collided when both reached for the seatbelt. "I'm sorry," Terry took hold of her hand, "I hope I didn't hurt you."

"Oh no." But she didn't want him to let go of her hand.

"Nice truck," she offered as they rode along the highway. "Umm, has that new car smell." Or, is it the scent of Terry I'm enjoying? Don't go there, girlfriend. Running her hand across the leather arm rest, "Much better than that electric blue tennis shoe you were driving."

He chuckled. "Yeah, I was a happy camper when I left that behind." He looked over at her, "You were right, of course, the dealer was happy to get it back to the rental company for me."

"That's right. I did say that, didn't I?" She looked out the windshield. "I'd forgotten in my sleepy stupor so early that day."

"I hope you'll tell me the story behind that morning some time."

"Sure," she agreed, studying her hands. "Some time I will tell you about it."

"Sounds serious." He glanced over at her.

"It was, very, but it turned out okay in the end. However, like your story, it isn't over yet."

They were quiet for a few minutes, and Willow noticed him glance at her.

"So how did you find the house? How did you even know it was for sale?"

"My mom's a realtor in Santa Barbara, and once she was sure I was serious about moving to Wyoming, she got online to check out what might be available. I think your house was the first one she saw."

"Had you ever been here before?"

"You're still having a hard time believing I just moved here to write, aren't you?"

"I am in no way wanting to sound suspicious of your motives."

She didn't believe him and didn't understand where his suspicion came from, then she remembered he didn't tell her his name when they first met. Why did he need her to clarify how she came to live here? Is he worried she wants to dig up his past? "I've never been further north than Colorado," she explained, trying not to sound annoyed.

He shook his head. "It's just that I find it so coincidental you moved here to start a new life, and I returned to start over and I'm lucky enough to meet you."

Willow was surprised to hear him say he was lucky to meet her, causing her stomach to curl. "Like you said, somebody had to buy it and that somebody was me."

"Yes, and if your novels were set in Montana, we wouldn't be having this conversation."

She raised her eyebrows and gave him a grateful smile. Willow made that decision long ago, but he was right. She could be living in Montana if she hadn't chosen Wyoming as the setting for her novels.

On the way through town, Willow spotted a mattress store. They pulled in and Terry helped her out of the truck, his hand on the small of her back as they walked into the store. After looking at their options, they decided on a queen size instead of a king bed since the bedroom was small. "We also need a bed frame," Terry told the salesman. "If you'll get it all together, we'll be back to pick it up in less than an hour."

Terry offered to pay for the bed, but Willow reminded him, "When you move on, I'll still need a bed for the apartment."

They drove to the big box store to buy linens, pillows and anything else they thought he might need to turn the small apartment into a temporary home. Heading back to the mattress store, streaks of lightning lit dark clouds, thunder quickly followed.

Willow flinched, "Wow, that was right overhead."

Terry nodded, "Looks like we're in for some rain. I'd like to buy you dinner, but why don't we get something to-go before it starts to pour?"

She agreed and called Red Kettle to place their order before picking up the bed.

When they pulled into Willow's driveway, there were light sprinkles on the windshield. "I'll get dinner in the oven to keep warm, then come help you get the mattress upstairs."

"Okay, I'll take these bags up," Terry said as he opened the door, rain coming heavier now.

Willow fed the kittens as both reached up to grab her hands. They buried their little faces in the food, and she promised to spend some time with them after dinner. She hurried out the door as Terry came down the stairs.

Pulling the mattress out of the truck bed, Terry instructed, "I'll go first, you just hold it by the bottom and try to steady it. You sure you'll be able to handle it?"

She nodded and they started up the steps in what had become a downpour. Her feet automatically found the next step without having to look down. After some wrangling at the small landing, they got the mattress inside, which was now dripping with water.

"I'll get one of the kitchen towels to wipe down the plastic covering," Willow said, "along with my face," feeling water running into her eyes. While at the counter, she tried the faucet. No water came out. She uttered an expletive and mopped up water as Terry used his pocketknife to cut the plastic away from the new mattress.

Willow went to the bathroom and nothing came out of that faucet either. "Terry, never mind," she said, walking back into the living room.

"What do you mean?"

"There's no water. I'll have to call the utility company tomorrow."

His shoulders sagged. "I'll go see if the water's shut off outside."

"No, let's eat dinner. I don't know about you, but I haven't eaten since breakfast."

"Okay, you go eat and I'll get this bed platform set up and figure out the water. I'd rather sleep in my truck than go back to that motel."

"No, come and eat while the food is warm." She gazed at him, their clothes and hair soaking wet. She reached for his hand, and he held on as though she were his lifeline.

"You can stay at my house tonight, and we'll deal with all this in the morning."

But he stayed where he was, his thumb caressing her palm, obviously surprised at her invitation to spend the night in her house. A flash of lightening lit up the room, and a loud clap of thunder broke the silence. "Okay," he said, resigned. "Let's go."

Chapter 7

Terry was a little overwhelmed as they headed down the stairs. Things weren't working out as easily as he expected. Then he thought about that beat-up old pickup on the cattle station. There was always an assortment of tools rattling around in the bed ready for any emergency. He made a mental note to buy a few of the basics for his new truck: screwdriver, wrench, maybe a hammer.

Now she wanted him to spend the night in her house, the house he grew up in. She didn't say 'sleep with me' so that meant he'd most likely bed down in his old room. He wanted to tell her no, remembering the last time he'd slept in the house before his mother died. But, hey, that was a long time ago, it's just a bedroom, and only for one night.

Except Willow would be sleeping in her bed down the hall which conjured up some pleasant images he didn't need to be thinking about right now.

By the time they stepped into Willow's kitchen their clothes were soaked and Willow's shirt clung to her breasts and stomach. She plucked at the wet fabric. "Are your bags still in the truck?"

"Yeah, I'll go get what I need." But he stayed put, eyes fully focused on her.

Looking up at him, she tilted her head to one side. "What?"

Without a word, he exhaled then went out the door into the rain. He wanted to help her out of her wet clothes hoping she wanted to help him out of his.

Willow was checking on dinner when he walked in with bags in both hands. "The guest room is just there," she said, pointing to the door at the end of the hall. "I'm going to put the sheets in the dryer and take a shower to warm up. We can make up the bed after we eat."

Yup, that was where he'd slept when growing up. "Right," he said and moved on carefully to keep from hitting the wall with his bags as he went.

Terry was grateful to be in the house he once lived in, though it didn't resemble the old house by any stretch. Except for the basic shape. He knew his mom and dad would appreciate that someone had taken care to renovate it but didn't think it was Willow.

Thoughts of happy times in this house filled his mind: blowing out candles on the birthday cakes his mom baked, twinkling lights on the Christmas trees in the living room and his dog Henry sleeping on the floor next to his bed. He couldn't help wondering how many people had owned the house in the last thirteen years. It didn't matter, living here was in the past, and he wanted to move on.

Peeling off his wet clothes he heard water running knowing Willow was in the shower.

Willow. Her soft, gentle touch and kind words had a calming effect on him. Unlike the past year he'd spent with Harley, where he'd always been on guard. A chill swept over him, grateful she was no longer part of his life.

After a quick shower, Terry arrived in the kitchen where Willow was preparing the table for dinner.

"Feels good to be warm and dry, doesn't it?"

"It does that for sure," he agreed, noticing her hair not completely dry and tucked behind her ears.

"I have beer and wine, red or white. Or," she added as an afterthought, "I have whiskey if you'd like."

His eyebrows arched in an agreeable expression. "Whiskey is tempting."

She didn't wait for him to add anything. "How about a shot to warm our insides before we eat? Then we can have wine or a beer if you want."

"Okay. I'm up for a shot," and ran splayed fingers through his damp hair.

"Sounds good to me too. It's in the cupboard." She pointed to the one on the left, where she kept liquor and bar glasses.

He liked that she gave him a task, making him feel useful. He poured whiskey into two shot glasses and held one out to Willow. "It's been an interesting day." He'd never imagined sleeping in her house tonight.

She nodded and stepped closer, then peered up into his eyes. "What shall we drink to?"

Terry was drawn in by her smile. Her expression held nothing back. He saw only kindness and caring. There's no way she would intentionally hurt him. He stared into her blue eyes that sparkled with laughter at the edges. A man could get lost in those eyes.

He realized she was waiting for him to speak, so Terry held out his glass. "Thank you," his voice sounding huskier than usual, so he tried to clear it. "Thank you for listening today and for renting me the apartment. Cheers," he said, then slugged back the shot as Willow did the same. He was impressed.

"You're welcome," she said, sincerely. "We're ready to eat."

~

Earlier, when Terry stepped in the kitchen, Willow thought he looked like a kid with his hair still damp and uncombed. A really cute kid. She relished spending time with this man as he held her chair, a man she hardly knew, but felt that would change. It already had. He'd shared parts of his past with her he might not have told anyone else. He confirmed there was more to come. She'd be patient, wanting him to feel comfortable opening up to her as she felt comfortable having him sleep in her house tonight. She could hear Norma ask why she didn't invite him to sleep in her bed, but it was too soon for her. She could see the longing on his face, and maybe he could see it on hers as well. If they were meant to sleep together, it'd happen under other circumstances and not because both were lonely and thrown together like this. As she thought about it, did they need a reason other than passion?

"I don't mind staying in the apartment tonight," he said. "I could have gone without water for the night."

Was he giving her a second chance to change her mind? Maybe, but Willow liked knowing she wouldn't be alone in the house. Norma was right; she wasn't one who could live on her own, not for long anyway.

"We'll get the water sorted out tomorrow and I have an empty guest room you may as well use." The whiskey had left a warm trail from her throat to her toes, heat rose up into her face and it wasn't just from the shot. Terry triggered sensations she hadn't felt in her body for way too long. She switched to beer and took a swig, hoping it would cool her off.

"I appreciate it." He exhaled, "I do look forward to sleeping without the sound of TV in the motel room next to mine."

Terry pulled a chair out for her at the kitchen table and they ate their chicken dinner, mashed potatoes with gravy, and steamed broccoli. "Have you and Norma been friends for a long time?"

She nodded, "Yes, we've been besties since middle school. Norma is brilliant. I'm encouraging her to pursue a doctorate in psychology."

"It's good to have a longtime friend you can always depend on, like my friendship with Tommy."

She wanted to stay put and continue to talk, but felt it'd been a long day. She reminded herself it was just this morning that Norma left.

They cleaned up the dishes, both stifling yawns, knowing it was time to say goodnight. The evening had been easy, they worked well together. She enjoyed doing things for him even if she was reheating take-away food.

"You know, when I was a kid, I dried the dishes mom had washed and set in the dish rack to drain. You store your silverware in the same drawer she did."

She reached over and laid her hand on his arm. "Well, that's pretty cool."

"You must be exhausted."

"I was just thinking to myself, 'it's been a long day,' but I've enjoyed your company. Thank you for buying dinner," she said, setting the towel down she'd been drying her hands with.

"Of course," he nodded gazing at her.

Willow thought he was going to say something more until he stepped closer and kissed her lightly on the corner of her mouth, his hand on her arm.

The kiss caught her by surprise, so soft, and sensual and way too brief. She wanted more, but warned herself, now wasn't the time.

She touched her arm where his hand had been. I'm in big trouble.

"Sleep well," he said, his voice warm and tender now.

Watching him head down the hall, she felt weak in the knees. Then let out a breath, "Terry, we forgot the sheets," she called after him. "I'm sure they're ready, I'll give you a hand."

"Right. Thanks, I can manage," he replied, then turned into the laundry room.

"Okay, kittens, let's go." She scooped up their dishes and they followed her into the bedroom, meowing the whole way.

Standing in the hot shower, Willow began rinsing her hair and thought she heard the door open and close. She turned then watched Terry strip out of his T-shirt and pajama bottoms before stepping into her shower.

His lust-filled eyes swept over every curve of her body, "You are so beautiful," he crooned, his voice full of passion. He pulled her silky wet body to him and began kissing her tenderly then more eagerly, holding her tight against him.

"Oh, Cowboy," she moaned, wrapping her arms around his neck.

Willow's eyes flew open, and the sound of footsteps in the hall brought her upright. Breathing hard, she fell back on the bed, thinking how vivid that dream had been, disappointed it was just a dream. She was so sure he'd been in the shower with her and could still feel him kissing her and her kissing him back.

"Wow, I've got it bad. Either that or I'm just horny," she murmured. If he looks as good naked in reality as he did in my dream...okay, let's refocus.

Her cell said seven-thirty when she opened a text from Norma, who seemed to be enjoying her road trip east. She shot off a brief reply then threw back the comforter. Willow quickly dressed, brushed her teeth and tried to tame her snarly bed-head hair, pulling it into a ponytail before stepping into the hall.

The guest room door was open, but there was no sign of Terry. She put coffee on and saw his truck still parked beside the garage. Heading to the apartment, she sprinted up the stairs, deciding to knock instead of walking in unannounced. She heard him approach and open the door.

"Good morning," she said in a groggy voice.

He stepped aside to allow her to enter. "Hope I didn't wake you."

She absolutely loved the way he looked at her in that suggestive, admiring way. And that sexy voice, he does know how to turn a girl on. She couldn't help seeing him naked in her shower dream this morning, then reluctantly shook the vision from her head. "I have coffee brewing and I'll see what I have to go with it."

"Or, I could take you to breakfast. I need a screwdriver to put the platform together, but I was able to turn the water on outside and both faucets work fine."

"Oh, great." She was relieved it was easily resolved. "I just might have a screwdriver. I'll go have a look."

"Wait. Come and see if you think I have the bed in the right place."

It felt like they were moving into this place together, sending a warm glow into every nook and cranny of her body. Taking in the position of the closet and bathroom door, Willow said, "Yes, I think that's probably the only wall you can put the bed against." She continued to survey the room. "It really is small now that the bed is set up, might be enough room for a chest of drawers."

"It's perfect for now, I appreciate you offering it to me."

They were quiet for a few moments, gazing at each other before Terry ran his hand across his mouth, "I'll help you find that screwdriver."

"Yes, we should go." Is it warm in here or is it just me? She thought. "Coffee will be ready too."

He followed her out the door and down the stairs.

The warm kitchen welcomed them with the smell of freshly brewed coffee. Willow filled the mugs she'd set out along with the last of the homemade chocolate chip cookies on a plate. "Help yourself. There's almond milk in the fridge. I'll check on that screwdriver."

Off she went to the laundry room and found two she hoped would work for him. "Are either of these what you need?"

He looked at her and grinned. "You're amazing and this one," he took the small Phillips from her hand, "would be perfect if it were a little bigger."

"Darn," she exclaimed, hands on her hips. "Guess we have to go to town."

They drank their coffee and ate cookies while Willow made a short shopping list of things Terry thought he might need. By late morning, the sky was dark, and hinting of more rain. Both grabbed a jacket before heading outside.

As they rode along Willow was aware that Terry had glanced at her a couple of times. She looked over at him and said, "What?"

"I can hear the wheels turning."

Willow's eyes narrowed while she listened. "But that's good isn't it? The wheels turning, I mean. I don't hear any weird noise."

Terry chucked, "I meant the ones in your head."

"Oh," her brows furrowed, and she giggled. "Was it that obvious?"

"Uh huh. Want to share?"

She tipped her head not sure she wanted to tell him what she'd been thinking. Willow was enjoying being with him in a big way. They were only out shopping for a screwdriver, but it felt more than that to her.

"For the past two months I've spent most of my days and sometimes evenings writing. It's lonely work. Just me and the kitties," she sighed. "Then I started using 'voice' in my writing program so I could hear a voice other than my own reading my words back to me. I like the reader with the British accent."

"Wow, that's interesting."

"What I'm trying to say is," giving him a sideways glance, "I'm enjoying being out with you."

"I'm glad," he said reaching over to touch her hand. "I feel the same."

The hardware store had everything on their list. Willow thought about her dad when she watched Terry take two more trips around the store, just to make sure he saw every tool on display. The kid in the candy store thing. As they walked to the truck, Willow suggested they stop at the supermarket since her cupboard was looking bare.

"How about a drive out to Pine Lake first? In case you buy anything that needs to be kept cold," he said.

"I'd love that."

"Why don't we pick up some fast food before we head out of town? An early picnic lunch, since we didn't have much breakfast?"

"Sounds great," she replied, feeling content being with Terry. She could get used to spending more time with him. Willow had work to do, but things would go back to normal tomorrow, and she could easily catch up.

After placing their order at the drive-up speaker, Terry paid the fresh-faced kid who handed over their food.

There wasn't a soul at the lake when they arrived under cloudy skies, only a shaft of sunlight shining on the alpine lake village. "This is beautiful, and so quaint," Willow said, taking it all in.

"It is beautiful and has many memories for me. All good," he added. "I've been out here almost every day since I got back. I feel connected here, a feeling I don't really have in town since so much of it has changed." He rolled down the window and took a deep breath. "It just smells good out here."

Willow rolled down her window and took a breath, too. The earthy scent of damp bark and pine needles was refreshing. "I had no idea this existed, or I would have come here to write."

"It isn't a good idea to come out here alone. Wait until the store opens, there'll be more people around, just in case a bear or mountain lion are out looking for food."

"Oh, I hadn't thought about that." Willow felt a shiver run up her spine. She looked out the side window to see if a bear might be watching them.

She understood why he loved it here. Besides being picturesque, it was peaceful and inspiring. The perfect place to write. She sighed as a family of deer stepped out of the dense forest and walked toward the water's edge. The lake was obviously special to Terry, and the fact he wanted to share it with her made her feel special.

"What about the people who still live here? Have you reconnected with anyone?"

"Tommy Logan, the sheriff who pulled you over. I stayed in touch with him while I was gone, called every year on his birthday. And, there's Brenda at Red Kettle. The three of us went through school together. I've yet to see Sheriff Bonner, and I have to stop putting it off. He became my legal guardian before I left."

He was quiet then, and Willow allowed him time to relive whatever it was he was thinking about.

"His wife died a couple years ago, and I heard he has Alzheimer's. Part of me wants to remember him the way he was, but that's pretty selfish of me."

"Maybe, but it's understandable." She watched him nod as he stared out the windshield, seemingly deep in thought. "Hungry?" she asked, getting his attention.

"Sorry. Yes, starving." He unbuckled his seatbelt, opened the door, and reached for the bag of food.

Chapter 8

*H*ow's this?" Terry asked pointing to a picnic table just ahead then turning to look at Willow for approval.

"It's perfect. Lovely view of the lake and the mountains."

They sat opposite one another and Terry opened the bag out to use as a tablecloth. They dug in, savoring every bite.

"I haven't had fast food in so long," Willow declared. "I try to stay away from it, but this tastes really good."

Terry chuckled at her, enjoying the first of his two burgers.

"Are you an only child?"

He nodded as he chewed.

"Me too. I always wanted a brother. Dad thought my ex-husband would be the closest he'd come to having a son." She looked over at Terry, "Might be the reason he didn't see through to the real Chet."

Terry arched his brows, "Yeah, maybe. I wanted a brother too. It would've helped. I probably wouldn't have gone away."

"Where did you go and why did you leave if you love it here so much?"

"Australia. I went back to the cattle station where I worked during my 4-H trip. When I got home, I saw Noreen Purvis was living in my parents' bedroom. I couldn't stand the sight of her, so I moved into the barn." She'd been way too comfortable taking his mother's place. "I tried to talk to Dad about it, but he said I'd understand when I was older. I couldn't imagine what in the world he saw in her.

"About a month later, when I got home from school, I saw a phone message Noreen left me. It said I was needed out at Durant Farms, ASAP." Terry told her he searched for his father to tell him where he was going but couldn't find him even though his truck was there. He didn't trust Noreen to tell his father where he'd gone.

"It's fifteen miles to the farm so I road my motorcycle, and when I got there my friend Josh didn't know who would've called and left such a message. He thought it must've been a mistake. All the hair on the back of my neck stood on end. I lit out of there and raced home.

"When I reached town, I could see smoke off in the distance and assumed it was a forest fire. The closer I got to the house, the faster I went. I turned onto the driveway and saw the barn engulfed in flames." Terry swallowed hard; his voice shaky. "I slammed on the brakes sliding to a stop."

He took a breath and raked both hands through his hair to keep from screaming, reliving that awful moment.

"I ran to the barn and tugged on the door, but it wouldn't budge. I couldn't understand why it wouldn't open and then I panicked. The door had to be blocked somehow. I had to make sure my dad wasn't inside, so I rammed my shoulder against the door, kicked it, but it wouldn't give. Cell reception was terrible in those days, so I ran to the house to call for help and saw Noreen standing on the porch with her arms folded, a smirk on her face." He'd shoved her aside to get into the house then heard sirens. He turned back and grabbed Noreen by the shoulders, shook her and yelled, "What in God's name have you done?"

"She just stood there with a hideous look on her face and said, 'I guess it's just you and me now, sweet boy.' I started toward the barn again as the sirens got closer and the roof caved in." He remembered falling to his knees, retching, holding his head in his hands, rocking back and forth, feeling helpless and totally lost.

He laid his hand on Willow's. "Thank you. I know this isn't easy to hear, but I appreciate you listening."

"Of course," she said, nearly in tears. "What a horrible thing to go through by yourself. You were so young."

He continued, "When the fire trucks pulled in, the barn was a total loss. They hosed down the side closest to the house to keep it from igniting." He sat up straighter, aware he was slumped over the table.

"When Sheriff Bonner showed up, I told him about the note and driving out to Durant Farms then finding out it was all a scheme. They wanted to get me out of the way so she and Billy could murder my father."

"Oh God, Terry. Was your father in the barn?"

He nodded and let out a ragged breath. "I was able to identify the Saint Christopher dad wore."

Her eyes glistening with tears, Willow reached over and took his hand in hers, "I'm so sorry."

"I couldn't save him," he said as that old guilt and despair resurfaced.

"Terry you did everything you could."

"Yeah, I guess," he said and hunched his shoulders. "But I've hated knowing it wasn't enough."

She agreed, "I can imagine," then released his hand. "So, who's Billy?"

Terry gave a wry chuckle, "Noreen's stupid brother." He saw movement out of the corner of his eye and pointed to one of the pine trees nearby. "See that squirrel?"

She turned, and watched it race up the tree.

"That squirrel has more brains than Billy had." He shifted on the bench seat. "He'd been helping round the property while I was gone. Dad kept him on, said Noreen thought it would be good for him to stay."

"Okay, but what about Noreen? Did they arrest her after what you told them?"

He appreciated her inquisitive mind and wanted her to hear about the trial from him instead of town gossip, if there was any. His feelings for Willow grew stronger each day, and he didn't want to keep anything from her.

Clearing his throat, he continued. "They questioned her, but she didn't make any sense. She changed her story several times within a few minutes. I told the

Sheriff to ask her where Billy was and she said, 'Yes, it was Billy who did this. He murdered my husband.' Another lie; they were never married. But she said it without any emotion. They took her in and began a manhunt for Billy Purvis, but he just disappeared. I was hoping he'd died in the fire too, but they didn't find a second body. No one knows to this day where he went." He shook his head, "I guess he was smarter than anyone gave him credit for."

"And was she charged with murder?"

"Yes. After giving my statement and talking with a few people in town, she was charged and went to jail over in Cody until the trial. Investigators could see where the barn door had been blocked to keep anyone on the outside from opening it. They found the origin of the fire and it'd been deliberately set."

"Did you testify at the trial?"

"Yeah." He was quiet for a few minutes. His expression turned almost menacing as he remembered sitting next to the prosecuting attorney, listening to Noreen testify. "She lied, and I couldn't stand to hear her anymore." Again, he sat quiet, then, "I stood up and yelled at the judge that she was lying. He slammed his gavel down and warned my attorney to keep me quiet or I'd be removed from the courtroom." He raised his voice, "It seemed so unfair that she could lie like that, and I had to be quiet."

When Willow put her hand on his arm, he pulled away, positive it was the attorney trying to get him to sit down.

He exhaled a deep sigh. "Noreen told the court we were in love and that I helped her set the barn on fire. I helped her kill my father!" He scrutinized Willow's face for some consolation. He needed to know she couldn't believe he would ever do such a heinous thing.

"She said we wanted to get rid of both my parents so we could be together and have the house and property."

"But no one believed her, did they?" Willow said quietly.

He turned his focus on her, puzzled by what she'd said then realized he had been seventeen again, reliving that day.

"No. No one believed her. But she'd said something so unthinkable, so disgusting right out loud in the courtroom for everyone to hear." He stared at something beyond Willow's shoulder. "That's the reason I had to leave," he spoke as though he'd never thought about it that way. "I couldn't face all those people who just might wonder if it were true." His gaze fell to his tightly clamped fists wishing he could go back and tell that young boy everything would be all right.

"Terry," Willow spoke softly, "You said Noreen wanted to get rid of both your parents. Are you saying she killed your mother as well?"

"It was never proven, but, yes," he said. "I'd bet my life on it."

"Why do you say that?"

"Mom had been ill with a bad case of flu. She went to the doctor and he gave her a prescription. She seemed to improve until Noreen came to visit and made tea for her."

He sat up straight looking off in the distance, recalling every detail as if it had happened yesterday. He slowly shook his head then relaxed, "I don't know how, but I think she put something in Mom's tea. Noreen washed their cups, dried them and put them back in the cupboard. Mom told her not to bother, she'd done enough to help her, she'd said. But Noreen insisted and maybe it was just a neighborly thing to do, but it made me suspicious."

"Yes. I can understand why you'd think that. It doesn't matter now though, does it? Since she's in prison, I mean."

He shook his head, "No. It was premeditated. She's in for life. In the end she confessed to plotting my father's murder. She revealed every detail of how she and Billy lured Dad into the barn, blocking the door and buying two cans of gas to start the fire." When the station owner recognized her photo in the paper the following day, he called the police and told them she bought the gas from him."

Terry ran a hand down his face, then arched his back. "My attorney thought she confessed to appear clever and smart."

"She sounds like a sick woman."

He nodded, needing to get the rest of this nightmare out in the open. "Even though I was perfectly capable of taking care of myself, I was underage. It was just six months before my eighteenth birthday and high school graduation. So, Sheriff Bonner and his wife Jody took me in without even asking. One of them was always with me. They became my court appointed legal guardians and I moved into their house."

Terry had protested, wanting to go back to his home and stay, yet not really wanting to go into the house. Not after Noreen had poisoned it for him.

"Sheriff Clay Bonner said, 'the law is the law' and social services would see to it that I was at the Bonner's for dinner every night and wake up there every morning. No exceptions." Terry smiled, remembering their kindness when he needed it most.

He didn't see the tears rolling down Willow's face, her hand covering her mouth as she quietly sobbed.

"I was told I could go back to the house when I needed to get stuff I might want; music, some photographs and my clothes, of course. When I went, I couldn't get out of the house fast enough. She not only killed my parents, but she took away my home." He was numb thinking about that moment when his life didn't resemble even one aspect of what it'd once been. He hung his head, not liking that feeling of hopelessness he thought he'd left behind.

Willow stood and stepped around the table to sit beside him, wrapping him in her arms. He responded by leaning into her when she pressed her cheek against his face.

Putting his arm around her, he pulled her close. "You're shaking," he said. "Are you cold or are you upset by what I've told you?"

"A little of both," she said with a weak smile then took his hand again. "You should be proud of yourself for what you've accomplished the past thirteen years. Not many young men could've succeeded after what you'd been through. But, that's all behind you. You're home now and you have a wonderful future ahead of you."

She's right, Terry thought. I can't do anything about what happened thirteen years ago. No point in carrying that tragedy around any longer. It will always be in my mind, but I'll only focus on good times with Mom and Dad from now on.

A huge weight lifted off him. Willow had listened without judgement and helped purge him of the awful guilt and memories he'd carried far too long.

He turned to look at her, smiling in agreement. "The other day when I said I was lucky to meet you, I meant it."

She laid her head on his shoulder, "I appreciate that."

"You have no idea how much better I feel." She was right, he was home for good and would build a life here again.

Cold air swirled around them as a stiff breeze kicked up, ruffling Willow's hair. She looked beautiful, so natural, he thought.

"Maybe we better go," he said, realizing the sun was hidden by dark clouds, but for a moment he wasn't even sure what day or what time it was. He stepped over the bench seat and helped her up, then pulled her into his arms. He looked down into her light blue eyes glistening with sweet anticipation. He gently kissed her lips for several seconds, then she put her arms around his neck and kissed him back.

He was a goner. Lost in the sensation of her body pressed against him, lost to the pleasure she evoked in him. He tightened his hold on her, enjoying the warmth they generated.

They flinched as hail pelted them. Terry gathered the remains of their picnic tossing it in the trash as they ran to the truck.

Once inside, the sound was deafening as hail came down in a deluge. They gazed at one another and started giggling. "You just need some flowers in your damp hair, and you'd look like a wood nymph," he said before smoothing some stands away from her face. He so wanted to help her out of her clothes. "You are something else, Willow James."

~

Willow pulled her jacket tight around her while
Terry started the truck and cranked up the heater.
She couldn't remember being kissed with such sweet,
eager passion. He'd turned her into a gelatinous mass;
she was thankful he had a firm hold on her when her
legs felt weak. She wanted him, but caution lights
were going off in her head until she realized it was
just lightening. She giggled, and Terry leaned toward
her taking her face in his hands and kissing her deeply,
their tongues dancing.

When he pulled back, she sighed, "Oh, don't stop.
We were just getting started."

"Why did I buy a truck with a console?"

"We're not teenagers," she said playfully, gazing into
those dark blue eyes set in that very handsome face.

"Right now, I feel like one," he said, and fastened his
seat belt, not taking his eyes off her.

Willow's body was buzzing with desire. She was
definitely falling for this guy and wanted his hands all
over her. For now, she'd settle for her hand in his and
rested her arm on the console.

She watched him chew on the inside of his mouth,
his gaze full of lust. He sighed, put the truck in gear
then reached for her hand and held on all the way
back to town.

They stopped at the supermarket and bought steaks,
veggies, potatoes, and a bottle of bubbly. Her eyes lit
up when he put the champagne in the shopping cart.
"Umm, my favorite."

"I feel like celebrating. I'm not as apprehensive about being back in Elk Valley as I was. I feel better about everything, and I have you to thank for that."

She was pleased he felt that way. "I'm a good listener. Something I learned at the paper, but more importantly, I wanted to hear your story."

They headed for the truck with two grocery bags of food. He made quick time getting back to her place, too quick apparently. Sheriff Logan was behind them lights flashing, and siren blaring.

"Bloody hell, that's just what I don't need right now," Terry pulled off the road abruptly and came to a stop then opened the door to step out, forgetting to unbuckle his seatbelt.

"Shit! Sorry."

Sheriff Logan was beside the open door as Terry struggled to step out. "Good afternoon," he offered, bending to peer in at Willow, and tugged on the brim of his hat.

"Sheriff," she nodded. Terry was seething, and it made her smile.

The sheriff closed the truck door and leaned on the window frame when Terry rolled it down. "Nice truck, Terry," he offered, checking it out.

"Hey Bud, what's up? Are you going to give me a ticket for driving five miles over the speed limit? I know you didn't pull me over just to admire my truck."

"Well, no, as a matter of fact I pulled you over to give you a friendly reminder to drive careful in this storm. Supposed to get more hail and maybe some snow in higher elevations."

"Mighty thoughtful of you, Sheriff, but I believe I have things under control."

Tommy reached in and gave Terry's shoulder a squeeze. "Yeah, I believe you do." He eyeballed Willow again. "You two have a nice evening now." With a tug on his hat brim, he turned and walked back to his patrol car.

Terry started the truck, "Sorry about that." He signaled and checked for traffic then pulled back out on the road.

"He certainly is dedicated to keeping the roads safe in this town." She was amused by the brief exchange these two old friends shared.

"Oh, yeah, he's a real do-gooder."

"Maybe he did just want to admire your truck."

"He admired it yesterday morning when we had breakfast together. What he wanted to do was admire my passenger." He glanced over at Willow's smiling face, "Are you sure you can't get any closer?"

She rested her arm on the console again, and he covered her hand with his. This guy melts my insides, she mused to herself. He knows just the right thing to say in that sexy drawl with that sexy smile. She noticed he'd picked up the drawl recently, replacing the slight Aussie accent he'd had the first day she met him. She was anxious to hear the rest of that story, but for now she was happy just to be with him and couldn't help wondering where it would lead. No matter, enjoy this time with him. Norma was right, she didn't need to be in a hurry to get into a relationship, but it seemed like that's what it was becoming, and she felt good about it.

Chapter 9

The kittens were excited to see them when they stepped into the kitchen. Willow put her purse on the counter and sat on the floor to play with them, but what they really wanted was dinner. They'd already grown some and she needed to feed them constantly to keep up with their energy and growth.

Terry set the grocery bags on the counter then watched while Willow played with the kittens. He stooped and scratched the top of Midnight's little head. "They sure are cute. I'm glad you have them to keep you company."

She looked up at him as he stood. "They're so much fun. Ouch," she said, startled as Stormy grabbed at her hand with those needle-sharp claws. "Okay, I'll feed you."

Terry chuckled. "You okay?" he asked, offering his hand to help her up.

"Yeah, just a scratch."

"I'm going up to the apartment. Be back in a bit to help with dinner."

When Terry closed the kitchen door Willow thought about the story he shared with her out at the lake. She couldn't imagine losing both her parents when she was a teenager, especially in such a violent way. Hearing those lies Noreen told in court must have been unbearable for a seventeen-year-old boy.

She thought about him running away from the home he loved and returning to Australia where he had friends and happy memories. Who could blame him? He seems to have all the confidence in the world now that he's back home planning his future.

When Terry stepped back into Willow's kitchen, she had the champagne on ice and was preparing the vegetables to roast. "Did you get your bed set up?"

"Yes. It's beginning to feel like home to me," he added.

She turned toward him, her hip against the counter. "You were cautious about your name and your background when I met you. Was that so folks here wouldn't associate you with what happened thirteen years ago?" Now that she'd heard more of his story, she was beginning to understand his logic.

"I was," he paused, searching for the right word. "Paranoid about coming back and having all that old stuff dredged up again. Foolish, I know. It was a long time ago. I didn't want to relive any of it again with a new audience." He was quiet a moment while Willow continued to cut up potatoes.

"You may remember I was evasive when I met you, and you said you were a writer. I'd always worried someone would write a story about what happened. I know I couldn't stop it, but I don't have to participate in it."

"Yes, I remember. It made me want to know more about you. Had you heard someone wanted to write a story about your father's murder trial?" She was intrigued.

"Yeah, Tommy told me a few months ago someone was poking around, asking questions, which is one of the reasons I made the decision to come home."

"Was it difficult for you to leave everything you'd come to know and return to the U.S., to Wyoming?"

"Very, and mostly because I didn't know what to expect. I had a nice life there. I had friends, I was a partner in the cattle station, which I loved and a couple other ventures as well. But I felt if I didn't leave when I did, I might not ever come back and couldn't imagine that."

"Did you have a girlfriend there?" She was curious to hear the answer.

"More of a friend. Her name is Harley, but I was ready to end the relationship. She was a bit rough around the edges and had become possessive." He crossed his arms, settled against the counter.

So, he didn't bring Harley with him because she was possessive, Willow pondered. Then thought about the past couple of days hoping she hadn't sounded that way. But what does possessive sound like? Hmm. I'll remember that...But I can only be myself.

"I don't miss my life there. I'm happy to be home. This is where I belong."

"I'm sure your parents would want you to be back here as well."

"I think so. I certainly feel a connection to them here."

She watched his gaze hit the floor, most likely wishing his parents were here to welcome him home.

Willow hadn't meant to make him feel melancholy and decided to change the subject.

"So, Terry, what are your plans?" Willow gave him a sideways glance as she began cutting a tomato for their salad. "You mentioned wanting to buy property. Will you raise cattle like you did in Australia?"

"Yes," he said eagerly. "Grass fed beef. Thanks for asking. I'm going to see some acreage tomorrow and having a second look at property I'm very keen on. If I buy it, we'd be neighbors."

Willow liked hearing the excitement in his voice. "Neighbors would be nice," She said. Unless they had a falling out, then it'd be miserable. She didn't want to believe all men were a disappointment like Chet had been. And still is, she reminded herself. Don't bring that into my friendship with Terry, she scolded that negative voice in her head.

"Was your father a cattle rancher?" She didn't think so since he'd never mentioned it.

"No, he came from three generations of farmers in Southern France."

"Really? What did they farm?" He does have a fascinating background.

"Lavender. My grandfather, aunts and uncles, and several cousins grow lavender and they have a farm stand selling everything lavender; Honey, jam, something called potpourri, tea, and soap." With a wave of his hand he added, "Other things I can't remember right now."

His description left a charming imprint in her mind. "So, you've been there and seen the farm and everything?"

"Uh-huh. I was twelve when we last went there."

"That's wonderful." She was happy to learn he had family even though they were an ocean away. "What brought your father to the states?"

"Dad and his older brother came over to expand the family business. Since much of what they export comes here, they decided to establish a lavender farm in Michigan, and once it was producing, my uncle went back to France. Dad managed the farm for several years then sold it. He traveled until settling in Wyoming after meeting my mother in a gift shop in Grand Teton National Park. They were married, bought this property, your property, and the rest is history."

Willow pulled in a breath, "How romantic."

"Yeah. I guess it is." Terry said. "I don't think they knew each other very long."

Willow felt warm and cozy in her kitchen listening to Terry while preparing their dinner. Then she reflected on what he'd said and realized the extent of owning Terry's former family home, and what it might mean to him. Surely, he doesn't expect me to sell it back to him. I love my house. I've done some of my best work at the kitchen table, and out on the deck. She searched Terry's face for a sign of regret that she owned the house, adding to the despair he already felt at losing both his parents, then his home.

"Terry," she said, feeling prickly. "How do you feel about me owning your family's home?"

He shrugged his shoulders, "Well, knowing you gives me a chance to be here in the house. Even though it's changed. I like that you've made it your home, and you seem happy here."

"I love this house. It's perfect for me, and you're welcome to come here anytime."

"Well, I think we should drink to that," he said reaching for the bottle that had been chilling on ice.

Willow handed him a small towel and watched as he wiped it down. The smattering of dark hair on the back of his hands caught her eye as he untwisted the wire cage and removed the foil. They were the hands of a man who spent most of his time outdoors, tanned and calloused. She could still feel those callouses when she'd taken his hand yesterday. Then she tried to remember what his hands felt like when he held her in his arms at the lake. She wanted to tell him to stop what he was doing and hold her, like he was holding the bottle of champagne.

Terry rotated the bottle until the cork popped out, making an impressive sound for a small object, bringing her back to the moment. Her body heated and she felt a little lightheaded without even tasting the champagne.

"Well done," she said enjoying the sound of the champagne cork popping. "This isn't your first time," she added.

"No, it isn't." He filled each flute to one-third, letting the fizz die down before topping off the glasses.

"You don't seem like a champagne kind of guy." She eyed him curiously.

"Something I picked up on my trip to Australia."

"That must mean you didn't fly."

"You don't miss a thing, do you?" he grinned. "No, you're right. I hopped a freighter out of Galveston,

Texas and the captain had champagne almost every night. I developed a taste for it and learned how to open it the way the French intended."

"Sounds like quite an adventure for a young man." She wanted to hear more but knew it had already been an emotional day for him. Time to chill.

"I look forward to hearing more about your journey sometime."

"Sure, maybe later."

She wanted to kiss him in that moment and knew he could see it on her face.

Willow cleared her throat, "Let's go outside and make sure the barbecue fires up. I haven't used it since I bought it," she revealed before opening the refrigerator to pull out the goat cheese she'd placed on a small tray.

He reached for both their jackets, as he helped Willow with hers, his hand brushed against her neck sending chills down her body. He rubbed her arms through the jacket, "Are you sure you want to go outside? If you are already cold, I can handle the grill."

"No, I'm fine." Willow was definitely feeling warm.

He took their glasses while she carried the cheese and small basket of crackers as they stepped out the kitchen door into the chilly evening.

Terry and Willow moved toward the covered grill, setting their drinks and tray on a small table then pulled the cover off draping it over the deck railing. Willow opened the cabinet under the grill and turned on the propane tank, and Terry lit all three burners.

"Looks like we're good to grill," he said feeling heat begin to rise across the burners before closing the lid.

He handed her one of the glasses then took hold of his glass when she spoke.

"I'm really pleased for you, Terry. You went through so much as a young man, losing everything you had, everything that was familiar. I'm sure your parents would be very proud of you."

"Thank you."

They clinked glasses and took a sip.

"It's lucky we both like coffee or we might not have met."

When Willow shivered Terry took the glass out of her hand, and set both glasses on the railing. He pulled her close, enclosing her in the safety of his arms, running his big hands up and down her back in an attempt to warm her core.

"Mmm, thanks," she said, snuggling against his chest.

"No, thank you for being cold," he said.

She looked up at him with dreamy eyes as his warm exhale floated across her ear. He took her face in his hands, planting his hungry mouth on her soft, warm lips. She kissed him back with the same eagerness.

"You have too many clothes on," he whispered, his lips still on her mouth.

"You are dangerous, Thierry Du Champs," she said, pronouncing his name with a French accent. Feeling warm in all the right places, pretty sure she was ready for what might come next.

She felt his body go ridged.

"Why am I dangerous?" He said, pulling back. "I would never hurt you."

"A little danger is good; don't you think? Keeps you on your toes." Okay, you're being too flippant for him, she said to herself. You're not in California. Ratchet back a bit.

"I have a different view of danger."

She cringed, "Yes, I know you do." Wanting to smooth things out she added, "I haven't been intimate with a man for nearly five months. I'm just nervous."

"Okay. No need to be nervous," he said, holding her so he could look at her face. "It's just you and me here," pulling her close again.

The look of lust on his face did crazy, wonderful things to her insides. "I find you very comfortable and easy to be with. I like this, being in your arms, but it also scares me."

"The last thing I want to do is scare you. Do you want me to leave?"

"No, of course not." She wanted to continue to get to know him but didn't want to be disappointed again so soon after her divorce. She could hear Norma, "Stop talking and let the man have his way with you. You know it's what you want. Go for it, girlfriend." So Norma!

He was silent a moment. "Okay. Are you saying you just want to be friends, no hugging or kissing or any of the other really good stuff? Because I want it all. I want all of you, but not if you don't want me in the same way."

"No," she quickly said and reminded herself, You're not shopping for a groom, forget what happened between you and Chet. "I want those things, too. We're adults and definitely attracted to one another. Why shouldn't we see where this goes?" If it goes further, great. If not most likely one of us will be very unhappy.

But shouldn't we at least find out? Again, she heard her friend, this time yelling, "Go for it, girlfriend!"

"Terry." She jolted back to the moment.

"What?"

"I want to rip your clothes off as much as you want to rip off mine. You and I have a strong pull to one another, not unlike the scenery that brought you back here," she said, sweetly. "I sense it and I believe you do too."

"Well put." He kissed her lips with desperate need and she melted into him. He released her from his grip to turn off the grill then steered her toward the kitchen door, his arm firmly across her back, in a protective way.

The heat from his hand felt like a hot summer day through her jacket. She half expected to find a scorch mark. They stepped inside and hung their jackets on the hook by the door.

"I'll just cover the steaks and put them in the fridge." Willow said, her voice cracking slightly.

He could only nod then saw the champagne in the ice bucket. "We're taking this with us," he said wickedly. "Crap. Our glasses are out on the railing. I'll go get them."

Willow stopped him before he headed back outside. "There are more where those came from," she said playfully.

Terry went to the cupboard where he'd gotten the shot glasses the night before. With two clean glasses in his hands, he went to her, pulling her close, glasses clinking behind her back. She put her arms around his neck and stood on her toes to kiss him tenderly. He let out a groan and they walked down the hall arms around each other.

"These glasses won't be of any use without the champagne," he said with a goofy grin.

She laughed and hurried back for the ice bucket, setting it on the chest of drawers next to the two glasses after closing the bedroom door. Terry sat on the edge of the bed and pulled his boots off, not taking his eyes off Willow. She kicked off her shoes and started to pull her sweater off, but he stopped her.

"No you don't," he said, slowly shaking his head. "That's my job." He stood and began kissing her again, his hands roaming over her, then finding warm tender skin under the sweater, his hand cupping her right lace-covered breast, all the while devouring her mouth.

Willow felt the sensation of floating, her head reeling, completely at his mercy. He was in control, she was only a passenger and what a ride. No man had ever caused such heat coursing through her body.

He lifted the sweater over her head then reconnected with her mouth as his hands found the button and zipper of her jeans. He tugged them down her slender hips. She didn't offer any help. She wanted him to undress her, but she wanted him to hurry. "No," she shook her head, "don't hurry."

"We're not going to rush this," he whispered reassuringly, his lips on hers.

She wasn't aware she'd spoken out loud.

He continued kissing her, moving to her neck and the hollow of her throat, sending thrill bumps all the way to her toes.

He let out a guttural groan when his hands moved lower and brushed the thong she was wearing. He continued kissing her while caressing her bare bum, then reached up, unhooked her bra, and she shook herself out of it. Tugging his shirt out of his jeans, she ripped it open before realizing it had buttons and not snaps like most western style shirts. A button hit the chest of drawers. There was silence, then giggles. He pulled the shirt off while Willow was busy with his belt.

Terry turned her around, laid her on the bed, and pulled the jeans off from around her ankles. She watched while his eyes slowly roamed over her before pulling a condom from the pocket of his jeans then yanked them off.

Willow rose up on her elbows to take him in. *He's more magnificent than in my dream.* The tan on his perfect physique rivaled any Chippendale stripper she'd ever seen and could now erase her bachelorette party from the fantasy file in her head. He was ready for her, big time.

"You have a gorgeous body," he said each word with importance, placing one knee on the bed supporting himself over her. She knew she could trust him when he asked, "Are you OK with this?"

She reached up, laced her fingers through his hair pulling him close, "Yes." That became her favorite word long into the night. Her thong stripped away, they began slow, sweet love making until their pace became blistering. She was glad not to have neighbors when she heard herself shout Terry's name. More giggles in the darkness.

So much for taking things slowly.

They dozed on and off in between getting their legs and arms intertwined, enjoying each other. They even stopped for a sip of champagne, but it took away from what both really wanted. There wasn't much left of Willow that Terry's tongue hadn't tasted. Her little sobs of ecstasy let him know she was as satisfied as he felt.

~

Terry gathered Willow into his arms and rolled her over on top of him where she lay like a puppet who'd lost its strings. She was completely spent. Her head on his big chest, she mumbled, but he couldn't quite make out her words. Something about lost count of orgasms. He chuckled, feeling pretty much the same. He was totally at peace and loved that she seemed to be as well. Is this what love feels like or it is lust being sated? He wanted it to be both. Doesn't matter right now, he thought and drifted off to sleep.

Chapter 10

erry woke as daylight lit the windows. His left hand was asleep, his arm extended serving as a pillow for Sleeping Beauty.

What an amazing night, he reflected, grinning like a fool, feeling incredibly happy. A night I'll never forget. No matter what happens between us.

He slowly withdrew his arm from under her head, pulling a pillow in for her instead. She didn't move a muscle, so he stayed put, watching her sleep. He couldn't stop looking at her and smiling, enjoying how perfect her body fit into the curve of his.

Okay, time to get up, he reminded himself. Sitting on the edge of the bed, he pulled his clothes off the floor and quickly dressed then shoved his feet into his boots. He lightly kissed her on the cheek and quietly, but reluctantly, left her to sleep.

Terry stepped out the back door with his duffle bag and headed up to the apartment, but part way up something caught his eye. Some slight movement and a sound he couldn't identify; not a deer or coyote. It was the sound of a bigger footprint. He stood still, looking behind him, out across the yard to the house and down the driveway. He saw nothing. The only sounds now came from birds on the hunt for breakfast, but still, he felt uneasy.

"Harley," he whispered, continuing to survey the yard and beyond. Still nothing. Terry thought he'd gotten over worrying about being back in his hometown, but the idea of bringing something into Willow's life that might cause her harm, was intolerable. You're not making sense bud. Harley wouldn't know where to find me, he thought, trying to be logical and reassure himself.

Probably a bear or big cat he decided, but it wouldn't hurt to go lock Willow's back door. Dropping his duffel on the landing, he hurried down the stairs, letting himself into the kitchen, turning the lock in the knob. He checked the front door before stepping back outside then locked the deadbolt in the kitchen door with Willow's key.

Terry could hear his father, 'Locks are for honest people.' He realized how foolish it was to double lock the kitchen door since breaking the window would allow anyone to easily unlock it by reaching inside. But his overactive imagination kept him from leaving the door unsecured with Willow inside alone.

While living on the cattle station in Australia, he hadn't confided in anyone his fear of Harley, and what she might be capable of doing. During the months they were together, she had become more aggressive and possessive. He knew he'd have been razzed by his station mates, so he laughed off her obsession with him. Frankly, he had been anxious about her behavior and didn't sleep well.

He'd never known *anyone* who took such delight in killing an animal. She seemed to enjoy the cat and mouse game with a possum or other small animal. It made his skin crawl just thinking about it.

It was a huge mistake allowing her to stay after she moved her gear into his living quarters, uninvited. He should have ended it long before it got as far as it did.

Harley was not the soft tender woman he'd imagined curled up in his arms.

He sprinted back up to the apartment, locking the door before turning on the shower and stripping down. He hurried through his shower, toweled off, and pulled on clean clothes.

Grabbing his gray leather jacket and hat, he locked the door, pausing to scan the yard again before heading down the stairs to the house, just in case that bear or mountain lion was still wandering about. He let himself in, making his way down the hall then sat on the edge of Willow's bed, smoothing a thick strand of hair away from her face.

"It's too early to get up," she said in a sleepy voice, rolling onto her back.

He gently kissed each of her eyelids. "It's a beautiful, sunny morning."

"No, it's still dark," she said blissfully.

"If you'd open those baby blues, you'd see how bright it is."

"But I want it to still be nighttime with you lying next to me."

He snickered at her silliness. "I'd like that too, but I have an appointment with the realtor at nine, and I'm going to have breakfast before I meet up with her." He kissed her lightly on the mouth. "I'm starving. Last night's workout left me with a giant appetite and not just for food," he added, nibbling on her bottom lip.

Willow reached up to run the back of her fingers down his cheek before kissing him.

"You're gonna make me late," he said, kissing her back.

"That's my plan."

"Come on, I want you to lock the door when I leave."

Willow squinted up at him, puzzled, but sat up, realized she was still naked. "My robe is hanging on the door of the closet," she said, raking fingers through her hair.

She stood up so he could help her with the robe but wouldn't let her pull it closed. He stood there and admired her, then looked at his watch wondering if they had time for a quickie but knew it might turn into a couple of quickies. "Later," he resigned himself. "I need to get going."

They kissed again at the back door. Terry said he wanted her to see the property next door. "I should be back around eleven thirty."

"Yes," she smiled up at him. "I'd like to see it."

~

Willow watched him glance around while he walked to his truck, wondering what he was looking for, puzzled by his sudden concern to lock the doors.

An hour later, after showering, drying her hair, and applying mascara, she sat at the kitchen table, making notes about what she wanted to tell Sheriff McCauley in Santa Barbara. She found it difficult to focus on anything but Terry. Just thinking his name caused her insides to go all gooey. Even the kittens had to remind her they were part of the family, too.

She still had Mac's phone number in her cell and touched the screen, putting it on speaker so she could take notes, if needed.

"McCauley," the deep male voice barked.

She smiled. "Mac, it's me, Willow."

"Sorry, I don't know anyone by that name," he teased.

"I've been a busy girl, writing and settling in." And, falling for the most wonderful man, she wanted to add.

"Is this a social call or official business?"

"It is business."

"Can you talk to one of my deputies? I'm about to go into a meeting. I'll be a couple of hours."

"I'd prefer to talk with you."

"Can I call you later this afternoon?"

She and Terry would most likely be thrashing around on her mattress later today. Her cheeks heated, even though there was no way Mac knew what she was thinking. She cleared her throat, "Yes, I'll be available."

"OK, good to talk to you." He disconnected.

"Another man of few words," she said to the kittens when they came into the kitchen to lay at her feet. "But, a great guy in the perfect job for him. The citizens of Santa Barbara are lucky to have him protecting them." Willow rolled her eyes and leaned back in the chair, remembering the embarrassment of her high school crush on Mac.

As senior class president, she'd introduced Mac at the assembly where he spoke to the graduating class about zero drug and alcohol tolerance on grad night. She was captivated by his boyishly handsome face set in a serious, no nonsense expression.

There was an air of confidence and authority about him. His wide stance was all business; feet planted firmly on stage, pistol on his hip and that shiny star over his left breast pocket. He was prepared for whatever came his way. The Kevlar bullet proof vest added to his naturally solid stature. Hearing applause brought Willow out of her dreamy-eyed trance. She remembered some of her classmates laughing and a few guys let out jeering remarks.

Over the next couple of years, Willow and Sheriff Mac ran into one another at a number of city functions where he introduced her to his wife and children. She wanted to tell Mrs. McCauley she was a lucky woman, but seeing them together, Willow was pretty sure she already knew that. It wasn't until her senior year at UC Santa Barbara that she was finally able to say hello to him without blushing.

As an investigative reporter for the local newspaper, Willow responded to traffic accidents, robberies or other incidents that came over the police scanner on her desk. Mac got to know her, trusted her no frills writing style. He would give her a little bit of information he hadn't shared with any other reporter, reminding her, "You didn't hear it from me."

She had a good rapport with Mac but knew she couldn't share her suspicions with one of his deputies.

Willow gathered up her iPad and a fresh cup of coffee before stepping out onto the deck where she settled in to write until Terry came for her.

Her heart fluttered. "I can't wait," she said.

She was fully focused on her writing, closing in on the last quarter of her novel when the sound of Terry's truck racing up the driveway and sliding to a sudden stop on the gravel got her attention. She set her work aside and went to the railing as he took the stairs two at a time. Without a word, he took her by the hand and pulled her into the house, pressed her up against the closed door, his mouth all over hers.

She giggled and unbuttoned her jeans while he did the same, pulling a condom from his wallet before casting his shirt off then helping her out of her T-shirt. They continued to strip down not taking their eyes off one another until Terry led her into the kitchen, and reached for a chair where he sat, pulling her astride of him.

She looked into those sexy dark blue eyes, and demanded, "Just who do you think you are barging into my home thinking you can have your way with me?" She moaned with delight as his mouth found her right breast, his hand on the other. After several minutes of enjoying her, Terry's hands moved to her bottom, he slipped inside her, pulling her tight against him.

"Why Miss James, I do believe you are happy to see me." He kissed her passionately while her hands gripped his muscular back. They began to move together until both were propelled to the edge of oblivion, collapsing against one another.

Willow pulled back, exhaling deeply. "How did you know that was just what I needed?"

"Cause it's just what I needed," he confessed with a slow exhale. He turned his head abruptly at the sound of a vehicle pulling up outside.

"What is it?" she asked, startled.

"I heard a truck."

Whoever was there turned the engine off.

Willow stepped off him with a surprised expression, shaking her head. Then it dawned on her as she went after her clothes. "It must be the hot tub guy," she said in a near panic since she was standing in her entry with no clothes on. Not that he can see her, but she felt, well, naked.

"Hot tub guy?" Terry questioned, also reaching for his clothes.

"Yeah, I bought a hot tub, and they need to make sure the deck can support it."

"You bought a hot tub?" He said over his shoulder as he headed for the guest room with his clothes.

"Norma thought it'd be a good idea, so I bought one." The doorbell rang and she called out, "I'll be right out. You can follow the deck to the back and—"

"Okay." Footsteps disappeared while she hurried into her bedroom to finish dressing.

Willow was giggling when she stepped into the hall just as Terry rounded the corner. He wasn't as amused as she was until she leaned into him, kissing his pursed lips.

"Come on, you have to come out with me."

The guy was under the deck with his flashlight then walked back up the steps as they approached. "Whoever built this deck planned for a hot tub because it's already reinforced," he told them. "So, you're good to go. We can install on Saturday if that works for you, and actually, you don't even need to be here. All the hookups we need are outside the house. It'll be a slam dunk deal."

"Great." She looked at Terry for approval for some reason and he shrugged, playing along.

"Sign at the X, just in case you aren't home. We'll be here about ten in the morning."

Willow handed back the signed form, thanked the guy, who waved his clip board at them before heading to his van.

"Okay, my little sex kitten," Terry said, and Willow felt goose bumps while his eyes roamed over her body pausing to give each of her luscious curves his full attention. His gaze landed at her tall, sexy city boots. She sighed thinking about him kissing her ruby polished toes last night before working his way up to the soft tender flesh on the inside of her thigh.

"Let's get moving or we're going to have to get naked again." Neither of them could hide the intense desire they felt.

It took Willow's breath away when he blatantly leered at her, letting her know what he'd rather be doing right now. She kissed him and off they went.

Terry's right. We'd be neighbors if he decided on this property, she thought during the five-minute ride. In less than a mile, they turned onto a dirt road lined with trees. In a quarter mile, the property opened up to reveal what must be acres of land. There wasn't a house or any other structure, though she was sure Terry saw it finished in his head.

"The barn will be there and maybe a bunk house."

"Where will you live then? Of course, you can stay in the apartment as long as you want," she hastened to add. Except he'd yet to stay in the apartment, she reminded herself.

He smiled and nodded, "I'll show you," and he turned the truck around, drove a short distance and stopped, shut the engine off. "I haven't given much thought to a house. I figure I'll be too busy for a while to have anything more than a cabin."

"That makes sense. Can we get out?"

"'Course we can." He kissed her tenderly, his hand on the back of her neck. "I can't keep my hands off you. Have you noticed that?"

"Yes," Her beautiful smile letting him know she was okay with it. He might be the best thing that's ever happened to me, she pondered, and it's not just because we've had our clothes off a couple of times. Although she couldn't deny that had been pretty amazing. There was more going on between them than just physical attraction. She loved that he wanted her to see the property he intended to purchase.

Chet had never asked her opinion, he was demanding and made decisions without consulting her. Terry was kind and thoughtful, trusting her with information he might not have told his closest friend.

Stepping out of the truck, Terry came around to open her door. He took Willow's hand, didn't let go while he mapped out the area in his mind, looking toward the road then back where the barn would be. "I'd say the cabin will be right here," letting go of her hand he gestured arms out.

"There's plenty of room to build a bigger place in the future."

"I think you've already made up your mind about buying this property."

"Wait 'til you see the one I looked at this morning. It's beautiful with lots of trees." He strode off, surveying the vacant land again. Willow felt excited energy, her scalp tingling, knowing Terry was probably visualizing his ranch up and running.

He walked toward her after picking up a couple of large stones and a broken tree branch, placing them where the front of the cabin would be.

"You're right. I do like this property. It feels right to me but more importantly it has lots of pasture. I've had an expert check it out and he gave it good marks as well." With a happy grin and feeling settled, he took her hand once again, "Okay, let's go eat.

As they neared the Red Kettle, Willow said, "This will be the first time we've been out together as a..." She stopped herself before saying 'couple', but that was how she felt. She wanted to be with him. How could she not after what they've been doing the past twenty-four hours? Yikes! Hard for her to believe it's only been twenty-four hours. Probably way too soon to be in a relationship. Took me longer to get involved with Chet and look how that turned out. But we're just dating, right? Oh yeah and sleeping together.

"Couple?" Terry ventured.

"I was going to say that but thought it might sound a bit presumptuous of me."

He reached over to lay his arm across her shoulders. "If I asked you to be my Shelia, would you say yes?"

"Yes," she said, without hesitation, knowing he meant the Aussie slang for woman. She'd seen Crocodile Dundee. "It already feels like that to me," She giggled as a sense of euphoria rippled through her.

"You aren't pushing me into saying that." He glanced over at her briefly before turning back to traffic. "If that's what you're thinking."

"No not really, we're adults and we want to be together." Surely, she'd learned something from Chet's disgusting behavior to recognize it in Terry if she saw it. She wanted to believe Terry was sincere but then, she'd never questioned Chet's sincerity. When they were married, she saw what she wanted to see. She nudged those silly thoughts aside.

Norma's right, we need time to get to know one another.

She looked out the window a moment before turning toward Terry. "Just be honest with me, and I'll be honest with you. If you ever decide you don't want to be with me, I want you to say so. Okay?"

"Willow, I'm crazy about you. You must know that. I'll do my best to be honest with you. Just kick me if you ever think I'm not." He reached over and took her hand, "Like I said last night, I'd never do anything to hurt you."

Willow gazed at her new boyfriend, "I know you wouldn't." In her heart, she knew he meant it.

Chapter 11

$\mathcal{T}$erry found a parking space up close where he pulled in next to Tommy's cruiser. Nothing like letting the cat out of the bag, he thought, walking around to open the door for Willow.

He knew this was a defining moment for them and wanted it to mean something. Terry wanted to remember it was a sunny spring day and Willow looked especially beautiful. She wore a healthy glow from their earlier intimacy. He felt rather arrogant knowing he was responsible for putting it there.

"Everyone in here is going to know we've been sleeping together." She teased, since he parked next to the Sheriff's car.

"They can all eat their hearts out," he said, leaning over to kiss her, feeling like he had the world by the tail. Terry's heart swelled with pride as he escorted Willow inside. He seemed to stand taller, his self-confidence returned for the first time since he'd been back. This could be the beginning of the life he longed for.

Tommy stood, hoping they'd join him in the booth in the back corner of the restaurant. Terry asked Willow if she minded, but she didn't.

"Hello, Miss James, Terry," He motioned them to sit opposite him after shaking Terry's hand.

"Please call me Willow, Officer Logan." She wanted to be his friend too.

"Only if you call me Tommy," he said as the waitress brought menus to the table. "Brenda, have you met Willow?"

"Hello," Willow said.

"Nice to meet you," Brenda nodded. "I've waited on you a couple of times."

"The three of you went to school together, right?" Willow asked.

Almost cringing, the two guys shared a look, before turning their attention to the menu, hoping Brenda wouldn't expose them for the horny teenagers they'd been.

"Yes, we did," she offered.

"I'll bet you have some stories to tell about these two troublemakers."

"A few that would curl your hair," she said, leaning forward before getting back to business. "What can I get you today?"

While they waited for their food, the guys nodded when Willow asked if they'd played football. She listened as the two friends began talking about particular games that stood out in their minds. They were responsible for their school winning the championship two years in a row.

Local press had fun with their names referring to Tommy and Terry as TNT. The Saturday morning sports page headline would read, "TNT destroys North Cody High in a landslide victory" or "TNT demolishes..."

After a long lunch, they said good-bye and headed for the property Terry had seen that morning. In ten miles he turned onto a dirt road lined with trees, then in a half mile the narrow road gave way to acres of pasture butting up to a mountain forming a box canyon.

He stopped the truck, but didn't turn it off, just sat there taking in the view. "This is a great piece of property, but I can see it's in shade right now and will be until tomorrow morning. Might not be the best choice unless I wanted total privacy. It is secluded," he observed.

"Yes, it's beautiful."

He turned toward her. "But..." He knew there was a 'but' and maybe she wouldn't speak it, not right now anyway.

"Well, it looks like a great place to ride horses."

"Nothing else?"

"I don't want to influence you," she offered quietly. "You want to build a cattle business which I know nothing about, and you need to have what you think is the best property for that."

He turned away and shut the engine down. "You're right. I do have to think about my business." Again, he held her hand as they walked around.

When she rubbed her arms and shuddered, he said, "Come on, let's go. It's getting cold."

~

Driving back through town, Willow's cell rang. "I have to take this call. Do you mind?"

He saw her expression change. "Do you want privacy?"

"No, I was going to tell you about this anyway so you may as well listen. I won't put it on speaker though."

"Hello, Mac," she said, "I appreciate you calling me back. I'm sure you're busy so I'll get down to business. Have you had any complaints from women who think they might have been slipped a date rape drug? Maybe, Ketamine or ecstasy?"

Terry shot her a startled expression.

"Why do you ask?" Mac questioned, cautiously.

"Because a good friend was obviously a victim of date rape in Santa Barbara and after hearing her story it reminded me of an incident I experienced and couldn't explain."

"Do I know this person?"

"Yes, and I know you can't go by my hearsay, but my friend is ready to come forward and file a complaint."

"Okay, Willow, we have had a couple of complaints from two women who, like you said, couldn't quite explain their behavior after having a glass of wine in a bar here in town."

"Was it the bar in Riccardo's?"

"Yes, one of them was. Is that where your friend had her experience?"

"Yes."

"How about you? Where did your situation occur?"

"In my condo and I may as well say right now, my ex-husband was the only person with me."

"Does your friend also think it was Chet?"

"Yes, and Mac—" Willow felt a chill roll over her body. This all felt so disgusting, and she wanted it to be over. She watched Terry's brow furrow, hands wringing the steering wheel.

She'd needed to be strong when Norma arrived and dropped the bombshell that she was pregnant and suspected Chet. Willow had shoved her own suspicions aside and now Mac tells her there were other woman who were assaulted by him?! Choking back tears, she was unable to speak.

A feeling of brutal betrayal hit her hard. She became enveloped by racking sobs at the realization that not only did her ex-husband drug and rape Norma, he did the same to her and other women in her hometown. It was all too much.

Mac waited patiently.

Terry pulled off the road, parked, and shut the engine off.

"You okay, Willow?" Mac asked.

She dropped her forehead into her hand. "I'm okay. It's just..."

"I know, take your time."

"Chet got Norma pregnant!" She shouted to get the words out. "He didn't even have the decency to use a condom!"

Terry leaned toward her with his reassuring arm across her shoulders, shaking his head.

A deep exhale filled her ear as Mac digested what she'd said. "Okay. That substantiates one of our complaints. I'm going to bring him in for questioning and let him know I have other accusations if you and Norma will give us your statement."

Willow reached over to lay her hand on Terry's shoulder. She needed to touch him, to feel grounded to something good and decent. The reality of this situation was anything but, and she had to deal with it.

"I'll check with Norma again, but I'm pretty sure she will agree. And Mac," She didn't wait for a response, "Norma had a miscarriage while she was here visiting me."

Another exhale. "I'm sorry she had to go through that. Chet needs help. Between you and me, he's a sick man."

Willow nodded and sniffled.

"Kiddo, why don't you think about writing an article on date rape and the drugs most often used? Apparently, we need to get this information out there again. Write about the drugs, what they can do to you and how to keep yourself safe from this happening. Include a description of the drugs. Call Mike at the paper and see if he isn't interested."

"Mac, you're brilliant, that's a great idea. I'll give him a call." Mike Polazzo was editor of Santa Barbara's newspaper; he and Willow had worked closely on a number of stories when she was a reporter.

"Okay, Willow, I'll keep you posted."

"Thanks, Mac." Her voice shuddered, "I appreciate it."

"It's my job. Take care of yourself." He disconnected.

Tears rolling down her face, Willow looked out the side window. She had an urge to quietly open the door and bolt. Instead, she reminded herself she couldn't run away from this. She wanted to stop apologizing for allowing Chet into her life.

Releasing a frustrated exhale, she held her cell to her forehead then turned to see the hard set of Terry's jaw.

"What the hell was that all about?" He questioned in an angry tone.

She filled him in on Sheriff McCauley's side of the conversation. Terry's back molars took the brunt of his anger at hearing what had happened to Willow and her friend Norma.

"Guys like that need to be castrated, without anesthesia."

"That would be too good for him," she said, "but, Mac is right. He needs to be stopped."

"So, Norma seemed to be all right when we met for coffee. Is she okay?"

Willow liked that he showed concern for her friend, even though they'd only met that one time. "She is and feeling better once she decided to go public, so to speak. By the way, I don't think she'd mind that you know about all this. If I thought so, I would've had this phone call in private."

He dipped his head. "I liked her. She seemed like a no-frills person. What you see is what you get."

"Well, she thought you were to die for," she said leaning toward him. "In fact, Norma told me you seemed like a decent guy who had good vibes, and I better act fast, or she might horn in on my territory."

"I knew she was smart." His face couldn't hide an embarrassed grin. "What will happen to your ex? Do you think he'll do jail time?"

"I don't know. I've never been in a situation like this. When I was at the paper, there were occasional stories about date rape, but they usually came from Los Angeles."

"He must be good at deceit or you would have seen through him."

"This all happened after I filed for divorce," she said. "He's getting even with me," she added in a near whisper.

Both stared out the windshield. "Why did you file for divorce? If you don't mind my asking."

Willow hugged herself, hands running along her arms. "I knew he'd been sleeping with his secretary before we met, I suspected he continued to do so after we were married." Her eyes narrowed as they met his, "And, you better believe I felt stupid, embarrassed, and ashamed I'd allowed such a disgusting character into my family, and my friends' lives and it's only gotten worse. My best friend was raped by him and ended up pregnant. How horrible is that?" Willow brought her hand to her forehead wanting to compose herself. She didn't want to cry about this anymore.

"I'm sorry." He cupped her face with his warm hand, wanting to hold her close. "I didn't mean to upset you like this."

"No, I know you didn't." Willow struggled to hold back tears. "We're trying to get to know each other, and we're doing the crash course. Get all the ugly bits out in the first few days and if we stick around, we just might make it to the end of the month."

He raised his eyebrows, along with a slow nod in agreement. After some thought and wanting to change the subject, Terry asked, "So, that morning I ran into you dressed in pink polka-dot pjs. You were coming from the hospital?"

She smiled hearing him describe her pajamas. "Yes, I'd taken Norma there at two that morning and stayed until she was in a room resting after the procedure."

"And there I was being so self-centered, flirting with you after what you'd been through. You must have thought I was a complete idiot," he said.

"Actually, playing word tag with you kind of lightened my mood." She cocked her head, "Do you know how close I came to going to Cody with you?"

"You had more important matters to contend with than my trip to buy this truck, which by the way, is out of gas. But I'm happy you even considered it."

With a puzzled expression, she asked, "What do you mean? We're really out of gas?"

"I intended to stop before we left town, but I was trying to follow your one-sided conversation and forgot. I can't remember the last time I did that."

"You have a lot on your mind," she offered quietly.

"Hell, apparently, we both do. I'd like to get my hands around your ex's neck. He's complete scum. If he needs his knees busted, I'm your man." He unbuckled his seatbelt and leaned toward her. "I've never had a more beautiful, exciting distraction. Under other circumstances, I'd be breathing fire right now."

"I'll keep that in mind," she said, then looked at their surroundings. "Fortunately, it's only a short walk from here. We'll take my car and get some gas."

~

Terry and Willow left the truck and darted across the road, turning onto the gravel driveway. They walked toward the house until Terry stiffened, slowing his pace. "What the hell?" he said under his breath, his gaze on someone standing beside the flower garden with their back to them.

"Were you expecting someone?" He quietly asked Willow. When she shook her head, he wondered if it had been Harley lurking around the property. His heart rate kicked up a notch, eyes narrowing, his gaze fixated on the figure. Several thoughts filled his mind; How did she know where to find me, and what's her motive for coming here? They were roughly 300 feet from the house, so he couldn't tell if she was carrying her hunting knife.

A few steps further, he exhaled, momentarily relieved the person he saw was obviously male. Noreen's brother, Billy Purvis, was next on his short list of nefarious characters. But, why would he be standing in the garden, and why come back now? There wasn't any sign of a truck or car, only adding to his puzzlement.

The man was crouched down, unaware of the couple approaching. Terry stopped abruptly, tightening his hold on Willow's hand. "Stay here until I find out who this is," he whispered. He was completely focused on the stranger.

Terry continued on alone, taking long strides wanting the element of surprise on his side but the gravel gave him away. The man heard him coming and stood, shading his eyes as he watched him approach.

This man is too tall to be Billy, Terry whispered to himself, then wondered if it was Willow's ex. His suspicious mind could only imagine this person as an unwanted intruder. As he drew nearer, he was suddenly freaked out by how familiar the stranger appeared.

Terry's pace quickened, this man was tall and lean like his father had been. His hair was heavily grayed, like his father's might have become, if he were alive. But his father wasn't alive, he'd been trapped inside the barn when Billy and Noreen set it on fire.

"It can't be," Terry said, emotion clutching his throat.

A smile began to form on the older man's face. He stepped forward as Terry closed in on him.

"Poppa, it is really you?" Terry choked back tears now, as he enclosed his father in his arms.

Alain Du Champs held onto his son as if his life depended on it. "*Mon fils*! I knew you would come! Where have you been? I have missed you so."

Terry heard the anguish in his father's trembling voice knowing he'd been robbed of seeing his only son become the man he saw before him. Alain stepped back to take him in. "So handsome and tall," he commented proudly.

Terry gripped his father's arms, peering deep into his eyes. "Father, *what* are you doing here?" he pleaded. "How can this be you? The police showed me your Saint Christopher still on the chain. They found it in the barn after the fire. I identified it. How can you be here?" he demanded in a rush of words.

He released his father, stepped back to look him over. Then, feeling a little dizzy he looked for some place to sit. One of the large rocks surrounding the garden would have to do.

Was this really his father, and why was he returning now? Had he been in Elk Valley all this time while Terry was in Australia? Questions he desperately wanted answers to.

Alain sat next to him and put his hand on his son's shoulder. "*Mon fils*, I am so very sorry to have deceived you. I had to get away quickly before the trucks came to put the fire out. I couldn't be found, I had to make them think I was dead. I had a gunshot wound in my right thigh and had to get away without leaving a trail of blood. I saw Noreen through the smoke standing on the porch with her arms folded, staring at the flames, knowing I was inside frying."

"But who was inside? Whose remains did the police find?" His expression filled with outrage.

Alain leaned closer, not wanting anyone to hear even though they were alone. "Billy, Noreen's brother."

Terry exhaled, wanting to slow his racing heart. "But why? Why couldn't you testify that Noreen wanted you dead? Do you know what I went through?" He tried to keep his resentment in check, but he was on a roll. "I was seventeen-years-old, my mother was dead and then I thought you burned up in a fire." Terry needed to say those things to his father, somehow hoping he could make it all better.

"Billy lured me inside the barn. He told me there was a hole in the roof that needing fixing. He pointed above us and when I looked up, Billy turned back to the barn door all the time talking while he slipped a board through the door handles. Next thing I knew he was pouring a can of gasoline on a bale of hay, ready to ignite it. I knew I had to get out fast." Alain spoke rapidly, using some French words in his excitement.

Terry's head was reeling.

"He had a gun. We wrestled with it and it went off. I was hit in the leg." Alain's eyes narrowed as though he were trying to recall something. "Remember that box of motorcycle parts I was always after you to put on a shelf? Well, when Billy stepped back, he tripped on that box and hit his head on the car jack. I saw blood pooling on the ground and reached for the gun, but thought I better leave it." He paused a moment, "Thank you for not putting those things away."

Terry let his head drop, "But he tried to kill you. You did nothing wrong."

"I panicked, Thierry. I had to get away without Noreen seeing me. I didn't know if she had a gun. Besides," he leaned closer to his son, "I wasn't an American citizen."

Running a hand down his face, Terry nodded.

"Where did you go, and why did you stay away so long?"

"I went back to Australia. When the trial was over, I had to get as far away from here as possible. I couldn't bear to be here and not see you. Mother was gone, then you. There was nothing for me here." he said, his voice full of anger and regret.

Chapter 12

Terry looked up and saw Willow standing at the base of the kitchen steps. He appreciated her giving them some space, then offered a half smile motioning her to come forward.

He put his arm around her and introduced her to his father. "Poppa, this is Willow. She lives in our old house."

Terry gave her a quick nod when she gasped.

"Yes, this is my father. Alain Du Champs." Terry watched her pull in a sharp inhale, her eyes glistening as she covered her mouth.

Quickly regaining her composure, "Bonjour, Monsieur Du Champs," she managed, extending her hand. "C'est un plaisir de vous rencontrer."

Alain's face lit up, and he kissed her hand. "Merci, ma belle. You speak French."

"Thank you for saying so."

Terry wiped away tears with the back of his hand while Willow leaned against him.

"Come inside."

The two men followed her into the warm kitchen. Father and son sat across the small table from one another, feeling emotionally drained, and almost giddy at the same time. Neither spoke, both adjusting to this sudden, totally unexpected discovery.

She never ceases to amaze me. "Thank you for making coffee, he said when he noticed three mugs on the table and cookies on a plate. The room was quiet, the scent of coffee was a welcome comfort.

Terry and his father couldn't take their eyes off one another out of fear of them disappearing again. Both turned toward her when Willow laid her hands on each of theirs. They'd almost forgotten she was there, then offered a smile at her kindness.

Eager to hear more, Terry asked, "Poppa, how did you get out of the barn?"

They listened as his father spoke of dropping his Saint Christopher in the barn next to Billy hoping it'd prove he, himself, had died in the fire. But Alain was able to get out of the burning barn without being detected since the fire would destroy his exit. He'd built the barn before Terry was born, adding crawl space and an exit at the back so the cat and dog could come and go.

Terry spread a hand over his chest and nodded. "Dad, you can stay with me in the apartment tonight."

"I cannot stay. I must leave before it gets dark."

"What'd you mean?" he asked, incredulously, knowing he sounded like a small child whose parent was leaving him behind. It occurred to him he hadn't asked where his father was living and how he got here. "Poppa, where do you live?"

"Just across the border in Montana." He placed his hand on his son's arm, "I will come again and we will talk about everything, but I must leave soon."

"This is so unfair," Terry said, his arms in the air. "I can't believe you're going; we have so much to talk about." Again, a light came on in his head. "Is someone waiting for you? Will they be worried if you don't return before dark?"

"Yes, Thierry."

"You drove here?"

He nodded, "I'm parked on the property behind the house."

Willow stood at the sound of a car and saw the Sheriff's cruiser through the kitchen window. "It's Tommy," she said over her shoulder.

"What is this, Grand Central frickin' Station?"

"I'll see what he wants."

"Don't let him in. It wouldn't be good for him to see Dad right now."

~

Willow turned and went out to head him off. "Hi, Tommy," she said, closing the door behind her before walking down the steps.

"Hey, Willow. Everything okay? I saw the truck parked across the road thought I'd see if I could help in any way."

She watched Tommy eyeing the door, expecting his friend to step out any moment.

"Yes, as a matter of fact we ran out of gas and came to get my car when Terry's phone rang." She turned and gestured toward the door. "He's on the phone. With his realtor. I think he's close to making a decision about which property he wants."

She thought she was doing a good job of fibbing, but there was doubt on his face. Clearly, he was ready to storm past her to make sure his friend was okay. Talking fast probably made her sound like she was covering something up. She was speaking to an officer of the law for heaven's sake, not to mention he's Terry's best friend.

"So, you need gas?" Tommy asked, tentatively.

"Yes. I was just going out to get a can of gas while Terry's on the phone."

"I have five gallons of gas in my patrol car you can have," he offered. "Just replace it as soon as you can."

"Oh, great," she said with more enthusiasm than needed. "I'll get Terry's keys and my purse." She quickly turned, taking the stairs two at a time, stepping into the kitchen.

"Would you stick your head out the door so Tommy can see that you are all right? I don't think he believes me. I told him you were on your phone. Oh, and I need the keys to your truck. He has a can of gas with him."

A tender smile formed at the corner of Terry's mouth as he watched her. He pulled keys from his pocket and walked to the door with her, his cell in hand. "Thanks, Tommy. We'll replace the gas later." He kissed Willow then waved at his friend, who was at the bottom of the stairs now, before retreating back inside.

After holding the door for Willow, Tommy slid in behind the wheel and headed out to the road and the waiting truck. "I expect the two of you to let me in on what just went on here. I don't believe either of you for a second. Something's up and I don't like being out of the loop."

Spoken like a man wearing a badge.

Willow batted her eyes at him, "Why, Sheriff, whatever do you mean?" She playfully used her best southern accent, loving life, but also feeling as though she was in the Twilight Zone. Who would have imagined Alain Du Champs would come back from the dead and walk into his son's life? It was all she could do to keep from telling Tommy, but it wasn't her story to tell.

Tommy flashed his dimples at her. "Don't play innocent little miss cutesy poo with me, Miss James."

~

"Do you realize we are standing in the middle of our kitchen?" Terry said, as they waited for Tommy and Willow to pull away from the house. On one hand, it seemed so natural to see him there but on the other, he never entertained the thought of seeing his father again.

"Willow's kitchen now, but this is like a dream and I don't want to wake up to find you gone."

"Everything is good," Alain said, with a reassuring smile, gesturing with his hands. "We can only go forward. I want to hear all about your years in Australia and everything you've been doing. I am pleased you have Willow in your life. I can see you are in love."

"Whoa, let's not rush things. I'm in a heavy case of 'like'. Too soon for us to be in love. We've only known each other a short time, little over a month."

"I knew your mother a month before proposing, we were married two weeks later."

"You and Mom were special."

"No more than you and Willow."

They stood in the kitchen, silent for a few moments. "I read everything I could about the trial, feeling...mm, desespoir, at not being there for you. When the trial was over and Noreen was in prison, I began making secret trips to the house to tend the garden." He leaned closer to his son. "I thought if I kept the garden going you would know I was still around. Those trips helped me feel a small connection to you, hoping to learn where you'd gone."

Terry couldn't imagine what that must have been like for his father not knowing where his son was. "What about your brothers? You must have let them know."

"Yes. After several months, I called Sebastian and Gabriel in France to tell them I was alive and well. I asked them to come and take ownership of the house as next of kin. I never gave up hope of seeing you again, and here you are," he added raising his arms.

Terry chuckled and heaved a sigh. "Well, that clarifies some stuff I've wondered about," he said then wrote his cell number on a piece of paper from a small pad on the counter. "I'll walk to your car with you." Alain folded the paper and put it in his breast pocket. They stood at the kitchen door waiting until the cruiser was out of sight. "Okay, let's go."

Walking down the stairs, Terry asked his father how he had escaped unnoticed with fire trucks and police swarming around the house and barn.

"I hurried away from the barn when the trucks came down the driveway. Everyone was busy watching the fire. I hid out in the overgrown brush for hours until they all left then waited a little longer. I had a feeling the fireman would come back to make sure there were no flare ups and I was right. They did return and left half an hour later."

Alain continued, Terry by his side, eager to hear the rest of the story. "I was numb with cold when I made my way to the house. I tended to my leg, just a flesh wound," he added, when he saw his son's pained expression. "But it bled some so I made a bandage and changed my pants, packing the ones I took off along with as much as I could fit into a small bag. I found my passport, took some food from the fridge, grabbed my jacket and drove away in Billy's car. You know how he always left his keys in the ignition."

As if Terry would remember that.

They walked through the trees and thick brush, ending up at the property next door. "Poppa, this is your old truck," Terry said, astonished. "How did you get it?"

"I will tell you everything when we meet next time." He opened the door, "I will call you when I know I can come." He pulled his son into a hug. "I love you my boy. I am overcome with happiness to find you at last."

Terry blew out a breath, emotion rising in his throat again, "I love you father. Please call me when you get home, I'll worry until I hear from you."

Alain cheek-kissed his son then stepped up into the old truck, started the engine before rolling down the window. "Au revoir."

Terry reached in to give his father's shoulder a light squeeze before Alain pulled away, waving out the window. He watched the old blue truck bounce along the uneven ground until he disappeared.

~

Willow thanked Tommy again and drove Terry's truck down her driveway. She was beside herself with joy for Terry to have his father back. What an amazing story. The softening of his face warmed her heart, knowing that finding his father had never been an option for Terry.

She parked his truck in the spot where he always parked and made sure it was locked. While walking toward the house, Willow heard Terry call her name from across the yard. Turning, she waited for him to reach her and when he did, he pulled her into an embrace that caught her off guard. She nearly lost her footing, but his big, strong arms kept her steady.

They walked into the house, arms around each other and Terry slumped down in a chair.

"Do you want to stay here tonight?" she asked, hoping he would say yes but his bewildered demeanor caused her to think he might want to be alone.

"You mean a great deal to me; I can't tell you how much I've enjoyed these past few days with you."

Uh-oh, is this going to be the brush off? Am I in the way now that his father is back in his life? she wondered. You're being silly, she scolded. Why wouldn't his focus turn to his father right now?

"Feels like I've been up for days," Terry stood, "I think I'll go shower and call it a night."

"We still have steaks in the fridge and vegies all cut up, marinated and ready to cook."

His knitted brows emphasized his conflict. "Oh, yeah. Steak and vegies," his voice trailed off. "I don't think I'd be very good company tonight," he admitted, one hand on the doorknob.

"We both have to eat, and those steaks won't keep much longer." Hmm, hope I don't sound like I'm nagging. He did say Harley was possessive. "I understand if you'd rather not."

He continued to gaze at her, "No. You're right. I'll shower and come back in an hour."

She nodded, not wanting him to leave but what he'd experienced this afternoon was so deeply personal. He needed some time to himself.

In forty-five minutes, he was back, smelling like soap and fresh laundered clothes, his hair still damp. She leaned into him and took in a breath. "Umm, you smell nice."

He kissed her soft lips, "That's supposed to be my line."

She eyed him carefully, "Are you okay Terry?" she said, then rested her head on his chest, her arms around him. He seemed distracted, but otherwise fine for someone who had experienced the shock of his life.

"Confused as hell, but, yeah, I'm fine." He ran a hand through his hair. "I just don't know what to think. Dad came to this house to tend mom's garden hoping I'd be here. He did that for thirteen years!" He couldn't hold back a spontaneous laugh. "So much jumbled stuff in my head that I need to let go of."

"Would a shot of whiskey help you to chill?"

He shook his head, "I don't think I could stop at one."

"I opened a bottle of really good red wine if you'd like some. You can pour me a glass." She turned back to the stove to check on the roasting vegetables.

He sniffed the open bottle of wine. "That does smell good." He poured the large glasses a quarter full, "These are the biggest wine glasses I've ever seen."

She smiled, "A gift from a relative." She left out the part about them being a wedding present. Most of her and Chet's gifts had been used by the time he found his clothes piled on the doorstep of her condo, and his key no longer fit the lock. She didn't return any of them. Eventually, she gave him all the gifts from his friends and family, and she kept the ones from hers.

He handed her a glass and held his out, "Thanks for today, for being so thoughtful and well, for being here."

"Of course, I was glad to be part of such an extraordinary revelation." She laid her hand on his arm, "It's unbelievable, and wonderful to see the love and admiration on both your faces."

He smiled in agreement. "I'm very happy you were here to witness this..." he couldn't find the right word, then "... miracle, after hearing so much of what happened." They clinked glasses and sipped the wine. "Umm, great wine," he complimented her. "Did you choose it or was it also a gift?"

"Yes, I did choose it at a wine tasting in Santa Barbara." She turned the oven off after confirming the vegetables were done. "Okay, I think we're ready to grill those steaks. I'll take your glass if you'll carry the platter."

They stepped outside just as they'd done last night, but tonight they managed to get the food on the grill and back in the kitchen to enjoy.

"You're a good cook, Willow," he said sincerely when they sat down to eat. "Is your Mum a good cook?"

"Yes, both my parents love to cook and are avid grillers." She thought it was cute that he used the English term for mom. Every now and then his Australian experience came forward.

"Did Norma drive back to Santa Barbara?" he asked after chewing and swallowing a bite of steak.

Willow set her fork down on her plate, "No, she didn't like the idea of going back there right now. She drove to Chicago to stay with her cousin, Sydney, for a while. She thinks she might want to settle there."

"It was a long drive to come here by herself especially being pregnant and all. Did you think it was odd?"

"For her, yes, it was out of character." She felt the back of her eyes stinging. It's been an emotional day. My tearful conversation with Mac and then the incredible gift of Terry's dad showing up out of thin air it seemed.

"I drove here by myself, too, my car packed with everything that didn't go on the moving truck. I cried for the first two hours, feeling sorry for myself as I fled the only home I'd ever known. I know it sounds dramatic, but that's how I felt."

His eyes narrowed, "Why do you say you fled?"

Willow's shoulders drooped; her hands fell to her lap. "I really was running away; I didn't think so at the time, but I had to escape."

"You mean because of your ex-husband?"

Willow nodded and they ate in silence a few minutes before Terry said, "Willow, I want to change the rules a bit between us." He set his fork down, leaned against the chair back. "I was out of line becoming so familiar with you without us getting to know each other first." He leaned forward and looked her in the eye, "Even though a stampeding herd of beef couldn't have kept me out of your bed last night."

Her face lit up and she ran her bare foot up the inside of his pant leg under the table. "You didn't hear me say stop at any point and I would have if I thought I wasn't ready to have a physical relationship with you. I hesitated, if you remember, but I wanted you too." Her gaze hit the table, "I still do."

He released a guttural groan, "I'm so happy you feel that way," He reached over and took her hand. "But now I want..."

Apprehension gripped her body, she felt woozy hoping this wasn't the end of the beginning. But, maybe it's best. I'm so falling for him and don't want to regret it tomorrow or the next day. Wish I'd had this conversation with myself when I fell for Chet.

He brought her hand to his lips, kissing each slender fingertip. "I want to do things properly and I want to begin by asking you out to dinner tomorrow night."

She watched him for several seconds waiting for what would come next. "You're asking me out on a date?"

"Yes, ma'am," he grinned. "I happened to see what appeared to be a nice steak house over in Cody when I was there buyin' my truck. I would be much obliged if you would say yes." His sapphire eyes pierced her light baby blues.

Willow relaxed some. He sure did have that western thing going on. No wonder we women find cowboys sexy, then decided to join in. Leaning forward, she fluttered her eyes at him, "Why, that's mighty neighborly of you, cowboy."

"My God, you're fun to be with besides being beautiful and as my father might say, magnifique." He cleared his throat, "Is that a yes?"

She propped her left elbow on the table and rested her chin in her hand, "I can only think of one other thing I'd rather do with you," she replied with arched brows. "But for now, I would be pleased to have dinner with you tomorrow evening."

He leaned over the table and kissed her tenderly. She didn't want him to stop, but also didn't want him to feel guilty for needing time to himself.

"Okay." He said, slapping his hands down on his thighs. "I'll call for you tomorrow evening at six-thirty."

He stood, took the remains of their dishes to the sink, offering to help wash and dry them.

"There're just a few, I can manage." She followed him to the door where he turned and kissed her lightly on her waiting lips.

"Oh," she thought, "what should I wear?" She hadn't been out to a nice dinner since moving here and wondered what would be appropriate.

"I don't think the place is dressy, but you always look great," he said in an admiring tone. He opened the door, sprinted across the yard and up the stairs before his whole gentlemanly approach flew right out the window.

She leaned against the closed door while the kittens were at her feet wanting attention. "Looks like it's just us tonight. Let's get you some food while I clean up these dishes." But that could wait while she sat on the floor for some kitty cat cuddles until they began to squirm. Willow rolled the little ball across the floor and was soon laughing as they scrambled after it. She felt better about cowboy's plan to court her before they got naked again. "It's good that Terry's sleeping in the apartment tonight. We could both use a little breathing room", she told the kittens.

After the dishes were dried and put away, Willow stepped out on the deck to look at the stars. 'Wow' was always her response when scanning the clear, immense backdrop for what must be a trillion stars. She loved that part of living out on the prairie, as she called it. She thought about her first week living alone in Elk Valley and hearing a woman scream. She had called the sheriff's office in a panic and was told it was most likely elk, but said they'd send someone to check on it. Now, that sound was a comfort, reminding her that she had four legged neighbors.

She turned to go back inside but couldn't help looking up at the dark apartment. A twinge of emptiness spread through her. Shivering from the chilly night air, she rubbed her arms, then closed and locked the door. In her room, she sat cross legged on her bed and wrote a note to call Mike Palozzo tomorrow and propose an article about club drugs.

Feeling exhausted, she snuggled under the comforter by herself. Nestling her head on her favorite pillow, she thought about her night with Terry. Once again, she was pleasantly surprised by how gentle he'd been for such a big guy. Smiling in the darkness, she replayed the sensual feeling of his lips all over her. Midnight jumped on the bed and curled up in the crook of her knee. "Thanks for cuddling. I wish Terry was here with me, but you'll do for now."

Sleep seemed impossible as she relived the events of the day. First, her emotional phone conversation with Sheriff Mac, then Terry's unbelievable reunion with his father. Tossing and turning for several minutes, she finally settled down, lulled herself to sleep with images of Terry, recalling every kiss, every caress sending tingly warmth throughout her body.

Chapter 13

Terry laid down on the new mattress and tugged on the blanket pulling it until his feet stuck out. "Oh yeah, short bed," he mumbled. He laid crossways then rolled over. That wasn't quite right, so he turned to face the other wall. Frustrated, he got up and went to the kitchen for a glass of water. He looked out the window at Willow's house, no lights. He wondered if she was asleep then took the glass back to the bedroom and made his six-foot-three frame as comfortable as the queen bed allowed.

The garage apartment was definitely better than sleeping in the motel, but he was still by himself. So was Willow. They could be curled up together right now if he hadn't tried to be so chivalrous.

"Kinda putting the cart before the horse don't you think, bud?" he said into the darkness.

When he left Australia, the long flight back to the states had allowed Terry plenty of time to think about living on his own in Elk Valley, Wyoming. He saw himself on the ranch he would build, only going into town for supplies. Mostly living alone, just his ranch hands and cattle for company. And his horse, Brumby, of course. He'd have few friends; his childhood buddy Tommy would be at the top of the list. He'd be happy to live in his house without a woman, not wanting to risk another relationship like he had with Harley.

Terry snickered at those foolish thoughts. There was no way he could deny how he felt about Willow and believed she felt the same about him. He rolled on his side, finally able to sleep, dreaming first of Willow then of his father. He woke up a couple of times, once with images of the fire and his father screaming as he tried to escape the burning barn. The most painful nightmare came in the early hours of the morning, bringing him upright in a sweat. In the dream, he called out to his mother and father who were standing beside the garden. His father told him he was mistaken; their son Thierry had perished in a fire. Nothing he said convinced them he was their son.

Terry laid back down after getting his breathing under control. He couldn't imagine anything more depressing than his parents not recognizing him. He forced the "what ifs" and "if onlys" from his mind in an effort to find sleep again.

At six-thirty he sat up on the edge of the bed, ran his hand over his face, hoping he'd hear from his father today. He checked his phone and reread the text message Alain sent last night letting his son know he'd gotten home safely.

Terry grinned, slowly shaking his head, then felt melancholy that he wasn't the one to teach his father about electronic devices. He was right, of course, they could only move forward. Knowing the regret he felt living in Australia while his father worried about him was pointless.

Heading for the shower, his thoughts were on the beautiful Willow and their date tonight. He sighed, thinking about her after sleeping alone without her hot body next to him. He didn't like the idea of spending another night without her. She was so soft and round in all the best places. He felt a quiver in his solar plexus, remembering how she'd responded to his touch. But for now, he had to focus on today's plans. There were decisions to make and he didn't want anything to adversely affect his judgement.

Stepping out the door he hurried down the stairs, eyes averted from Willow's house for fear of caving in and going to her. He sat in his truck fantasizing about kissing her awake, feeling heat rise as he lifted the comforter to slip in beside her.

"Later," he said aloud, then fired up the truck and drove out to the road. Pausing there he decided to have another look at the property next door before meeting Tommy for breakfast.

Terry stood with his hand on the open window frame taking in the view, remembering the confinement he'd felt deep in the gold mine in Australia month after month. His determination to succeed helped him fight claustrophobia until striking gold on his nineteenth birthday. During the trip from Galveston to Melbourne, the sea captain had told Terry about an old friend who had won a gold mine in a poker game and was sure there was gold to be found. He could use the help of a strong young man if Terry was interested. He jumped at the chance since he didn't have a hard plan except to eventually make his way to the cattle station where he'd worked during his 4H trip.

The man was sixty-five but looked eighty from years of mining and breathing in dust. When Terry chipped his way into a healthy vein of gold, the miner made him a fifty-fifty partner, said he didn't have any family and neither of them could have gotten to this point without the other.

After they sold the mine to a large mining operation, Terry was happy to be breathing clean air on the cattle station with miles of open space. The fact there wasn't a mountain or pine tree in sight didn't bother him at first until he began dreaming about Wyoming, longing to be surrounded once again by the mountains he grew up loving.

"Yes," he said, when nothing negative jumped out at him while scanning the acreage. He felt a strong connection to this property having ridden his horse here and his dirt bike when he was a little older. One of his favorite memories was the time his mother packed a picnic supper and the three of them rode to the top of the hill on horseback. And, now he would own that hilltop.

The property outside of town was beautiful mostly because it was secluded. He lightly shook his head, but I'm not hiding from anyone so why do I like the idea of seclusion?

"Besides, Willow thought it was cold."

~

Willow woke during the night after having another dreamy dream about the man she was falling in love with. Actually, she was already there but would try to take things slowly from now on. She wanted to be sure of her feelings for him and not dive into a relationship just because he's a sexy guy who makes her feel special. "Duh. Who wouldn't fall for a guy like that?" She said in the darkness.

Terry was sensual and calculating in his love making, putting her desire and passion before his own. No man had ever made love to her so thoroughly or so lovingly. Was he that way with Harley? She doubted it, after he'd told her how aggressive Harley had been.

She fell back to sleep then woke with the sun, lying in her cozy bed thinking about what she would wear on her date with Terry. She threw back the comforter and went to her closet pulling several things out. Some went back on the rod, but she laid a few on her bed for consideration. With hands on her hips she decided she didn't like anything.

"Stormy, I don't have a thing to wear," she said when the kitten jumped up on the bed circling to find just the right spot to settle and have a nap.

In the kitchen, Willow filled the tea kettle, added a tea bag to a mug, then decided against it. "I don't want to sit here by myself this morning," she said when Midnight rubbed against her ankle. She couldn't help checking to see if Cowboy's truck was there and was a little disappointed when it wasn't. "He got an early start, wish I'd been invited," she said to the kitten.

Dressing casually then pulling her hair up in a ponytail, Willow added a navy blue UCSB ball cap before walking out the door.

It was late morning when Willow sat outside with her coffee and morning glory muffin at Elk Valley Roasting Company. Spring was definitely here she thought, with wildflowers popping up everywhere and new leaves sprouting, bringing life to bare trees. She looked forward to seeing more of this beautiful area, wishing Terry could show her around. But she knew he'd be busy over the next several months getting his cattle ranch up and running.

Willow loved the idea of Norma living nearby or at least close enough to visit occasionally. She knew her friend loved the big city, but Chicago probably wasn't more than two hours away by plane. She made a mental note to check it out before calling Mike Palozzo at the paper.

After a few pleasantries, he said he was interested in seeing what Willow had in mind for an article on club drugs.

"Email me a rough draft or the finished article, whatever you want. I know it'll be good, Willow." They chit chatted for a few minutes then said good-bye. She'd write something tomorrow and email it to Mike.

Willow tilted her face to the sun while thinking about the busy newsroom. She kind of missed being in contact with people all day. As much as I love being with Terry, having a women friend would be nice, she thought to herself, before taking a sip of coffee.

The barista came out to tidy up the tables after the morning rush and Willow called to her. "KC…"

KC glanced over at her and smiled as she finished wiping off a table.

"I'd like to find something nice to wear tonight but I don't know where to shop. Do you have any suggestions, or do I need to go to Cody?"

She straightened, shook out the towel she was using. "A new shop opened up here in town, and if what the owner was wearing is any indication of what she's selling, I'd check there first."

Willow looked up at her through shaded eyes, "Do you know where it is?"

"She left a few of her cards. I'll bring one out as soon as I'm finished here."

"I'll follow you in and get it." The name on the card read, Green With Envy, owner, Shannon Kelly. "Cute name, thanks KC," she said, fingering the card.

"Sure, let me know what it's like."

Willow stepped back outside to finish her coffee before driving to the new boutique. She recognized the street name on the card and easily found it and the shop. The front door of the quaint older home was painted a fresh shade of spring green and a sign out front announced a pre-grand opening. She liked the look of it even before opening the door and stepping inside.

"Welcome."

"Good morning," Willow responded, searching for the source of the voice.

A shock of gorgeous, curly ginger hair emerged from behind the counter which was covered with boxes. Willow stepped forward, smiling at the pretty face with a flawless, porcelain complexion and the greenest eyes she'd ever seen. Bottle green, she thought.

"Hi I'm Shannon," she said with an engaging drawl. "As you can see, I'm not completely set up for business but thought I'd open so anyone who stops by can get an idea of what I have here," she explained, sweeping a strand of hair from her forehead then exhaling.

"Nice to meet you, I'm Willow. I was intrigued when I pulled up," she said. "I love your sign and the light-hearted feel of the door."

"Thank you. I wanted it to have curb appeal."

"Are you a realtor?" Willow asked, thinking of her mother using that phrase so often.

"No, but I recently put my condo up for lease and that's a term my realtor used."

"Was that here?"

"No, in Jackson Hole."

"So, you recently moved here?"

"Yes, three weeks ago," she replied, setting a few boxes on the floor so there wasn't such a barrier between them.

"I've only been here two and a half months myself," Willow said, thinking back.

"Where did you move from?"

"Santa Barbara, California. What brought you here?"

"Difficult breakup," Shannon said. "He's a ski instructor and mountain bike tour guide in summer. I had to leave to get on with my life. I didn't want to keep running into him and my former massage therapist."

"Your story's not unlike mine. I'm here to get away from gossip and embarrassment since divorcing after just seven months of marriage." And she continued to explain the reason for the breakup and her desire to come here to write.

"Ouch. I'm sorry to hear that, but at least we both have our careers to keep us going. These days it's important for us gals to have our own money."

"Did you have a store in Jackson?"

"Yes, still do, the Whole Closet."

How clever, Willow thought.

"Are you shopping for anything in particular?"

"Yes. I'm going to dinner tonight with a cowboy and I want something sexy, and fetching, without being too obvious of course." She wanted to remind Terry what he was missing by sleeping above the garage.

Shannon stepped out from behind the counter and led Willow to a rack of skirts pulling a few out, hanging them on a large antique hall tree. She flipped through a round rack of blouses, chose three, then arranged them with the appropriate skirt before stepping back.

"Wow, you're good. I like all these."

"You're easy to dress. You have a great figure," she said, studying her with an educated eye. "You've got those long legs and a curvy shape. Are you wearing a push-up bra?"

Willow's hands moved up to her breasts. "No, this is me. *You* sure aren't wearing a push-up bra," she added, admiring Shannon's double E's.

"No, you're right, but if I did, I wouldn't be able to see over them," Shannon said wryly. "They can get in the way in more ways than one. You're very well proportioned, but I'm top heavy and so often men's eyes never see mine."

Willow thought that was probably true. In the dressing room, she pulled her cap off, then tried on the two pieces she liked most and felt she needn't go any farther since the day was rapidly whizzing by. The long, black gored skirt hugged her hips, flaring out at the hem while the white blouse with its ruffled neck plunged deep revealing just the right amount of cleavage.

Willow saw a different woman in the mirror than she'd been when she first moved here. The emotional strain was gone from her face, as though she'd been on vacation, but knew it was because she was enjoying life again, thanks to Thierry Robert Du Champs and how she felt about him. Excitement buzzed through her, knowing she'd be seeing him in a few hours.

"Wow, you're going to knock this guy's socks off," Shannon said as Willow stepped out of the dressing room. "That's the perfect outfit for you."

"Okay, I just need a pair of cowboy boots, and I'm good to go," she said, giving her shoe size then twirled around, watching the hem of her skirt swing.

"Let's open a couple of these," Shannon said, pointing to the large boxes against the wall. She grabbed the box cutter and pulled out all the boot boxes, finding black in Willow's size. "These might be just right," holding up a boot for her approval. "The silver-gray design is subtle but will add some interest to the monochrome look of the skirt and blouse."

Willow pulled them on with the help of a boot horn and went to the mirror again. "I love these," she commented, turning to Shannon. "They feel great, and you're right, they're perfect with what I'm wearing." She had a big smile on her already happy face.

Shannon stood behind her seeing both their reflections in the long mirror. "I wouldn't wear any jewelry; you don't want to distract him, maybe a pair of simple earrings."

She wrote up the sales slip, ran Willow's credit card then wrapped the skirt and blouse in green tissue placing them in a bag with glitter shamrocks surrounding the name of the store.

"You have to promise to come back and tell me your date's reaction," she said, handing her the bag. "Since you're my first paying customer, here's a coupon for ten percent off your next visit."

"That's nice of you. I really appreciate your help, and thanks for having such nice things to choose from. I'll definitely be back." She headed for the door then turned, "Shannon, let me know if you ever want to meet for coffee before or after work. I wrote my cell number on the slip. I enjoyed meeting you and chatting."

"Yes, I'd like that."

Willow sang with the music playing on the car stereo as she hurried home. Pulling into the garage, her gaze automatically went to the spot where Terry always parked. It was as empty as she felt and not just from hunger.

It was one-thirty, so she grabbed a protein bar before taking the shopping bag and boot box to her room, hanging up the new skirt and blouse while mentally planning the rest of the afternoon.

At three o'clock she filled her bathtub, which reminded her that the hot tub had probably been installed this morning while she was out. Willow looked forward to she and Terry having a soak when they got home. The mere thought of slipping into hot water with him caused a sweet curling sensation in her stomach. She was crazy in love and couldn't imagine spending her life without him.

She'd been happy working as a reporter at the newspaper, receiving accolades and awards for articles she'd written. Leaving after four years to focus on her fiction was an easy transition for her. Her father, and a few of her friends wondered if she'd made the right decision. When she learned Chet was having an affair with his secretary, she too had her doubts blaming herself since putting so much time and effort into her second novel. Chet was usually too busy, he'd said, to travel with her to book signings or to receive an award. Most likely too busy between the sheets with his secretary.

Willow stepped out of the tub after wrapping a towel around her wet head. She dried off and applied the first coat of burgundy polish to her toes and pale pink on her fingernails. After blow-drying her hair, she added rollers so her long hair would be curly when pulling it up in a clip. She spritzed perfume on her wrists, hollow of her neck and between her breasts before slipping on the one push-up bra she owned and was surprised at the effect, hoping her cowboy would be duly shaken to his core.

She checked her image in the bathroom mirror one more time, adding lip-gloss when her doorbell rang.

Chapter 14

Standing at Willow's front door Terry heard her footsteps, and his jaw dropped at the sight of her framed in the doorway.

"Oh, you are so not playing fair," he said, gently shaking his head. His eyes swept over her as he blew out a breath. "I'm speechless. You are beautiful, and I feel privileged to have you for my dinner date."

"Well, thank you Terry," she said, then saw the white roses in his hand.

"Oh, yeah," he said, blinking several times to ease the erotic images he'd been enjoying to another corner in his mind. They'll come in handy later. "These are for you." He held the flowers out to her, "but you put them to shame."

Now she giggled, "Thank you, how thoughtful." She sniffed them, "They smell yummy."

"You smell mighty nice yourself."

"Would you like a drink, or do we need to go?" she asked, on her way to find a vase.

"I think we better go," he was feeling warm around the collar and everywhere else.

"You're extra handsome this evening," Willow said and placed the roses in a vase of water on the coffee table. They walked out to the waiting truck and headed for Cody.

Terry did his best to keep his eyes on the road, but Willow's breasts were making it difficult. "Have you had that outfit in your closet or did you go shopping today?"

"I found a great new boutique in town, and yes, I bought this today."

He loved seeing the delight in her eyes when she talked about something as simple as finding a clothing store she liked. "Good, I wouldn't want any other man to have already seen you in that."

"Shannon will be pleased," she said, turning toward him with a sultry gaze.

He raised a questioning eyebrow.

"She just moved here, opened this great store and helped me put this together."

"She's to be congratulated."

They listened to a country and western station on the drive to dinner while holding hands. "I have something to tell you, but I'll wait until we get to the restaurant. Although I will say, I called my friend Ian Digby in Australia. Before I left Oz, I told him he'd be my first choice for ranch foreman. So, when I talked to him today, he said, 'Okay mate, when do I start?'"

Willow giggled hearing him speak with an Australian accent.

"I'm making arrangements for my horse to be brought over and Digger, Ian's nickname, will see that Brumby gets off all right."

"Wait," Willow said, "You're having your horse brought over here?"

Again, using an Aussie dialect, "Yeah, a man's gotta have his horse."

She giggled again. "That accent is kind of sexy."

"Well, expect to hear it more often then."

"But, how will your horse get here?"

"He'll fly," and explained there were companies with specially equipped planes that transport horses and other animals all over the world. "I've already spoken with a shipping agent and I have the necessary import paperwork set to go." Terry looked over at Willow with a big smile, "Just waiting for the barn to be completed. I want everything in place before he gets here."

"That is so exciting."

He nodded, "And, when Brumby does arrive, quarantine is a minimum of forty-two hours. Ian will be ready with a truck and horse trailer to haul him here."

"It sounds like you have thought of everything. So, how did Brumby get that name?"

Terry spent a moment thinking about the stallion and how much he missed him. "Brumby is Aussie slang for wild horse, but since he isn't close to being that, I thought I'd help out by naming him Brumby. Give him a little clout, street cred, so to speak."

It was obvious he couldn't wait for his horse to arrive.

"Tell me about him."

"He's part Arabian; light gray with dark gray tail and mane," he smiled at the thought of him. "He's macho."

"My gray cowboy has a gray horse! Sounds like I may have some competition."

"No worries, Sheila." Terry was on a roll with the accent, "He doesn't mind sharing me." He'd wait to tell her the rest of the good news when he could focus on her and not the highway.

The Cody Ranch Steak House was dimly lit, and Terry held tight to Willow's waist in that protective way he had, not wanting her to stumble in the dark entry. But mostly because he loved having his arm around her. When she leaned into him, he knew she felt the same.

Terry had reserved a corner booth and the hostess showed them to their table.

Willow slid into the center of the booth and Terry sat as close to her as he could, pressing his muscular thigh against her leg. When he turned to look at her, he knew she felt the same electric jolt he had.

He ordered a bottle of red wine from the wine book their waiter handed him, along with menus and a promise to return with the wine. After approving his selection, the waiter poured a glass for Willow then added wine to Terry's glass. He also ordered a light appetizer of crab stuffed baby portabella mushrooms.

"Miss James," Terry began, easing his arm around her shoulders, his wine glass in hand. "I am the proud owner of two hundred-fifty acres of land that adjoin your property with an option to buy a hundred more." He was beaming, "and, I am proud to be here with you this evening. You are *the* most stunning woman in this restaurant."

They clinked glasses, then took a sip of wine. "Terry, that's wonderful news. So that's what you were up to today. I'm happy for you and excited about being neighbors."

He nodded, savoring the wine, setting his glass back on the table. "Yes, I left early this morning and drove back over to the property, and it was clear to me I should buy it." His expression of wonder intensified. "Can you believe my father has parked his truck on that property for the past twelve years when he came looking for me and to tend my mother's garden?"

"That's amazing. Gives me goose bumps. Knowing you'll be seeing your father regularly is one of life's unexpected treasures. Do you remember thanking me for taking care of your mother's garden?" She didn't wait for his reply, "Well I didn't have the heart to tell you it wasn't me, but I never imagined it could be your father."

He kissed her hand, his eyes locked on hers when their starter arrived. They dug in hungrily.

Setting her fork down in between bites, Willow laid her hand on his arm. "Terry," she began as he gazed at her, "Are we on this date because your father is back in your life?"

Once again, he was amazed by how insightful she was. "Yes, but only because I don't think my father would approve of my not courting you before I got your clothes off. Not that I regret one second of our first night together," he quickly added, kissing her hand.

"I admire my father, always wanted to be just like him. He never complained and was eager to help anyone who needed an extra hand. And, I want to have the same loving relationship my parents had."

"What a nice sentiment," she offered, fork in midair. "I, too, wanted to be just like my mom and dad, but I blew it when I married the wrong guy."

"It's not too late, is it?" He said, while his thumb gently massaged the back of her hand.

She gave him a half smile, "No, of course not. I just wanted to get it right the first time like they did instead of going through so much misery." She was thoughtful a moment, "Fortunately, we didn't have a baby before I realized who the real Chet was." She shuddered. "Then we would have been connected for life." She set her fork down, "I'm sure your father would be proud of the way you've always treated me."

He hoped that was true. "I know we've been busy, but how's your book coming?" he asked, taking the last bite of stuffed portabella.

"It's finished. Now I'll edit then send it to Sydney to edit, and she'll most likely send it back for some rewrites." She kissed him, "Thank you for asking."

~

Willow was impressed with the way Terry had taken control, ordering the delicious appetizer, and choosing the perfect wine to complement their dinner. He seemed to know exactly what he wanted. She wanted to be on that list too. Up at the top and her name in capital letters. Underlined, asterisks on each side.

When their dinner arrived, they ate offering murmurs of appreciation for the delicious steak. They decided against dessert and on the way home Willow said, "I think the hot tub was installed today. I forgot about it until I was in my bathtub, but never went out to look."

He glanced over at her with a twinkle in his eye while her fingers fondled his ear lobe then moved down his cheek. He took her hand, kissed her fingertips.

She was anxious for him to kiss the rest of her when they got home.

He parked in front of her house so they wouldn't have far to walk. Before going in, they walked down the deck to check on the hot tub and sure enough there it was, purring away.

Terry lifted the lid and steam escaped.

"Should we christen it?" she said, her eyes sparkling in the moonlight.

"Yes ma'am," he said with a lusty smile and a quirk of an eyebrow.

She took him by the hand leading him into her bedroom where they undressed, eyes trained on each other, then pulled the big towels around them before stepping back outside.

"Yikes, it's hot," Willow declared, sitting on the edge pulling her feet back out of the water.

Terry pulled on the tether holding the thermometer, "It says a hundred two degrees. It just seems hot because you're cold." He let his towel drop to the deck then sat on the edge, easing into the hot water while Willow did the same. When he sat on one of the seats across from her, she joined him, moving onto his lap and wrapping her legs around him.

An hour later, skin feeling waterlogged, they dried off and padded to her bedroom for more tender love making before falling asleep.

~

The next morning Terry left Willow to sleep and drove to the Red Kettle to meet up with Tommy, knowing this was his day off work and he wouldn't be in uniform. During breakfast, he broke the news, off the record of course, that his father was alive and well.

The news took Tommy so completely by surprise, his fork hit his plate with a clang. Every head in the restaurant turned toward the two guys in the corner booth.

Terry was wide eyed watching Tommy do his best not to cough with a mouth full of food after the involuntary inhale response of the news he'd just dropped on his buddy.

"I'm sorry, I should have waited until you'd swallowed."

After taking a drink of water, Tommy said, "That is some kind of miracle! What an amazing story. Man, I can't wait to see him."

"I'm grateful for your friendship Tommy, being able to tell you this takes a load off my shoulders. Willow knows of course, but she didn't know dad." He fiddled with his coffee cup, "I knew you'd be happy to hear that horrible day thirteen years ago didn't turn out as bad as we all thought."

Tommy's brow furrowed as he sat back. "Okay, let me think about this for a minute. Your dad was declared legally dead after the fire, and Noreen got a life sentence for murdering him. But it wasn't Alain in the barn, it was her brother," he said quietly. "What, if any, are the ramifications of this situation?"

"As far as Dad knows, no one's ever seen him at the house or anywhere else." He knew his dad had kept his visits to the house quiet, but Terry hadn't thought about any of that.

"You should probably talk to a lawyer about this. Did he have life insurance that paid a death benefit to you?"

"No. Dad didn't have an insurance policy that I know of."

Tommy nodded, "So there wouldn't be any fraud there." He looked at nothing in particular while he wondered if he was missing anything. "Even though your dad didn't die in the barn, Billy did. So, Noreen actually murdered her brother." He chewed on his lower lip a minute. "Would it make any difference thirteen years later? A lawyer's your best bet to make sure there wasn't any criminal intent."

"Thanks," Terry said, "I need a lawyer to get my business set-up anyway."

When he got to Willow's, he joined her on the deck as she emailed her article to Mike at the paper. It was a beautiful Sunday morning with a bright blue sky and those billowy clouds he knew Willow loved.

He filled her in on his conversation with Tommy, then told her, "I'm going to Montana to see my dad on Tuesday. I'll look at hiring a lawyer and run all this past him or her," he said, though only mildly concerned.

The following day Terry was tied up with the foreman in charge of building the barn while Willow kept busy editing her manuscript. That night she ate dinner alone after Terry called to say he'd be back late.

When he got home, he found Willow asleep in bed with a book on her chest. She stirred when he set the book aside before slipping in beside her. Pulling her into his arms, he kissed the tip of her nose.

Chapter 15

Tuesday morning, Willow's arm lay across Terry's chest, her leg draped over his when his alarm sounded at 5 a.m. He wanted to get an early start to drive to Montana and told her not to fix him breakfast. He'd stop for coffee along the way.

Since they hadn't had much time to catch up, she followed him to the apartment where he still kept some of his clothes. While he packed a few things, Willow said, "I'll make room for your clothes, so you don't have to come up here to shower and dress."

"Don't go to any fuss," he said, "I don't mind having my gear in the apartment."

She watched him for a few minutes, "Well, I can tell you're distracted so I'll leave you to pack."

Terry caught her hand before she left the room. "I'm sorry Willow. I am preoccupied with dad and hiring a lawyer and forming a business. I hope you don't mind me going alone. I feel I'd still be ignoring you. I need to focus on dad and the ranch right now."

"No. I get that, maybe I can go another time."

"Hey, why don't you take a few days and go see Norma or go out to California."

"Oh, I don't know. I really need to keep working on my manuscript." She kissed him on the cheek, "I'll be fine," she said heading for the door.

"Okay, I'll be down in a few minutes. I'm just about finished packing."

Standing beside his truck Terry kissed Willow long and hard. "Call me along the way," she said while he pulled the seat belt across his lap and clicked it in place.

"You know I will."

She walked around the front of the truck then saw him open the door and step out to take his jacket off tossing it on the passenger seat. He waved out the window and drove to the road.

Willow found it difficult to concentrate on her manuscript. "I'm not doing a very good job editing," she said out loud, after finding another mistake in a paragraph she'd read three times. She'd had enough of sitting alone on the deck and went back inside, feeling a little depressed. The kittens were good company, but her conversations with them were one sided.

"My house is empty without Terry," she said standing in her kitchen then glanced at the clock and saw that it was 11:30. No wonder I'm hungry. Reaching for her phone she checked for new text messages then rolled her eyes lightly shaking her head. "I'm such a dork. He's only been gone a few hours. But I was sure he would have called by now." She looked out the window above the sink. "I just don't want to believe I've stepped into the same kind of relationship I had with Chet," she said to the kittens.

Not liking the thoughts running through her head she pulled the key to the garage apartment off the hook and climbed the stairs relieved to find some of Terry's clothes and toiletries in the bathroom. "Well of course his things are still here. He didn't move out for heaven's sake. Can I really not get by without him for a few days?" She eyed a tee shirt laying on the bathroom counter. "Apparently not," she said and grabbed it holding it to her face, taking in his familiar male scent. She grinned, remembering an article about a famous Hollywood movie star who said she always slept with a pair of her husband's underwear when he was away on location.

Willow took the shirt and stepped back outside, locking the door before heading to her house, where she tucked the tee shirt under her pillow.

She couldn't understand why Terry hadn't called, which only increased her worry. Now her thoughts became dreadful images of Terry lying somewhere, injured, or sick and not able to call for help. She sent him another text and wondered if he just didn't have good cell service.

She sat on the floor in the kitchen to cuddle Midnight when he rubbed up against her leg. "Well, kitty this is what I get for falling hard for Terry in such a short time. But he seemed perfect for me in every way," she said pouting a little. Stormy joined in, reaching up to chew on her long hair.

"You know, I don't remember ever saying that about Chet. Boy, I really messed up. Wish I'd listened to Norma, she saw right through him. Now, I've got to keep my eyes wide open when Terry comes back."

Her cell rang, and she couldn't grab it fast enough, positive it would be Terry.

"Oh, hello Mac." She tried not to sound disappointed but was sure she'd failed miserably. Fortunately, she sensed he was too busy to notice.

"Chet's agreed to group counseling if no charges are pressed. He wanted to know who spoke up, I told him I couldn't give him names unless someone wanted to press charges. Said he thought he knew who it was, but I reminded him, he's the offender not his victims."

"Okay, Mac, we'll see how that works. I think I might fly out there for a couple days. I'll give you a call. Maybe we can meet for coffee."

He sounded distracted, but said, "Yeah, sure. Let me know. Bye Kiddo."

Maybe Terry is right. She hadn't seen her parents in three months. "Even they're too busy and can't come to see me, but I could fly there and spend a few days," she said. Now her spirits lifted as she crawled on her knees to the counter, grabbing her iPad.

Willow pulled up one of the travel websites, entered her departure city and destination then began checking her options. "Looks like I can leave Friday at eleven, but first I need to make sure Mom and Dad will even be home."

The kittens were bored with her and began a game of chase around the house. She quickly dialed her mother's cell and left a message. She's probably busy selling another multi-million-dollar house, Willow thought with a chuckle. "My mother is amazing," she said while touching her dad's photo, then hearing his familiar ring tone. Please answer, she pleaded.

"Hi sweetheart, how are you." She started to sniffle. "Willow what's wrong?"

"I'm fine, really, just happy to hear your voice."

"And...?"

Dad can read me like a balance sheet, she reminded herself. They'd always been close, there was never anything she couldn't tell him. "And, I'm coming home for a visit."

"That's great, when will you be here?"

"My flight arrives Friday at two-thirty and I'll take a shuttle to the house, if that's okay, of course."

"I think it'll be fine. I'll be home by four and your mother should be as well."

"I can't wait to come home. I've really missed being with you."

"But otherwise, you're okay?" he asked tentatively.

"Dad, I'm just lonely, and I need to come home for a few days. That's all. Really."

"Your mother will be happy to know you're coming."

"All right, I'll see you Friday. Love you."

"I love you too baby. Bye."

She set her cell on the floor as the kittens ran back into the kitchen sliding on the tile while Willow laughed. "You two are the best thing I've got going right now." Then it occurred to her, they needed to be taken care of while she's away. "Holy crap. Well, there must be someplace in town that boards pets, but first I need to eat something. I'm starving," she told them, before going after her purse.

"You guys be good, I'll be back in a while." She locked the door then headed to the garage and into town for lunch at the Red Kettle. Tommy pulled in the parking lot right behind her, and the two walked in the restaurant together, sitting at his favorite booth in the back.

"So, how's Terry doing, haven't seen him in days," Tommy asked, perusing the menu he already knew by heart.

"Fine. He's on his way to see his father. I haven't heard from him, but reception is probably awful."

His ears perked up, "Why didn't you go with him?"

"He needs time with his dad and he'll be busy hiring a lawyer and whatever else he needs to do."

Tommy closed the menu with a snap and dropped it on the table. "What the hell's wrong with him leaving you alone with wolves at your door?"

Willow laughed, "Anyway, I'm leaving."

He cocked his head as his eyes narrowed, "Leaving?"

"Yes. I'm going home for a few days. I want to spend some time with my parents." She shrugged her shoulders, "I thought this would be a good time to go."

Tommy watched her carefully, as a cop would, for any signs of stress or depression. "Why didn't you call me?"

She glared at him with arched brows and a you've-got-to-be-kidding expression on her face. "Really

Tommy? I should call to tell you I'm lonely?" She settled against the seat back. "I don't think so."

"What?" He sounded wounded, shoulders arched, arms out. "I'd be happy to come over to keep you company for a while or even all night." He waggled his eyebrows and gave her a goofy grin to let her know he was kidding.

At least she hoped he was.

"You shouldn't say things like that Tommy. Terry's your best friend, and I'm hopelessly in love with him."

"Yeah, I can see that, always have. You two are meant for each other." He reached over to put his hand on hers briefly then withdrew it. "No doubt about it."

"Did we order?" Willow asked, puzzled, "I don't remember ordering, but this is what I wanted." Glancing over at Brenda, "She's really good."

"She thinks she's doing herself a favor." Tommy said.

It took Willow a minute, but she finally got it. "You think, she thinks we're here together, as in *together*?" she asked, horrified.

"Yeah, she's the queen of gossip here in Elk Valley."

Willow's eyes grew wide, "Yikes, thanks for the warning."

They ate in silence for several minutes before Tommy asked, "When do you leave?"

"Day after tomorrow and by the way," she set her fork down, elbows on the table and fingers laced, "do you know where I could board my cats?"

"Humm, that's short notice." He mulled it over then offered, "Why don't I take care of them for you? I go by your driveway at least twice a day. I could check on them, make sure they have food and water."

"I couldn't ask you to do that," she said. "You're busy being a policeman but I really appreciate the offer." Out of the corner of her eye she caught Brenda staring at them. Willow resisted the instinct to reach over to touch Tommy's arm as a friendly gesture. She suddenly felt uncomfortable being here with him even though it was just two friends having lunch.

"Willow, I'm happy to do this for you. Like you said, it's only for a few days. Besides, I've missed having a pet since I had to put my dog down. I really don't mind."

"Okay, if you're sure it won't be too much of an inconvenience."

He shook his head, "Not at all. Why don't I follow you to your place, you can show me where everything is, and how much to feed them."

"Great. I'm ready to go if you are."

Tommy paid their check then followed her back to her house. Willow gave him a key and wrote out kitty care instructions showing him where fresh litter was stored and set out cans of food.

"I'd be happy to drive you to the airport."

"Thanks, but you're doing enough to help me, I don't mind driving. Oh, let me put my parents address and phone number on that note so you'll know where I am."

"Okay. Well, have a great time with your family," he said, dropping the key in his shirt pocket along with the note before pulling her close for a good-bye hug.

Hugging him back, she said, "Thanks Tommy, you're a good guy." It felt good to have a man's arms around her, but they were the wrong arms.

That night when Willow got into bed, she couldn't help wondering if Terry was even thinking about her. She sent another text message to him, this one a reminder that they could be curled up together skin on skin. She was not one who sent naked photos of herself, but she was tempted.

"But then, maybe our relationship is one sided," she said then groaned and punched her pillow before nesting her head on it.

When her cell rang, she saw Terry's familiar phone number and said "Terry, I'm so glad you called! I've been worried about you."

His words were choppy and then the call dropped. She immediately called back but got a busy signal, then sent a couple of text messages.

She fell asleep with the phone in her hand and tried calling and texting a number of times the following day. They were finally able to get a few words in before the call dropped again. "Yeah, I get it. He has rotten cell service."

Willow was up early Friday morning, ready to leave at eight. She double checked the kitten's food and water, knowing Tommy would stop by later in the day.

On the way to the garage, something laying in the dirt got her attention. She took a closer look picked it up, and realized it was a cell phone. Terry's cell phone. Looked as if he'd dropped it then backed over it. She could see where a small rock had pierced the back. The glass was broken, and it wouldn't turn on. So that's why he wasn't able to get in touch with me sooner. She let out a breath feeling a little better.

Chapter 16

Terry reminded himself to hold his speed down as he drove back to Elk Valley. When he'd discovered his phone was missing, he'd stopped in Sheridan, Wyoming to buy a new one and called Willow but it went right to voice mail. At least she'd know he'd left her a message. So frustrating. He was anxious to see her and tell her about his trip, especially the conversations he'd had with his father and his meeting with the architect. He wanted to hold her in his arms and tell her he loved her.

He couldn't help himself and drove a little faster. Then he heard his text message alert and pulled off the road. He smiled seeing it was from Willow sent earlier in the day.

When he pulled up to Willow's house and saw the sheriff's cruiser there, his heart rate kicked up a bit.

"What's wrong? What are you doing in Willow's house? Where is she?" Terry questioned his boyhood friend when he walked in and found Tommy in the living room.

"She's gone," Tommy replied, hands on his hips.

"Gone? Gone where?" There was a quiver in his voice, and fear had a strangle hold on his heart.

"She went home to see her family." He replied, calmly.

"Oh good. I'm glad she did that. But, how did you get in here?"

He pulled the key out of his pocket, "I have a key," Tommy said with a sly grin.

"Why don't you just tell me what the hell's going on here, so I don't have to ask so many bloody questions?"

"I'm taking care of her cats while she's gone."

"Well, I could have taken care of them," he said, sheepishly.

"Only if you'd been here. Where the hell have you been?"

"Up to my ass in lawyers, accountants and architects," he said, waving his arms. "Besides, Willow knew where I was. We just couldn't talk on the phone."

"Not a good enough reason to avoid Willow."

"I would never avoid the woman I love, as if it's any of your business."

"Terry, she loves you. Don't ask me why, but she does."

"You have no right…"

"Shut up for once in your life," he interrupted, raking fingers through his hair. "You can't neglect a woman like Willow. There are other guys waiting in the wings for the privilege of her love. And, if you love her like you say you do, you need to tell her, not me."

Terry collapsed on the sofa, "You're right, I'm over-reacting." He rubbed the back of his neck, "I lost my phone somewhere, I bought a new one, and was able to get a text off to Willow, but it couldn't send until I got near a cell tower. We had a brief phone conversation but reception is almost non-existent where dad lives. And, I've been preoccupied trying to build a home and a business as well as making sure my dad's okay. I drove to Montana to see him and meet his wife. I don't regret that. But now, I want to build a future for Willow and me. Nothing else matters except making a life with her."

Tommy clapped his hands, "Hurray! Now go tell her that, you jackass."

~

The trip from the airport seemed longer than Willow remembered. Guess I'm just anxious to get there, she thought. Stop-and-go traffic on Highway 1 reminded her how simple life was in Elk Valley. When the shuttle pulled up in front of the house, Willow's mother was unloading grocery bags from the trunk of her car. She thanked the driver with a tip before hurrying toward her mom.

"Darling, it's so good to see you," Frankie said, while they rocked back and forth in their hug. "You look wonderful, happy I would say," she commented, pulling back to look at her daughter. "I've been to the market, so we have plenty of food and won't have to leave the house if we don't want to."

As they carried the last of the groceries into the house, Willow's father, Patrick, pulled into the driveway. Setting the bags on the front steps, Willow ran to him, arms out, ready for a hug.

Then, stepping into the house she heard Rambo bark. Her dad took the bags and she darted out the back door to sit on the lawn and cuddle her dog whose tail whipped back and forth while he buried his head against her.

After several minutes she stood, then cringed when Rambo struggled to stand. His hip dysplasia had gotten worse. I'll bet Chet kept him outside, she thought. Her parents had a dog door installed that allowed Rambo to go in and out of the garage when they were at work. He followed her into the kitchen making himself comfortable on a big fluffy dog bed.

"We took him to the vet and got some pain meds which seem to help," Frankie said after Willow expressed her concern.

Once the food was put away, Patrick poured champagne to toast Willow's visit.

"We've missed seeing you!" He said, raising his glass, "And we're pleased you took time to come for a visit. We want to hear everything about your life in Wyoming."

Their welcoming words were just what she needed, causing her to blush. Even Mango, her mom's Maltese, was delighted to see Willow again, sniffing her pant legs full of the scent of her cats.

Willow observed her parents working together in the kitchen. Her mom humming and swaying to an Ella Fitzgerald standard while preparing steaks to grill. Patrick kissed her on the cheek then patted her on the behind before opening a bottle of wine. Willow was thinking about the life she imagined and wanted it to be with Terry. Of course, she wanted a wonderful, happy life with him. Her parent's words became muted as she imagined moving around her kitchen with the man she was madly in love with.

The three of them continued to prepare dinner, just as they'd done countless times before, talking incessantly as Willow told them how much she loved her house and the small town feel of Elk Valley.

She also told them she'd sent her third manuscript off to her editor and how glad she was to have Stormy and Midnight. Then she went on and on about Terry, describing in detail everything he'd told her about his life. She finished with how much she cared for him. Frankie loved hearing her refer to Terry as Gray Cowboy, and was anxious to meet him.

"I think I'm in love with him, but after what I went through with Chet, it feels like we're moving too fast." She sighed, "But, I can't help the way I feel about him. Being with him is so easy, we seem to want the same things in life."

She rinsed off the lettuce and put it in the salad spinner. "I miss him so much, and it makes me nervous."

"Just because your marriage to Chet was disappointing doesn't mean your relationship with this new guy will end the same way," her father said. "Trust and respect are as important as being head-over-heels in love. More so, maybe."

She nodded in agreement, "Wish I'd thought to question Chet's integrity. I know Terry has respect for me, but I have to be smarter this time."

The following day they sat in the backyard enjoying the sun and the abundance of flowers in full bloom, relaxing, glad to be together.

Willow enjoyed the sounds of the neighborhood: kids on skateboards whizzing down the street, a neighbor calling their dog and that familiar balmy whiff of the ocean. She'd missed those things.

Later, as they headed back into the house Willow revealed, "I always saw myself falling in love with a great guy and we would be the perfect couple like you guys. We would have a long, loving marriage but now I wonder if that is even possible for me."

She observed her parents, longing to be just like them. They've made successful careers for themselves and have an enviable life together.

"You know your dad and I aren't married, and it hasn't made any difference in our relationship."

Three of the lamps in the living room came on automatically as the sun headed for the ocean. The background music was deafening. And yet, the room was like a vacuum, one could most likely have heard a pin hit the plush ivory carpet.

"Oh, yeah. But you did have a ceremony, right?"

"Yes," Patrick said, "the three of us went to Hawaii when you were..." he turned to his wife for guidance.

"You were four months old, and we bought you a lovely frilly dress, and I made a halo of flowers for your tiny head and..."

"Anyway," he said, interrupting her.

And, Willow smiled knowing her mom would go on for ten minutes, taking a trip down memory lane and her dad would forget what he was saying.

"We went to Hawaii to attend a retreat where we were part of a mass wedding ceremony, albeit a mock ceremony, on the beach at sunrise. Sunrise because it represents a new beginning," he explained, using hand gestures in an attempt to make it more credible. He chuckled, "It all seems silly now but at the time we thought it was the way to go."

Frankie stepped up next to Patrick linking her arm in his, smiling, remembering that morning.

"Oh, you two are making me sick. I can't believe you didn't even have the decency to 'not' get married before I was born." Willow was teasing them, feeling good about her unconventional family.

Patrick, frowning slightly, slipped his hands into his trouser pockets. "Your mother and I didn't rush to get married because there was a time when we weren't sure we would stay together."

Willow swallowed hard. "Why, what happened?" The little girl in her thought she might have been the reason.

"Some things changed between us." He glanced over at Frankie who had moved to the couch. Patrick joined her.

"Okay, that's not good enough. I want to hear the real reason you didn't get married." Willow said, as she sat on the coffee table facing them.

Patrick held Frankie's hand. "Your mother was steeped in the cult we belonged to. I no longer thought it was healthy and wanted to get away from it, thought it would hurt my career."

"Yes, I remember you talking about that a few years ago. I was writing an article for the paper on religious cults." She'd thought it was interesting but couldn't imagine her parents becoming part of something so controlling.

Frankie nodded, "Your father made some valid points, so I decided to leave the cult. The leader made life difficult for a few months, but it worked out in the end."

"Well, I love the idea of being married. I want to make that commitment to a man I plan to spend the rest of my life with." Willow held up her hand, "I know, I botched it the first time, but Dad's right. I feel much different about Terry than I ever did about Chet. Why did I say yes to him just because he asked me to marry him?"

The little dog whimpered, apparently not appreciating the tone of the conversation.

Willow picked Mango up and stroked her soft coat, "I'm sorry, I didn't mean to make you nervous."

The door chime began its elaborate tune, but they chose not to hear it.

"Why didn't you get married then?"

"A few years later, I was offered a job in another state. Your mother was just starting out in real estate and didn't want to leave Santa Barbara or her family. I really wanted this job, so I went there for six months."

"You guys actually separated? I don't remember that."

"You were three or four at the time, and your Grandmother Desiree took care of you while mom worked, so you always had family around you."

The door chime sounded again. "I think we should answer the door," Frankie offered.

"No. It's probably just a kid selling magazine subscriptions. I want to hear the rest of this story. Maybe I'm not the failure I think I am."

Patrick heaved a sigh, "I missed you and your mother terribly and didn't want anything to keep us apart. So, I sent my resume to Pacific Coastal Bank, they offered me an interview, and here I am."

The door chime became annoying as their heads turned toward the front door.

Willow pressed on. "This means so much to me knowing you aren't perfect and that it's okay." She thought her parents looked relieved, yet weary.

Frankie noticed movement out the picture window with its view of the backyard. "There's someone in our yard. I don't think it's the gardener," she said, squinting to see who it might be.

"Oh, all right. I'll see who it is. Bloody hell."

Frankie raised her brows and mouthed the words, 'bloody hell?'

Patrick shrugged his shoulders as Willow stepped through the French doors into the backyard.

She spotted him immediately. She knew that gait, that muscular back and everything else about him. "Terry!"

He turned, dropped his duffle and stepped forward as she leaped into his arms, wrapping her long legs around him while he kissed her hungrily before coming up for air. "It feels so good to have you in my arms again," he murmured in her ear.

"I'm glad you're okay. I was worried when you called and I couldn't hear you. I was lonely and scared you didn't want to be with me anymore."

And he kissed her again, so there would be no doubt that he cared deeply for her. "I'm sorry," he said, stroking her hair then wiping her tears away with his thumb. "I love you Willow, and I need you by my side."

She gulped and felt all those luscious, familiar tingles running through her body. "Oh Cowboy, I love you too." She kissed him before releasing her grip around his waist.

By then her parents had come to see what the murmuring was about. Terry and Willow were in a tight embrace when Patrick said, "Hello. You must be The Gray Cowboy."

"Come in, please." Frankie smiled, gesturing with her hand, feeling a little teary eyed. Terry grabbed his duffle and followed Willow into the house.

If he wasn't touching Willow in some way, Terry's eyes were glued to her, watching her every move. It felt as if he was making up for not seeing her the past few days.

They made themselves at home in the living room only to migrate into the kitchen where Patrick opened another bottle of champagne. Willow and Frankie began setting cheese and crackers on a tray with other munchies when they settled in around the big island in the center of the kitchen as though Terry had always been part of the family.

Patrick was all ears when Terry began talking about the property he purchased and his plans to raise grass-fed beef and that the barn was under construction.

"Well," Patrick said, "as Willow may have told you, I'm President of Pacific Coastal Bank, and if you need financing for one of your projects, I'd be happy to help in any way I can."

Terry's eyes narrowed then gave him an incredulous stare. "That's very generous of you, sir. I appreciate that."

After dinner in the backyard, under the stars, Terry told Patrick and Frankie how much he loved their daughter and complimented them on raising such a wonderful woman. At nine o'clock Willow's parents said goodnight, and Terry and Willow moved to the double lounge chair to cuddle under the outdoor heaters.

The two wrapped themselves in each other's arms, kissing, hands roaming over their bodies. "I've missed this, snuggling against you." Willow clamped her arms around him, "But I'm glad you went to see your dad, I know you had a lot to catch up on."

His face lit up, "You know what? I know this sounds stupid, but I felt like an orphan with both my parents gone. It was wonderful to sit and listen to dad talk about how he met Aimee and now they raise goats like my mom did. He took her to France to meet his family. They even talked about moving there but dad said something kept him from going through with it. He was so sure I would show up one day and wanted to stay close."

"That's beautiful. A miracle, really."

"I missed having you with me, though." he said with a sigh.

"My sweet Terry," she said, cupping his face with her hands. "I love you so much." She kissed him tenderly.

His mouth devoured hers as he began to remove her clothes. "Wait, I'll go get a blanket," Willow said, kissing him before darting into the house. The backyard was secluded and the lounge, with its canopy faced the back wall. Willow returned with the blanket and Terry enjoyed watching her lust-filled eyes roam over him as he lay back, hands linked behind his head. She proceeded to strip for him in an agonizing, seductive way. He was all but drooling by the time she began unfastening his jeans.

"Are you sure this is okay with your parents for us to get naked in their back yard?", he whispered in her ear. "They hardly know me."

"I think that's why they went to bed early." She said helping him remove his jeans.

The two of them rolled around on the lounge giggling then tried to muffle their cries of ecstasy before wrapping up in the blanket, whispering their undying love for each other.

They stayed out on the lounge talking and planning their future until two a.m. when they went up to her room, falling asleep in each other's arms.

They woke to the sweet smell of bacon and coffee, then hurried to shower and dress, before joining her parents' downstairs. Terry admired the way Patrick and Frankie worked together. They seemed to instinctively know what each other was going to do next. He couldn't remember too many times when his dad was in the kitchen helping his mom. But he wanted that with Willow. He also made a mental note about the way the light came in the window brightening the kitchen thinking how it might work in the home they would build.

After breakfast, out on the patio, Terry said, "I can understand why people flock to California. This is amazing to sit out here," his eyes swept the yard, "and have breakfast in this beautiful garden." Purple, pink and coral azalea were in full bloom along with a variety of blue hydrangea. Frothy Australian tree ferns sat in two corners of the flowerbed framing the well-manicured, lush green lawn.

"Yes, we feel fortunate to live here," Frankie said.

"Mom, can I borrow a car? I'd like to show Terry around Santa Barbara and we're going to meet Sheriff Mac for coffee." She turned to him, resting her hand on his thigh. He covered it with his. "I hope you don't mind."

"Not at all."

Frankie stood, "I'll get my keys."

"And I'll put some shoes on and get my purse," Willow said, then kissed Terry before hurrying into the house and up the stairs.

When Terry was sure she was out of earshot, he leaned forward, "Mr. James..."

Patrick stopped him, "Terry please, call me Patrick."

"Okay, Patrick," he cleared his throat. "I want you to know that Willow means the world to me."

"Frankie and I are pleased to see how happy our daughter is. But, as you know, her husband of just seven months was a disappointment on so many levels."

Terry nodded, "Willow filled me in on some of the reasons she ended her marriage. As she may have told you, I lived in Australia for thirteen years. I'm glad to be back in Elk Valley and reconnect with friends. So much has changed though, I wasn't sure if I'd fit in." He hitched his broad shoulders, "It's been an adjustment, but the best part was meeting Willow and getting to know her over the past several weeks, then everything clicked into place. I want a life with her, a family and a home. She's made me feel whole again without any effort and helped remind me where I came from; a happy loving family."

Patrick smiled, "It's obvious she loves you as much as you love her. That's right isn't it darling?" he said when Frankie stepped outside.

"Yes, we think it's wonderful."

"Okay, I'm finally ready." Willow announced following her mom out the door.

Terry observed her every move as she kissed her parents, thanking them for breakfast. He was overwhelmed with love for her, knowing they would be married and live happily ever after. And, someday a young man would come to ask for their daughter's hand in marriage. He'd be as nervous as Terry had been. He couldn't imagine ever feeling as happy as he did in that moment.

"I'm the luckiest girl in the world to be loved by my three-favorite people."

Terry gave her a hug before they went to the garage where Willow fired up her mother's silver 760 BMW. "Nice car," Terry said, duly impressed.

"My parents don't do anything halfway. Mom likes to pamper her clients while showing properties."

As they drove along, Terry admired the homes on streets lined with mature trees, the mountain range as backdrop to the town as it met the coastline, but feeling a little closed in at the same time. He didn't think he'd be happy living in a big city.

~

Willow easily maneuvered the big car through the streets of her hometown, wanting Terry to see her high school and the newspaper where she'd worked.

When they arrived at the coffee bar Sheriff Mac McCauley, dressed in civvies, was seated at an outdoor table in a corner hoping for a little privacy. He stood when he saw Willow approach.

"Hello Willow," he greeted her with a hug and stuck out his hand to Terry, "Hello, I'm Mac McCauley."

"Terry Du Champs, pleased to meet you Sheriff. Willow has only good things to say about you."

"She just thinks she knows me." He smiled, "It's good to see you Willow. Looks like you are enjoying life in Wyoming," he commented, glancing over at Terry.

Her face flushed slightly, "Yes, meeting Terry has been the best thing about my move. How's your family?" she added when they sat down.

He proceeded to bring her up to date on his wife's part-time job at a daycare center, his son's second year in college and his daughter's final year in high school. They continued to chat, enjoying their coffee before getting down to business.

"I'm glad we were able to meet," Willow said. "I don't believe my ex-husband will do well in a group setting at rehab. I think he'll be intimidated and won't be able to speak honestly. He's very good at telling people what he thinks they want to hear."

Mac was thoughtful as he nodded. "All we can do is try, but he will be advised that we can still press charges." His phone buzzed on the table and he held up his index finger to the couple, silently asking them to wait while he answered the call. He stepped away, his back to them. After a brief conversation, he turned to Willow and Terry, "Duty calls, even on my day off."

They both stood. Willow gave him a hug, thanking him for taking time to meet with them. The two men shook hands, Mac held on, locking eyes with Terry. "Take care of our girl." Terry knew there were unspoken words in that look.

"You have my word." With the grip he has on my hand, I wouldn't want to mess with him, Terry thought.

"I'm glad you've had him on your side," he said, his arm around Willow as they watched the sheriff sprint across the street to his red 1969 Camaro.

"That's a classic." Terry remarked.

"Yeah, he's real proud on that car. Restored it all himself."

"I've never seen so many beautiful cars. Out on the station I only saw pickup trucks, mostly crusted with dirt."

"Come on. I want to take you to one of my favorite places." Willow said reaching for his hand.

Chapter 17

Willow drove them to the resort where she once worked. They followed the hostess to an outdoor table and Terry stopped abruptly to take in the view.

"I can see why you like coming here. Beautiful view of the ocean," he turned and added, "and the mountains."

She was pleased to see Terry enjoying the scenery while they waited for their iced tea. "Would you mind if I called my parents and asked them to join us here for lunch?"

"No, of course not." However, he did mind, he had a surprise for Willow and wanted it to be a private moment. Then reminded himself, they'd have the rest of their lives to celebrate special moments together.

It was a perfect day on the sunny California coast with the sound of the surf and sea gull's high-pitched call in the background. A balmy breeze kept them cool while the four of them enjoyed lunch. Terry told stories of his life on the station in Australia and his determination to conquer calf roping, "Or, at least get the rope around the head of the practice dummy and not have it come back off when I pulled the rope."

Willow and her parents laughed. This wasn't a story Willow had heard, in fact, he hadn't really told her much of anything about his life on the cattle station, except the little bit about Harley.

"My buddy, Tommy Logan, is a natural-born calf roper; he came in third in Junior Rodeo when he was thirteen." He, himself remembered being more concerned about the animal than throwing a rope around its neck.

When they finished lunch, Terry asked Willow's parents, "Would you mind if I took your beautiful daughter for a little stroll on the beach? It's something I've wanted to do since we got here."

"No, you two go ahead," they answered in unison, smiling at one another.

"Miss James," he said, pulling her chair out when she stood.

Willow raised her eyebrows at her parents, shrugging her shoulders slightly with a puzzled expression.

They walked to the gate that led out onto the sand; Terry took her hand as they walked down the beach a short way. "I've really enjoyed being here with you and your parents. They're very nice, easy to be with. Your mother is beautiful, your dad is smart and loves your mother very much."

"That's nice of you to say and all true," she said, hugging his big arm while they walked.

As though they'd reached the perfect spot, he stopped, took her hands in his and got down on one knee. Gazing up at her, he said, "Willow Desiree, you are the most wonderful woman I've ever met. You're thoughtful and kind. You've made me happier in the short time we've known each other than I ever imagined I could be. Will you please marry me?"

Her breath caught and she felt fluttering in her stomach. "Oh, Terry," her eyes tearing. "Yes. Yes. Yes. I love everything about you, and I want to spend the rest of my life with you."

He drew her to her knees, kissing her passionately before leaning back to reach into his pocket. He pulled out a small white satin box opening it to reveal an oval sapphire surrounded by diamonds, all set in platinum.

Willow gasped, hands flew to her chest, tears welling on the corner of her eyes. "This is the most beautiful ring I've ever seen." She was overwhelmed at the obvious extravagance of this token of his love for her. "It matches the color of your eyes perfectly."

He gathered her onto his lap before taking the ring out of its box to place on her finger.

She kissed him tenderly then held her hand out in awe of her engagement ring, feeling love for this man oozing from every pore of her body. "When did you have time to find this ring with everything else you had to do?"

"This was the first thing I did last week," he said, taking her hand in his and pressing it to his lips. "And, it was the most important thing I did. I wanted to let my father know my intentions as well. We can have it resized later."

"It's almost a perfect fit." Then it occurred to her, "Hey, how did you know my middle name?"

"Saw it on the internet," he said, squinting into the sun as he gazed at her. "There's a fair amount of information on you and your successes. You didn't tell me you won an award for a news article you wrote. There was also a 'New Kid on the Block' article about you and your first book. Very impressive."

She giggled with a shrug as though it was no big deal, then wondered where that framed certificate was. Probably in a box in my closet. "Come on, lets go tell my parents and show them my beautiful ring." He held her where she sat a moment longer for one more kiss.

Big smiles on both their faces held nothing back when the newly engaged couple walked into the hotel courtyard where Willow's parents waited. Her father stood as they approached.

Frankie's eyes were like saucers as she admired the lovely ring. She put one arm around her daughter and the other reaching for her future son-in-law.

Then Willow noticed her mother looking around the terrace and said, "No mom you can't invite everyone here to join in our group hug." They all chuckled before her parents offered congratulatory words, handshakes and more hugs.

Another champagne cork popped that evening and Frankie announced she and Patrick wanted to give Willow and Terry an engagement party in Elk Valley. "That way, we can see your home and meet your friends and your father, Terry."

"That's a great idea. We can celebrate Terry's birthday at the same time," Willow said looking up at him.

They decided to fly out two weeks from Friday. Terry was eager for them to meet his father and stepmother.

Since they were leaving the following morning, Willow decided to let her parents know what had happened to Norma and suspicions of her own about Chet. She wanted them to hear it from her before someone in town mentioned it. Their reactions were nothing short of what Willow expected; shock, disbelief, then outrage. They promised to keep the information to themselves since Chet was going to rehab.

They also decided it would be in Rambo's best interest to remain with Willow's parents. She didn't want to put him through any more trauma by caging him for the long flight to Wyoming in the luggage compartment. "Maybe I can fly out again and rent an SUV and bring him back with me," she suggested to her parents.

~

Once they were airborne Terry held his phone and brought up a photo to show Willow. "The barn site has already been graded." He pointed to the orange flags in the picture indicating the footprint of the barn. "And, I want you in on every phase of the design and construction of our home."

She was excited to hear the plans he'd already set in motion and happy to be included in decisions about the house.

"No cabin?" she teased and knew this was the beginning of their future.

"Actually, we could build a cabin on the hilltop above the property and make it our secret hide-a-way."

She arched her brows and held on to his hand. "I totally missed this the first time," Willow said.

Terry gave her a quizzical look.

"That feeling of being part of a two-sided relationship. I missed out on the *you* and *me* part of my former marriage. It was always about him and what he needed." She shuddered. "And that's the last time I will mention my ex again. You are all that matters to me now."

"I love you," He ran the back of his fingers down her cheek and kissed her, then kissed her again more deeply, as though they were alone on the plane.

They sat back holding hands, and Terry said, "When the house is finished, how about if we keep your farmhouse for our families to come stay for as long as they want?"

"Sweetheart, that's a great idea, it can be the guest cottage."

"I think it's important for kids to know their grandparents. I didn't have that opportunity. I was around my dad's family the few times we went to France, but I don't remember much about mom's parents. Her dad died when I was ten and my grandmother lived in Nevada and we didn't get out there very often."

"I was lucky to have wonderful times with my grandparents on both sides. My lovely Grandma Desiree was like my second mom. Dads parents moved to Florida when I was a teenager, but they did come to my high school and college graduations."

"I want to take our kids fishing at Pine Lake with my dad and your dad. And, you and your mum, of course."

She leaned over to kiss him. "I can't see my mom fishing, but I know she'd love to be there. She'll want to organize a picnic lunch."

They closed their eyes for a few minutes then Terry hauled in a breath when Willow said, "You know, you haven't told me much about your life in Australia, except the Harley part. What made you decide to return to the US."

"I read in the paper an American auto race was coming to Adelaide and decided to take some time off to go see it. It was a great diversion; I thoroughly enjoyed the excitement of the race cars as well as being around Americans." He smiled remembering that day. "I spent most of my time in the pit area listening to the team members and how they spoke. I realized I missed hearing my native dialect and was becoming an Aussie more and more every day. The only reason it bothered me was the possibility of losing my identity. I didn't want to forget my parents or my friends, as though they never existed."

"You went to the race by yourself?"

"Yeah. I needed some time away from Harley and didn't want to share my plans with her." He'd convinced her she'd be needed at the station while he was gone. It galled him to play a game of deceit to keep her from following him. He left some of his clothes and a few personal items sitting out to remind her he'd be back in a few days. Knowing how violent she could be, he simply didn't trust her.

"While in Adelaide, I bought a one-way, first class ticket to the states leaving in six weeks." He'd decided to add a layover in Honolulu to acclimate to the Western Hemisphere before flying on to the mainland.

"The urge to go home became too strong to ignore, so I called Tommy to let him know my plans and would ship a few boxes of personal things to his address." It creeped him out having done the same thing thirteen years earlier. Sneaking away to start a new life for himself once again.

"And," Terry said turning toward Willow, "I forgot to tell you. Dad remarried several years ago, her name is Aimee. She's also French and seems perfect for him; soft spoken, takes good care of him. I was happy to see that. She's looking forward to meeting you."

Since they arrived in Cody an hour late, they had a quick meal before heading to Elk Valley.

The following morning Terry was out of bed at six-fifteen, went to his former apartment to shower and dress. He'd move his things into her house later, he thought, then chuckled at renting the apartment, only staying in it one night and never paying Willow any rent.

Returning to the house, he sat on the bed and kissed her awake, "Willow, I'm going to check the progress next door, I'll be back in half an hour, if you want to go to breakfast."

She murmured in agreement then giggled as he lifted the comforter to admire her naked body before leaving the room.

Willow got up, and took a quick shower, before stepping out on the deck dressed in jeans, tee shirt, and a cardigan when Terry came up the driveway. She shouldered her bag and trotted down the steps, eager to spend the day with him.

Before fastening her seatbelt, she leaned over to kiss him, and his left hand cupped her face causing thrill bumps all over her body. "Just the sight of you excites me to no end. You're extra beautiful this morning." He sighed, before turning the truck around and heading back out to the road. "The lumber for the barn should be delivered today," he announced, with a big smile.

"That's exciting, sweetheart. I can't wait to see it."

He knew their life together would always be like this, crazy in love and something exciting on the horizon.

They stepped into the Red Kettle and Tommy stood to welcome them. Willow hugged him warmly. "Thank you so much for taking care of Midnight and Stormy." He hugged her back peering over her shoulder at his best friend with a shit-eatin' grin on his face.

Terry watched his buddy "Okay, you two that's enough." But, apparently, it wasn't. His scowl made Tommy smile. "Take your paws off my fiancée, you gorilla."

Both men knew this was the end of their rivalry over every girl in town. When they were teens, it was a game to see who would win the girl of interest. There were times when getting the girl was more important than actually wanting a date with her. Not behavior Terry was proud of and knew his buddy probably felt the same.

He was ready to settle down, get married and have a family, but was pretty sure Tommy wasn't and wondered if he ever would be.

Tommy released Willow but kept his arm around her, then extended his hand, "Congratulations, Terry. I'm happy for you both."

Terry shook his hand knowing he meant what he'd said.

The three of them ordered breakfast while Brenda jotted it all down.

Willow presented her hand to Tommy, wiggling her ring finger, he whistled at the sight of the sapphire and diamonds.

"Holy shit brother," he held her hand, eyeing Terry. "I guess you do love her."

She told him her parents were giving them an engagement party and would send an email invitation in a few days. "Please bring a date if you'd like," she added.

"I'm not seeing anyone at the moment, but I'll let you know if that changes."

When it came time for Terry and Willow to meet with the architect, the three of them walked out to their vehicles where Tommy gave his longtime friend a bear hug, then hugged Willow who seemed to be a little emotional.

Once Willow was in the truck, Terry called out to Tommy before he got into his cruiser to make his rounds.

Terry pulled out a photograph from inside his jacket pocket, making sure his back was turned toward the truck.

"What've you got?" Tommy asked.

"Have you seen this woman around town recently? Wanting to be inconspicuous, maybe staying at one of the smaller motels?"

He looked long and hard at the photo of a tall woman standing between Terry and a giant dude. Tommy shook his head, "I'd have remembered her. Is this the woman you were with in Australia?"

He nodded.

"Are you concerned about her being here? You said she could be violent. Is she a possible danger to you?"

Terry knew his buddy was all cop now, serious, asking for information that would help him understand the motive behind Terry's concern and how he could help.

He shrugged, "I don't really know."

"You obviously don't want Willow to know your suspicions. What makes you think she's here?"

"I don't, but a couple times out at Willow's house I felt sure someone was watching me. I can't believe Harley would come all this way to harass me. It's a long shot, but if it is her, how did she even find me?" He shook his head and sighed. "I don't like the idea of her sneaking about."

"Got it." He studied the photo for a minute, "Have you said anything to Willow?"

"No. I don't want to worry her. As I said, it's just a hunch."

"Okay, but I think you should let her know your suspicions. I will ask around though, discreetly."

"I'd appreciate it." He gave Tommy's shoulder a squeeze and turned back to the truck, knowing Willow was watching his every move.

"Everything okay?" she asked out of curiosity, her arm across the back of his seat. He was surprised to see where she was sitting.

"Now everything's great," he said, sliding in right next to her, eyeing the seat back.

"I hope you don't mind me putting the console up. I wanted to be closer to you."

"I'll be damned; you are one smart cookie." He kissed her before starting the engine then put his beefy arm across the front of her, tucking his fingers under her right thigh, pulling her even closer. "Oh yeah, that's so much better."

Chapter 18

*B*abe," Terry began, once they were out on the road. "I want to go over a few things with you about the house. I went over most of this during the two-hour meeting I had with the architect last week, but I want to bring you up to speed with it." He saw the preliminary drawings three days later. It was one of the reasons he didn't make it back to Elk Valley until after Willow had left for California.

"Okay, tell me everything," she said, curling her legs underneath her.

"I gave him a rough idea of what we might want, like a big master bedroom and bathroom with two walk-in closets. I saw that your closet at the house is full to capacity, so the closets need to be big." He was seeing all of it in his mind's eye. "Also, on the second floor I think we should have three more bedrooms, each with their own bathrooms. What do you think?"

She was beginning to see it as well and nodded. "So, sounds like you're planning on a big family," she teased him.

He quickly turned to look at her, "You do want kids, don't you?" Then checked for traffic, which was almost nonexistent. "We've never discussed that, have we?"

"I love the idea of making babies with you," she replied lovingly. "When I was a kid my doll house family had four children. They became my family while my parents worked, and my nanny was reading. That's always been the number I've had in my head for myself."

He grinned like a fool. "I'm so glad to hear you say that. OK, four bedrooms it is." Reaching over, he pressed his hand to her cheek, she leaned into it, laying her hand on his.

Terry turned onto the dirt road and made his way to the heart of the property. He shut the engine off, got out, and went to open the door for Willow. He wrapped an arm around her waist and pulled her close and whispered into her ear, "Welcome home." It wasn't until the words were out of his mouth that he realized how much he needed to hear them, too. He had left Elk Valley in so much pain, then spent over a decade healing his emotional wounds while learning everything he could about ranching. He had returned home with the slightest hope of reconnecting with old friends and building a business. But here he stood with the woman of his dreams in his arms and a bright future laid out before them.

Terry remembered setting stones and a broken branch so Willow could see where the front door of the cabin might be and wondered what happened to them. But workman and their trucks had been swarming around the property preparing and pouring the footings for the barn. At least he hoped it was the workmen that had moved things around. He scanned the hillside and wondered if someone was watching them.

They walked around the new home site and Terry laid markers down where he thought the corners of the house would be.

Once again, he felt he was overreacting thinking Harley might be nearby. But what would he do if she was watching them. His body's fight or flight response kicked in as a prickly sensation swept through him. It was all he could do to keep from looking over his shoulder, but he wouldn't give himself away. If Harley thought he suspected her, it would put Willow in jeopardy.

He imagined her with a gun. She would pick me off first, then Willow. Hair on the back of his neck stood on end as the toe of his boot poked at an imaginary object in the dirt while he regained his composure. Harley never had a gun in Australia, he reminded himself. But she was never without that hunting knife. The one with the ten-inch blade. Walking toward Willow, he focused on her instead of scanning the brush for the possibility of a stalker he assumed was Harley.

"I think we should have a big kitchen, don't you?" Not waiting for her answer, he put his arm around her then moved swiftly to the truck. "I need to plug my phone in." Once they were seated inside, he continued. "The architect I spoke to last week will be here soon, if you want a different one, we can look around. We should probably find a kitchen designer, too," Terry added, hoping he sounded calmer than he felt.

Her mouth dropped open slightly, "We're having a kitchen designer?"

He loved seeing the look of delight on her face. Pulling her into a hug and kissing her helped him regain the peace he had enjoyed when they first arrived. "Yes," he answered when they came up for air then smoothed some wayward golden strands away from her face. "I want this house to last us the rest of our lives, so let's make it exactly the way we want it, without any regrets down the road." He knew he was filling her with a lot of information in a short time, but continued on, "I think we should have a guest room downstairs and offices for both of us. I want you to have a place where you'll feel comfortable writing."

She smiled, listening to him share what he had been thinking about for some time. "Will we have a deck? A wrap around deck, maybe?"

"Yeah, I think we should," he said, envisioning how it would look. "You really enjoy the deck at your house. How about an entrance to the deck from your office? That way you can step outside to write, or just take a break."

"I love that idea," she said, happily getting caught up in planning their future then wondering if they should wait to build the house. "Terry, all of this sounds wonderful, but it's also going to cost a fortune. I have a small savings account as well as money my grandmother left me. I'd be happy living in our farmhouse until the ranch is supporting itself. I just don't want you to spend all the money you worked so hard for in Australia."

Terry suppressed a smile, not wanting Willow to think he didn't appreciate her offer. "Sweetheart, we'll be fine. I know we haven't talked about financial matters, but trust me. The money I have won't run out anytime soon. Probably last another generation."

Dust floated above the dirt road announcing the arrival of another vehicle. Terry waved and let out a sigh of relief when the architect pulled in next to his truck, knowing whoever might have been there would probably take off now.

After an hour of jotting down ideas and must haves, the architect told them he had enough to continue his design drawing for their approval. They set up a time to meet again in ten days.

They stopped at the supermarket for supplies before heading home and a soak in the hot tub. It was there that Willow suggested it might be fun to introduce her new friend Shannon to Tommy on a double date. "She's beautiful with bottle green eyes and a figure that would stop traffic."

He nodded eyebrows raised. "It would be good for Tommy to meet someone new," he said, putting his arm around his future bride. "If she's as pretty as you say and has a great figure, I don't see why not."

~

The following day Willow sat outside in the sun and jotted down a list of marketing materials she'd need for her upcoming book launch, then felt pangs of separation anxiety at the thought of being away from Terry to do book signings. She sighed and picked up her engagement and birthday party to-do list which by now was rather daunting.

"Our party will be early evening," she said out loud then stood and walked to the end of the deck spreading her arms wide to determine how many tables would fit on the deck for their sit-down dinner. "Good thing I'm here by myself," she said under her breath.

"People might think I've been chewing locoweed." She chuckled and wondered if there was such a thing.

Willow was happy to check the caterer off her list since her mother was in charge of the menu. She made an appointment with a coordinator for the following day to discuss where the dinner tables would be set up out on the deck and where to place the bar and cake table. Feeling like she needed a break, Willow decided to do a little shopping at Green With Envy.

Shannon was blown away when she saw Willow's impressive sapphire engagement ring. "Wow, this guy must really love you," she said sounding genuinely pleased for her but also a little envious.

"Thank you, I'm thrilled," she said, admiring her ring. "I would have been just as happy with a cigar band." And she meant it. "So, I was wondering. What do you think about doing a blind date?"

"I don't know, Willow," she said, turning back to a blouse she'd been steaming. "I'm not sure I want to meet anyone right now. Besides, the two stores are keeping me pretty busy."

"It's just an evening out with me and my fiancé. We would invite his tall, handsome friend to join us." Willow arched her eyebrows for emphasis.

Shannon rolled her eyes and smiled, "Okay, sounds interesting."

"His name is Tommy Logan. He and Terry have known each other since grade school, so he's not just some random guy."

Shannon nodded.

"And, he's our town sheriff." She saved that for last not knowing how she'd feel about dating local law enforcement.

"All right, since your guy knows him and you'll be there, it might be good to go out and have some fun."

"Great. And to make you feel even better, Terry and I will pick you up and take you home." The two agreed that Sunday evening would be best, and Willow would let her know for sure once she spoke with Tommy.

Then she invited Shannon to their engagement party and to celebrate Terry's thirtieth birthday. "That's the other reason I want you to meet Tommy and Terry, so you won't feel like an outsider," she added.

Willow sent a quick text to Terry telling him about their double date on Sunday, then tucked her phone into her purse and began rubbing her hands together. "Okay, now let's get down to the important stuff. I want a new western shirt to wear with my jeans on Sunday."

"Okay, let's check over here." Willow followed her to the round rack of blouses where Shannon flipped through them pulling out four for her to choose from.

"These are cute," she said, as Shannon set them on the hook in the dressing room. Willow first tried on the lavender plaid with rhinestones on the cuffs and pocket flaps. She stepped out in front of the long mirror and turned under Shannon's watchful eye.

"Okay, let's get those boobs out there where they belong," Shannon said, playfully. She opened the blouse one more snap, "Yes, much better."

Willow laughed at her remark, nodding in agreement. While Shannon wrote up the sales slip, a hand tooled leather backpack caught Willow's eye. Thinking it might be time to replace the one she'd been using the past five years, she said "I love this. Is it the only one you have?"

"Yes, but I can order another one."

"I want it, but I've spent a fair amount of money this month, so I won't take it until I see where I stand."

Shannon put the blouse in a bag handing it and the sales slip to Willow. "I'm staying in one of the bedrooms temporarily," she gestured with her thumb over her shoulder indicating the location of the bedrooms, "so you can pick me up here Sunday evening."

Willow hugged her, "Okay, see you then."

She drove to the sheriff station and caught Tommy as he was getting into his patrol car.

"Hi beautiful," he said, eyes roaming over her.

"You have no shame, do you Tommy?"

"Just admiring a beautiful woman."

"Would you like to go out Sunday evening?" She teased, hoping to catch him off guard.

He stared at her, waiting for her to continue, "And..." he said.

"I'd like you to meet a friend of mine. She recently opened a boutique here in town and doesn't know anyone."

Tommy interrupted her, "You talkin' about the new shop on Poppy Lane? The one with the green door?"

"Yes, that's her shop. You've seen it then?"

"Sure, I've been by a couple times on my weekly rounds but didn't look like anyone was there."

"She has another shop in Jackson Hole and goes to check on it once a week or so. Anyway, she's also coming to our party and I just thought it would nice if she knew someone other than me."

"Okay. So, do you mean, like a blind date?"

"Exactly like a blind date, except Terry and I will be there, too."

He leaned against the cruiser door, arms folded. "What's she like?"

"Her name is Shannon, she's beautiful with gorgeous ginger hair and the most amazing green eyes I've ever seen." Tommy was about to say something, but she cut him off, "Yes, she has a great figure." She hated herself for saying that but knew he would ask. Can't guys raise their view eight or ten inches to look into a woman's eyes for a peek into her soul instead of instantly sizing us up by the size of our breasts? She wasn't going to tell him anything about Shannon's breasts, they'd speak for themselves when he met her.

"When would this double date take place and where would we go?"

"You aren't one for surprises, are you?"

"I hate surprises." He said it like she should have known that.

"Sunday evening at the Buckaroo. I've never been there and thought it would be nice since they have a dance floor."

"Okay, I'm up for an evening out," he said, pushing away from his patrol car. "What time and where do I pick her up?"

"How about meeting us there at six-thirty? We'll bring Shannon with us."

"Okay, it's a date. But I'm picking up the tab to celebrate your engagement."

"Well, that's very nice of you. You may have to take that up with Terry, though."

On her way home, Willow stopped at the market to buy a few things for dinner as well as cat food. Pulling into the garage, she saw someone move across the window on the opposite wall. She got out of the car and went to the window but didn't see anyone. She walked outside and surveyed the yard, listening for whatever might have been there.

Then she saw a dead rabbit right in front of the stairs that led to the apartment. "Oh no, poor thing." She must have interrupted a predator, not a person. She felt a chill and hurried to the house reminding herself that everything has to eat. As long as they didn't eat her or the kittens.

When she called Terry, he said he'd be home in half an hour. "Okay, I'll be in the hot tub waiting." In the meantime, she got busy making a salad and washing the vegetables, setting them on the cutting board for later. She went to the bedroom to undress, then wrapped one of the beach towels around her, grabbing another one for Terry.

Like clockwork, she heard his truck on the gravel drive. She listened as his boots echoed across the deck, until finally she heard his deep voice, "Having yourself a little soak are you, madam?"

She loved those lusty eyes checking to see if she was wearing a bathing suit, then rose up just enough to expose her bare breasts.

He ran his tongue over his lips before pulling his boots off. He tugged his shirt out of his jeans then began unbuttoning it while Willow giggled, catching her lower lip between her teeth, eager for him to bring his body next to hers.

But he continued to torment her. Dropping the shirt, he unbuckled his belt, then the button. He slowly unzipped his jeans, pulling them and his briefs down over his hips, revealing all his manliness.

Terry stood on the edge of the hot tub a moment before sliding into the steamy water, making his way over to her waiting arms, he slid his hands down her wet, slick body to her bum, pulling her tight against his hips. "I've been looking forward to this all day," Terry remarked in a husky voice.

After their love making in the hot tub, they went into the bedroom to dress, but decided since they already had their clothes off, they'd have dessert first.

In the kitchen after they finished dinner, Willow cleared the table and told Terry both Shannon and Tommy agreed to dinner and dancing at Buckaroo Sunday evening. He pulled her onto his lap, "You're pretty excited about this match-making exercise, aren't you?" He kissed her lightly, loving her so much it almost hurt.

"I want our friends to be as happy as we are," she said, arms around his neck, kissing him back. "If they don't click, at least they gave it a try."

"That's awfully sweet of you. What else did you do today, beautiful?" He punctuated his question with more kisses, and she was having trouble thinking of anything except the feel of his hands on her body.

"Oh, I forgot to tell you about the rabbit." She told him she found the carcass by the garage.

"What do you mean?" he asked, the hair on the back of his neck standing on end.

"I thought I saw someone outside the garage window. But I went out to look and found a dead rabbit, I realized it must have been a wild critter. Do you think a coyote or big cat dropped it when it heard me pull into the garage?"

He was quiet a moment then stood easing Willow off his lap. "Yeah, could be." He went to the sink and looked out the window thinking it might be wise not to use the hot tub until they find out if someone is watching them.

"I don't know much about wild animals, but that seems close to the house. I'll be more careful with my cats, make sure they don't slip out the door when I go out on the deck to write."

Terry nodded absently, "The rabbit's probably gone, but I'm going to go see." He stepped outside and got a flashlight from his truck before calling Tommy.

"Tommy," he said, when his friend answered his cell.

"Hey, Terry, what's up?"

"I was hoping you might have some news. Has anyone seen Harley?"

"I didn't have any luck at the motels in town, I'll check a few places out on the highway tomorrow. I did show the photo at the fast food joints, and one employee said he thought he might've seen her."

"Okay. Willow said she saw someone by the garage today and she found a dead rabbit. I'm going to check it out." Terry crouched next to the bloody lump by the stairs. He turned the carcass over and let out a string of curses. "Tommy, this wasn't killed by an animal. The cuts are too clean."

"Shit! Definitely looks like someone is stalking you."

Terry stood and looked out into the darkness. Harley was out there, and he was her prey. "I want some private security here at the house around the clock. I don't want any surprises and I don't want to alarm Willow. I don't believe she's in danger, but I don't want to assume anything when it comes to Harley," he added, glancing toward the house making sure she wasn't able to hear him.

"Do you want me to set that up?"

"Yeah, I'd appreciate it." His hand went to the back of his head then began rubbing his neck. "We have a house full of people showing up here and I don't want anyone hurt because of me."

"Right. Tell Willow not to worry, I'll get on it tomorrow morning."

Terry didn't respond. Willow wasn't aware of any of this. He pictured her smiling face while they had talked about their house and didn't want to do anything to dampen her joy. This was his problem. He would protect her.

"Terry, you did tell Willow we think Harley might be stalking you, right?"

"No, I don't want her to worry. She's so happy right now, and I don't want her to feel anxious about this."

"I think you're making a mistake not telling her. But, that's just my opinion."

Chapter 19

*T*erry was, once again, knocked back on his heels when he saw Willow dressed for their double date. "Do we really have to go on this blind date with those two? Can't they go by themselves, and we can stay here so I can undress you?"

She stepped into his arms and planted a light kiss on his pouty lips then wiped off the lipstick she'd left behind. "I want you to meet Shannon, and I can't wait until Tommy sees her," she said, eyes dancing with delight. "This is going to be a fun evening celebrating with our friends and there will be plenty of time to remove my clothes later."

When they arrived at Shannon's, Terry was pleasantly surprised how accurate Willow's description had been of her new friend. If his good buddy didn't become an arrogant fool, Tommy could end up as happy as he and the beautiful Willow were. Just like she said.

Shannon gave Willow a friendly elbow jab in her side and said, "Nice catch, girl."

Willow raised her eyebrows as if to say "duh."

Tommy was just stepping out of his truck when they pulled into the parking lot at Buckaroo Bar and Grill. "I've never seen him in street clothes," Willow said. "He cleans up pretty good."

"Tommy," Terry began, cupping Shannon's elbow, "this is Shannon Kelly. Shannon, Tommy Logan." They said hello then did a quick assessment of each other and offered the usual niceties before the four of them walked into the restaurant.

Following the hostess to their table, Terry could see Tommy's gaze glued to Shannon's bling-covered butt in those tight jeans tucked into high heel cowboy boots.

"I do believe you have steam rising from your collar, Bud," Terry told him, just above a whisper. "Take it slow or you might spontaneously combust before our very eyes." It was good to see him admiring a beautiful woman, other than Willow, that is.

The four of them slid into the big booth, girls in the middle, hunky guys flanking them. Tommy seemed a bit tongue tied as he caught sight of Shannon's ample breasts for the first time.

Terry picked up the slack, "I can't remember the last time I've been in the company of two such stunningly beautiful women." He smiled with a sideways glance at them.

"I was just going to say that," Tommy chimed in.

"Well, we sure do appreciate having you two bookends protecting us," Willow added.

~

Willow took a moment to soak in the atmosphere. This was a real cowboy bar and dance hall. The dining booths sat along three sides with the bar in the center. The stage and dance floor punctuated the rectangular room, taking up most of the space. Big screen TVs hung in both corners visible from the booths; one showing a rodeo replay, and the other playing Professional Bull Riding. She flinched when she saw a rider flip over the horns of an angry bull.

Cowboy boots and old pistols in holsters hung from the ceiling over the bar. The walls along the booths were dressed with photos and memorabilia of great western movie stars from the forties.

The waitress brought their beers and appetizers, then rushed off to another table. Arranging the plates and passing the food gave them something to do and Willow watched Tommy and Shannon visibly relax now that there was a bit of distraction in front of them.

Tommy held out his long-neck beer bottle and offered a toast to Willow and Terry, congratulating them on their engagement. "I'm very happy for you and wish you a long happy life together." The four clinked bottles and took a swig, Terry and Willow thanked them for their good wishes.

"And I have more good news," Willow said, and Terry's eyes narrowed. She hadn't even hinted about this.

"I received a contract today for another book series!"

"That's wonderful, sweetheart." Terry pulled her in for a kiss. They had agreed to keeping their hands and lips off each other until the evening was over, so they wouldn't make Tommy and Shannon uncomfortable. But this news definitely deserved a little celebration.

"I think this cowboy bar will be the perfect setting for my opening scene in book one."

Terry grinned at her, "I thought you might be creating a story in your mind when I saw that pensive expression on your face."

Her breath caught at his observation. It wasn't embarrassment, she certainly wasn't embarrassed about her great news. It was because he was proud of her. Chet had always belittled her plans to write romance novels. A lot of people didn't see the value in them, but she wrote for those that did. She wanted to bring stories of true love and a happy ending to the world. Terry understood that. He understood her. Not trusting her voice, she mouthed the words "I love you" to him and he winked back.

The band finished setting up and ran through a sound check. The couples hit the dance floor at the first strum of a guitar when they began playing one of two upbeat songs with a typical western story; one about lost love and the other, new found romance. Both Tommy and Shannon knew the Texas Two-Step, and Willow was impressed watching them strutting their stuff. She and Terry decided to stick with basic moves on the dance floor since neither was up to speed with the dance routine.

The next song was slow, and the guys pulled their ladies close, moving to the music. Willow was pleased to see that Shannon and Tommy were smiling and seemed to be having a pleasant conversation. When the song ended, they returned to the booth and ordered another round in anticipation of their dinners arriving.

Terry complimented them on their dancing skills and Willow said, "I definitely need to practice the Texas Two-Step. Maybe we can take lessons," she said to Terry, then watched his eyebrows reach for the sky. "Or not," she quickly added with a smile.

When they finished their meal, the ladies excused themselves and made their way to the restroom.

~

"So, what do you think of Shannon?" Terry asked, eager to hear Tommy's response. He thought they made a nice couple.

"She's pretty, easy to talk to, with the kind of body I've only dreamt about," his eyes lit up from the inside.

Terry smiled at his excitement knowing how it felt to meet someone who caused a stirring deep within. The girls came back with fresh lip gloss ready to dance again but Shannon suggested they change partners. Terry was reluctant to have Tommy's hands on Willow, but it meant he could get to know Shannon a little better.

"Thanks for coming out tonight to meet Tommy," he said, when they began dancing. "I'm afraid I've got two left feet tonight," Terry said and was happy when Shannon took the lead until he got the pattern. "You two look good on the dance floor."

"I'm enjoying myself, and Tommy seems like a nice guy. By the way," she smiled at him, "Willow's engagement ring is beautiful. I'm happy for you both."

Terry responded with a broad smile. "Thank you, I'm crazy about her and can't wait for us to get married."

He twirled her out then pulled her back in. "Willow looks great in the things she bought at your boutique," he told her. "Her birthday's coming up and I'd like to buy her something nice. If you can think of anything, I'd like to stop by and check it out."

"I know the perfect thing," she offered. "Willow was admiring a hand-tooled leather backpack the other day but didn't buy it. Said she'd think about it."

"That would be perfect." He'd be happy to see her with something nicer than that canvas bag. "Set it aside, and I'll come by for it next week."

At ten o'clock, Willow was fading while Terry stifled a yawn. "I hate to be a party pooper, but I'm pooped."

All eyes were on Shannon wondering what she wanted to do. Tommy spoke first, "I'd be happy to drive you home if you'd like to stay a while longer."

"I promised we'd take her home," Willow said, then glanced at her friend.

"I have to open the store by nine in case I have a delivery," she told them. "But since the lead guitarist said they'd do a line dance next, I wouldn't mind staying half an hour more, if you're sure you don't mind driving me home."

Oh yeah, like he's not going to want to drive you home, both Willow and Terry thought, as they eyed one another.

"Okay," Tommy said, and stood to shake Terry's hand when he slid out of the booth.

The two women hugged, and Willow couldn't help but ask, "You're sure?"

Shannon smiled and nodded; told her she'd call her tomorrow.

"Goodnight Tommy," Willow said after she hugged him. "It was a fun evening."

When they drove out onto the road, Willow said, "I think they had a good time together, don't you?"

"The fact that she wanted him to drive her home meant something." Terry paused then added, "Will she tell you how their evening ended?"

"Most likely. It's what we girls do, confide in each other for reassurance."

He looked over at her through narrowed eyes, wondering what she might have said about their love life.

She read his expression, "No, I've only told my two girlfriends how much I love you and that's all." She was quiet a moment, then, "Well, I might have told Norma how amazing you are in bed."

"Really?" He was a little bit shocked, but that just made him hurry home a little faster.

~

"Good morning," Willow answered in a sing-song voice when her cell rang at 8 a.m. She was anxious to hear Shannon's report. "How are you today?"

"Really good," she replied. "I had a great time last night, and Tommy was a perfect gentleman when we got to my front door. He kissed me ever so tenderly before saying good night, and I was a little disappointed. Then, wow, he pulled me right against him and kissed me like he was memorizing my mouth with his tongue." She sighed, "It was a very nice kiss, kind of sweet, really. However..."

Uh-oh, here comes the 'but', Willow thought, cringing slightly.

"Once I got inside, I started to cry. I almost wished I'd invited him in, but I knew I'd have been thinking about Kiren, my ex."

"Do you think you'll see Tommy again?"

"Yes, if he asks me out, but I need to make it clear I'm not ready for any kind of commitment, not for a while anyway."

"That's the way I felt when I realized I was beginning to fall for Terry, and look where I am now," she felt that electric buzz travel through her, "crazy in love with him after only two months."

"My business comes first and if he's okay with that, I'm happy to step out from time to time."

Friday Willow drove to Cody to pick up Norma at the airport then headed straight to a party store. With three bags of decorations, paper dessert plates and napkins, they drove back to Elk Valley. Terry was sitting on the wicker sofa on the deck with a beer when they pulled in. He set the long-neck on the railing and went down the steps to the car, opening the passenger door to help Norma out.

"Well if it isn't the Gray Cowboy," she said with a flirtatious smile as he pulled her into a hug.

"Nice to see you, Norma," he said, warmly. "Thank you for coming, it means a lot to us." He glanced up and saw Willow come around the front of the car. "She's been counting the days until you would arrive," he told her before stepping toward Willow. "Hi, gorgeous," he put his arm around her, and kissed her.

"Hi, sweetheart." She peered into his dark blue eyes thinking, our kids are going to have the most beautiful eyes. "How was your day?"

"Not nearly as good as yours by the looks of it." He took the shopping bags from her and set them on the deck, then went back for Norma's luggage. "Although, the trailer was delivered today," he said over his shoulder.

"Oh, good," she knew he'd be happy to put it to use on the property. "Well, we had the most fun! I told Norma I think we should open a party store and rent tents, and ponies, and have a catering service." Willow was glowing, eyes twinkling.

"I feel like I'm in a live action Norman Rockwell painting. This week might be a little too down home for me," Norma said.

"Noooooo," Willow said. "You're going to be so glad you came." With that, the three of them walked into the house, Norma heading for the guest room, Terry following with her bags.

Willow began putting a few appetizers together while Terry poured wine in three glasses. Norma joined them, one hand on the counter, the other on her hip. "Well isn't this just the picture of domestic bliss," she said with a little playful sarcasm.

Willow chuckled and Terry grinned. "She's been training me, so I don't embarrass her when Patrick and Frankie get here."

"That is so not true." She reached over to lay her hand on her friend's arm, "Mom and Dad love Terry. The four of us had a great time together."

Out on the deck with the tray of finger food and wine, they toasted and laughed while Willow took every item out of each bag to show Terry.

Then Norma said she'd been on the internet to check up on Dr. Bruce Fredrickson. "I found out he's single and hasn't lived in Elk Valley very long."

"What are you saying, girlfriend?" Willow asked.

Norma shrugged, "Nothing really. I was just thinking, I'll probably be the only single woman at the party."

Terry touched Norma's shoulder, "No worries, I'll have an empty arm you're welcome to."

Jerking her head back, Norma appeared caught off guard by his offer and seemingly at a loss for a snappy retort.

Willow's heart swelled with love for him once again.

~

The next morning Terry laid in bed listening to Willow's steady breath, in and out. She was sleeping peacefully. Then wondered if the noise that startled him awake was an animal or could it possibly be Harley sneaking around? He just didn't want to believe it and hated the idea of keeping secrets from Willow. He knew she trusted him, She'd asked him to always be honest with her. How will she feel if they find out it was Harley who killed that rabbit?

He only had himself to blame for his angst. He should have let Harley know his intentions. He should have told her good-bye. But he was never sure of what she might be capable of doing.

Now, he needed to protect Willow and both their families from a possible intruder, while hoping he wasn't eroding their relationship by not sharing his suspicions with her. Trust is an important factor in a good marriage, he reminded himself. But, Willow had enough to think about, this party was a joyous occasion, and he wanted it to end as happily as it would begin. He knew the police and security people would do whatever they could to make that happen.

Later that day, Willow and Norma drove to Green With Envy so Willow could show her the dress she had found for the party a few days earlier. The three young women chatted nonstop, Norma perusing the racks for a dress while Willow was in the dressing room. When she stepped out, Norma's jaw dropped, "Whoa," then turned to Shannon, "I want something just like that!"

With a big smile on her face, Willow asked, "You don't think it's too much cleavage, do you?"

"Can a woman ever have too much cleavage?" Norma asked, all three said "no" at the same time and giggled like schoolgirls. "Willow, you know your mother will be wearing something low cut, not to mention, gorgeous. In fact, I think we should all put 'em out there." More giggles erupted.

Norma tried on a pale orange tank dress with a deep scoop neck and a chiffon wrap splashed with flowers in shades of orange and yellow with just the right touch of green. "Wow, you look fabulous," Willow said, sincerely.

"She's right," Shannon chimed in. "Those colors are perfect on you and the cut is very flattering."

Again, Willow and Norma returned home with armloads of shopping bags. The two spent the afternoon deciding how they'd decorate the deck and railing before preparing their evening meal.

Chapter 20

Willow had suggested Norma go to see Dr. Fredrickson under the pretense of needing allergy meds. On the way home from shopping, they drove to the clinic where they waited for Norma's appointment. She was a little nervous but decided she had nothing to lose by inviting him to Willow and Terry's party.

When she heard her name, Norma followed the nurse to the examination room where the nurse took her temperature and blood pressure.

After adding the numbers to Norma's medical record, she said, "Dr. Frederickson will be with you shortly", then left the room.

Norma thought it would be fun to take all her clothes off and sit up on the exam table, but stayed in her chair. There was a light tap on the door before the doctor entered. "Miss Wasserman, it's nice to see you again and under more pleasant circumstances, I trust." He smiled down at her, extending his hand.

"Hello, nice to see you too, and with my clothes on." She enjoyed the look of surprise on his face as he sat in the chair next to her. He has a nice smile, she thought.

"How are you doing? Any problems?"

"Not really. But I seem to be allergic to pollen or grass and don't know what to take for it."

He pulled a small pad of paper from his pocket and wrote two options for over-the-counter remedies. "Either one of these should help with sneezing, watery eyes." He stood to check the nurse's notes and added, "Everything else looks good. Did you have any other questions for me?"

She stood pulling the strap of her handbag over her shoulder, "No. Um, unless you'd like to go to an engagement party with me next weekend." Norma watched as his eyebrows nearly reached his hair line, waiting for what she would say next.

There was a long pause. She realized he wasn't sure if she was serious.

As gently as possible, Dr. Frederickson asked about the guy involved in her pregnancy.

"Of course, you have a right to know since I am asking you out on a date, sort of."

She sat back down lacing her fingers together in her lap and began to tell him what had happened to her, giving him all the details that led up to Willow taking her to the hospital that night. When she was finished, her fingernails were digging into the palms of her hands. Her shoulders sagged when she released a deep breath, her bottom lip clinched between her teeth.

Norma finally relaxed her hands and looked up at him blinking away tears, expecting a lecture on how she could have prevented the date rape.

"I heard stories just like that as an ER intern at UCLA Medical Center." He clamped his jaw shut and lightly shook his head. "I'm sorry you had to go through that. You should have told me in the hospital."

"It's all good now. The sheriff in Santa Barbara has confronted the guy and he's going to rehab." She searched his face, feeling those all too familiar pangs of guilt her mother made sure she felt and couldn't help wondering if he thought she was to blame. Norma exhaled a sigh.

"I'm glad you're okay and thank you for telling me."

"I'm glad I told you, too." Norma felt a lot better than she had when he first asked the question. The guy was a doctor, it was literally his job to make people feel better. But this was different. He didn't blame her, didn't judge her, as far as she could tell. Maybe this tiny town had a few redeeming qualities after all. "So... back to the original question. The party is at six o'clock next Saturday at my friend Willow's house. I'd be happy to pick you up if you'd like." She knew that sounded too eager, but there was no taking it back now.

He gazed at her for several seconds, though to Norma, it seemed an hour had ticked by. "Yes, I'd like that."

She was thrilled to the point of bursting. "Wonderful. I'm glad," she added feeling giddy, her eyes glued to his face. He really was handsome. "This will be a small group of very nice people and it's not formal. I think you'll have a good time." I know I will, she wanted to add along with a big wet kiss. "The party is at..." Then she remembered, "I already said it was at six, didn't I?"

"I'll be there next Saturday."

"If you'll give me your number, I'll text you Willow's address." He gave her the number and she sent him a quick hello text. "There, now you have my number, too."

He grinned, and something inside her felt like a teenager with a date to the prom.

"Thank you for asking me. I haven't had much time to socialize since moving here."

"See you next Saturday then," she added, nodding at the same time.

"Great, okay," he stood and opened the door for her. "Have a good day Norma. See you Saturday."

Again, Willow and Norma returned home with armloads of shopping bags. The two spent the remainder of the afternoon planning how they'd decorate the deck and railing for Terry's birthday and their engagement party.

After dinner, Willow and Norma decided to barbecue the following afternoon, and Terry said they should invite Tommy and Shannon to join them. There was a party brewing so Willow suggested Norma call Bruce to see if he'd like to come too.

She couldn't get to her phone fast enough. He told Norma hc had rounds to make but thought he'd be able to leave the clinic around six.

The two had been busy all afternoon making poppers and nachos as well as hanging brightly colored streamers and lanterns along the deck. They were just finishing prepping the meat for the grill when Tommy arrived alone, he'd left a message on Shannon's cell when she didn't answer. Told her to join them at Willow's if she could.

Willow guessed she'd most likely gone to her store in Jackson.

When Terry introduced Tommy to Norma, she said, "Doesn't the state of Wyoming produce anything but tall, buff, handsome guys?"

"You aren't complaining are you Normie?" Willow asked, teasing her.

"No, I just want to make sure there's one left for me to take home." And, as if he'd heard her request, Bruce drove up the driveway, and Norma's demeanor brightened even more.

Norma left the group and headed down the stairs, smiling as she walked around the front of the car to greet him.

"Thanks for inviting me," he said, putting his arm around her shoulder as they started toward the house.

"I'm sure it will be my pleasure," she said, staring up at him. "Are you from Wyoming?"

"No. I grew up on the East Coast."

They walked up the steps where Terry thrust his hand out, introduced himself to Bruce then introduced him to Tommy.

Willow had her *Margaritaville* mixer, a bridal shower gift from Norma, set out on the kitchen counter. A pitcher full of liquid gold sat on a tray along with glasses rimmed with kosher salt. They set out the hors d'oeuvres, and the tray of margaritas on the coffee table outside, filling each glass before Terry made a toast to the group.

"When I decided to come back home," he began, "I never imagined I'd be having dinner with my beautiful bride-to-be and our friends on the deck of my former family home." He gazed at Willow and winked. "Tommy, we've known each other since grade school, and you made my return seem like I'd been away months instead of years. Thank you for coming," and he raised his glass.

They all chimed in with a rousing "Cheers!"

The guys stood out on the deck at the barbecue shootin' the breeze, grilling flank steak and chicken breasts. Willow and Norma were busy in the kitchen making a salad and all the fixings for their fajitas.

They were famous among their friends in Santa Barbara for the Mexican dinners they prepared. "Remember when we talked about opening a restaurant?" Norma said.

Willow laughed, "Yeah, but you squelched it," she turned toward Norma with a cheese grater in her hand. "You said you knew the day would come when you wouldn't be able to get out the door."

Norman nodded, and chucked.

The table was quiet for several minutes as they dug into the delicious food, words of praise spread around the table. Bruce was especially complimentary. He said he ate most of his meals out, since he sometimes worked eighteen-hour days at the clinic. He often slept on the sofa in the staff break room and had stopped buying food to prepare since it tended to go bad while he was busy being a doctor.

Willow had poured him a glass of iced tea when he declined a second margarita. He didn't have more than two sips of the first one since he had a cesarean section early the following morning.

They sat outside on the deck as the moon began its ascent in the sky, enjoying coffee and dessert, lanterns swaying in the breeze adding color to the evening.

At nine o'clock Bruce told Willow and Terry, "Thank you for a very nice evening and the delicious home cooked dinner." His gaze fell on Norma including her in his appreciation. "I have an early morning, so I need to get going."

Everyone stood, the guys shook hands, and Willow hugged Bruce thanking him for coming. He held his hand out to Norma, and the two of them headed to his car.

"Norma..."

She wanted to say, Yes. The answer is, yes, I just need to get my toothbrush.

When they stopped next to the driver's door, he peered down at her inquisitive eyes and sly smile. He held her at arm's length, taking her in. "Will you have dinner with me Tuesday?"

"Yes, I'd like that." Her insides were jumping up and down with joy.

"Monday always seems to be busy at the clinic and I need to be there for my patients."

"I understand, but I will look forward to..."

Before she could finish, he pulled her to him, his six-foot-two frame towering over her, even in her three-inch heels. Bending down to kiss her, she responded by holding back a little of what she was feeling. When he released her, she felt lightheaded, and put her hands on his chest.

"Wow, that was nice."

Stepping back, he opened the car door and gazed at her as if memorizing her face. "Sweet dreams," he offered, then buckled his belt and started the engine.

She gave him a seductive smile, wanting to put her hands on the open window, lean in with a sultry stare and tell him, oh no, they will be raunchy dreams, and if you're lucky, I just might tell you about them.

"See you Tuesday." He pulled forward to make a U-turn then headed toward the road. Norma stayed put until he was out of sight.

When she got to the front door, Tommy and Terry were on their way out. "Going over to check out the new trailer," Terry said, as they headed to his truck.

Norma found Willow in the kitchen wiping down the table and waiting for a full report.

~

Terry and Tommy stepped into the trailer where they were greeted by a State Trooper and three deputies dressed in street clothes. The group began strategizing about their plan to draw out the stalker they assumed was Harley. They had a bead on her hideout thanks to night vision gear.

Tommy was the first to speak, addressing Terry. "Do you think she has a gun?"

He shook his head, "I never saw her with a gun. She carried a knife and I expect she has one with her. Harley's an excellent tracker, hunts with her knife." He was thoughtful a moment, "Hell, she tracked me down."

Terry could only imagine how she'd found him and assumed she'd gotten on his laptop, or cell phone when he was in the shower. He'd been careless, never thinking she'd come after him.

'Never underestimate the power of a woman', his mother used to say. Especially one who's pissed.

Chapter 21

The following Saturday evening, Terry stepped out on the deck dressed in a pair of gray slacks, a white western shirt and his gray cowboy boots. He pulled in a breath of that fresh pine scent he loved and didn't think life could get any better. Once again, he reminded himself how lucky he was to have found Willow, and now family and friends were coming to celebrate their engagement and his birthday.

Terry squinted into the setting sun when he saw a car pull onto the driveway. He smiled as his father, Alain and his wife pulled up and parked. Aimee waved as Terry came down the steps to greet them, cheek-kissing her then his father.

When Tommy pulled in a short time later, he sprinted toward Alain almost lifting him off the ground in a hug.

"Coucou fiston. I am very pleased to see you."

"Not as much as I am to see you!" Tommy said with a catch in his throat.

Alain introduced Tommy to Aimee who had heard stories about him from Terry when he visited them in Montana.

~

Willow's parents had arrived earlier, and Frankie was standing-by watching her daughter put the finishing touches on her lovely face while Patrick stood in the bathroom doorway admiring his beautiful wife and daughter.

Hearing Alain's French accent Willow said, "They're here. Come on let's go greet them." She knocked on Norma's door and said, "Meet us out on the deck."

Willow's parents hung back while Terry introduced Willow to Aimee who embraced her then handed her a small box tied with ribbon. Willow inhaled a slight gasp of surprise by her thoughtfulness. She untied it, feeling a little nervous as she struggled with the lid which landed on the ground. Terry stooped to retrieve it while Willow folded the tissue back to see a linen handkerchief with the word "Amour" embroidered on it.

She used it to dab tears welling in her eyes. "Thank you, what a lovely gift," she said, wishing she'd thought to do that for the ladies today.

Alain gave Willow a hug before he and Aimee embraced Frankie and Patrick as though they were family.

Norma joined the group and received heartfelt hugs from Willow's parents. Bruce arrived and when everyone was acquainted they gathered on the deck, each with a glass of champagne before Patrick toasted his daughter and Terry, wishing them as much happiness as he and Frankie have shared.

"Have you set a wedding date yet?" Tommy asked and Terry turned to Willow.

She had everyone's attention, "I want to be married on the deck of our new home," she said, then kissed Terry on the cheek.

"But that won't be for several months," Tommy pressed, looking at Willow then Terry.

"I know, but we have so much to accomplish in that time, and I'd like to enjoy being engaged for a while."

Terry shrugged his broad shoulders. "You heard the lady! We'll be married at the new house and we want all of you to be there."

While they enjoyed their champagne, Willow was happy to see Patrick and Frankie chatting with Alain and Aimee. She was also pleased to see Tommy with his arm around Shannon.

When dinner was announced, everyone sat to enjoy a delicious supper of filet of beef with cherry cabernet sauce, wild rice and asparagus.

When dinner was winding down, Patrick stood then tapped a spoon on his wine glass to get everyone's attention. "This has been a delightful evening. Frankie and I have enjoyed meeting each of you and appreciate you for caring about our daughter. Terry," Patrick said, "We're thrilled Willow fell in love with you, we think you two are a perfect match." He looked around the table and added, "We all wish you a long happy life together."

Terry shook Patrick's hand and thanked him and Frankie for welcoming him into their family. "I didn't expect to feel so comfortable stepping back into my old life in Elk Valley when I made the decision to return home. But, meeting Willow..." Terry reached for her hand and brought it to his lips, "and falling in love so quickly and easily wasn't on the radar. Willow," he gazed at her with those sapphire eyes, "I love every moment we've spent together since I met you. You've brought clarity to my life. I'm very happy you said yes."

Tommy whistled and the ladies gave an approving "Awe."

Willow stood to put her arm around Terry's waist, and he pulled her into a hug. "It means a great deal to Willow and me to have you all here."

More toasts were given as laughter and amiable conversation filled the evening air. When the dinner plates were removed, the cake was placed in front of Willow and Terry who blew out his birthday candles. Everyone promised to take some cake home since they were too full to enjoy more than a taste. The guests broke up into two groups when Patrick produced five cigars and Terry, Tommy and Bruce walked down the front steps to solve the problems of the world while smoking their Montecristo No. 2 cigars. Alain had declined the cigar; he and Aimee remained on the deck to enjoy the evening light and happy conversations.

The ladies had formed a circle and were complimenting each other on their lovely dresses and Willow's engagement ring. She told her mother about Shannon's boutique, hoping to take her there before they flew back to California.

~

Terry turned to see his father and Aimee sitting on the wicker sofa enjoying the view from the Du Champ's former family home. He was overcome with gratitude and love for family and friends celebrating his and Willow's engagement. He could never have imagined returning home from Australia and finding such happiness after being away over ten years. Life is full of surprises. Not always good, his gaze hit the ground hiding the emotion he felt. They're easier to handle if you roll with the punches, and you have someone by your side cheering you on.

Alain and Aimee were ready to go up to the garage apartment so Willow walked with them toward the staircase. Terry caught up to them halfway across the yard. He was anxious about his father and Aimee being upstairs away from the house even though the security crew in the white van parked beside the garage was on alert for anything unusual.

"We leave early tomorrow morning so we will say good-bye now." Alain told them.

"Willow and I are going to make breakfast in the morning, please stay." Terry glanced from his father to Aimee, but he knew she wouldn't interfere. This was his father's decision.

Terry couldn't hide the disappointment he felt since they hadn't had much time to visit.

"You enjoy time with Willow's family since they live so far away. We will come back soon, so we can spend more time together."

Terry knew his father's decision was firm and wouldn't press the issue. "All right," he said, "until next time then." After good-bye hugs, they watched Alain and Aimee climb the stairs, open the door, then turn on a light before closing and locking it.

"You're very tense about something and it makes me feel uneasy." Willow told Terry when they headed back to the house, her brows furrowed. "You and Tommy have been checking your watches since dinner ended. What's going on?"

He didn't like seeing her anxious expression. "You know me so well. I thought I was doing a good job of keeping something from you, and I've only caused you worry."

Wrapping his arm around her, they continued toward the house while he told her Tommy was sure Harley was stalking them. They felt pretty certain she was hiding nearby and tonight they were going to attempt to draw her out to confront her.

"I don't like this," she said.

Terry stopped, hugged her tight, and kissed her on the forehead. Hearing voices, they saw Patrick and Frankie walk down the front steps ready to drive back to the B&B in town where they were staying. They were planning to leave the next morning for a little vacation in Jackson Hole.

"We hope you can come and stay for a day or two before we fly home," Frankie said as they headed down the steps. "It's only a few hours' drive, do you think that would be possible?" she asked.

"We'd love to." Willow hurried to respond. It was obvious Terry was preoccupied with what would take place later this evening. "I'll call you in a couple days after we figure out when would be a good time."

After more hugs, Willow and Terry waved to her parents as they drove out to the road. While Bruce and Shannon said their goodbyes to Norma and Tommy out front, Willow pulled Terry along the deck to the back of the house.

~

"I feel like I've been gut punched. I am totally blown away that you've kept me in the dark about this," she said turning to face him. "How long have you known your former girlfriend has been stalking us? Must be quite a while." Willow's hands flew in the air, "Nothing's changed for me. I'm right back where I was with Chet." She was furious with herself. How could I let this happen to me again? Are all men liars?

"Willow don't say that. We weren't completely positive it was Harley until recently. And," he huffed out a breath, "she was never my girlfriend."

"Well, you must have meant a great deal to her since she traveled across the world to come after you."

Willow paced, unable to stand still, turning her engagement ring around and around her finger. Someone has been threatening them and he didn't even tell her about it.

"Why would you keep this from me? I'm a big girl, I could have handled it. Now, I just feel betrayed." Everything she thought she knew about Terry was crumbling. This is a lousy way to start our life together. I knew we were moving too fast. Better to find out now.

"Willow, I only wanted to protect you and everyone that was here tonight. I didn't want anything to ruin our party." Terry took hold of her shoulders and looked her in the eye. "You have to understand Harley is psychotic and she's not going away on her own. I didn't want you to worry. I am so sorry."

He pulled her close to him and for the first time since they met, she didn't hug him back. She broke from his embrace and backed away from him. "Oh Terry," she said lightly shaking her head as her gaze hit the ground.

"I should have told you." His voice was unsteady. "I never meant to hurt you. I just wanted to protect you."

How could they have been so happy just an hour ago, and now Willow's heart had a fissure running through it as wide as the Grand Canyon.

They stared at each other, not sure what to say next when they heard a short crisp whistle.

"That's Tommy. I have to go. They're waiting on me."

"What are you talking about?" her high-pitched voice was shaky.

"I'm walking over to the trailer with a deputy as though she were you hoping to draw Harley out into the open."

"No," she pleaded stepping closer to her man. "You can't be involved in this. You aren't a policeman." She tried not to sound hysterical but wasn't doing a very good job.

"I have to. It is the only way." He quickly told her everything that had been discussed in the trailer a few days earlier.

"You might get hurt. Please don't go." Willow begged through anger and tears.

Anger at Harley for coming all the way from Australia thinking she could get him back.

Anger at the unfairness of putting him in danger.

She'd finally found the man she wanted to spend the rest of her life with and didn't want it to end abruptly. The thought terrified her.

"Willow," he said holding her arms, peering into her frightened eyes. "She has to hear my voice, or she'll continue to hide out and plot her attack when we least expect it. I want to get this over with. The team is waiting for me."

The back door opened, and they turned to see Norma joining them on the deck. "If that was supposed to be a private conversation, you should have closed the windows." She made her way to Willow's side and put her arm around her.

"Sweetie, let's go make some coffee and see if the kittens need water." Norma gently steered her away so the Gray Cowboy could go join the posse and catch the bad gal.

Willow held on to Terry's hand, her fingers trailing across his palm as she allowed herself to be led away. She didn't look back at him.

Once in the kitchen, Willow did everything Norma suggested including throwing back a shot of Jack. She was anxious about Terry's safety, but at the same time still furious at him for keeping this from her.

"How could he have done this to me? I thought we were partners. I don't want another relationship like the last one. I can't believe Terry lied to me like Chet did." She walked around the room running her fingers through her hair. "I never saw this coming; I thought this time around would be better."

"Technically, Terry withheld information he thought would protect you." Norma said, "So, he's not really a liar. Chet, on the other hand, flat out lied to you, but you can't punish Terry for what Chet did."

"I'm just so disappointed," she said then threw back a second shot.

~

Deputy Maggie Brown was in command now. "Okay," she handed Terry a stab resistant vest since they were sure Harley would be carrying a knife. "Get this on and secured." Then she spoke into her shoulder radio, "We're on our way."

The two of them set out across the property and the deputy began chatting about how much fun the party was, but Terry didn't hear her until she nudged him, and he came to life, remembering what his role was.

Fortunately, he became more animated with his arm around her shoulder while reminiscing about the party and their friends wishing them well. He tried his best to sound convincing while his heart was back at the house.

Terry, with Willow's stand-in, continued toward the new property chatting, hoping to sound happy and giddy. Both felt relief when the corner of the trailer came into view. Deputy Brown tensed at the sound of rustling brush, her pistol ready. She turned to see a large, tall figure dressed in camo pants and jacket, lunge at her with an equally large knife, poised and ready to strike.

Terry let out a startled gasp.

The deputy quickly stepped sideways but not before Harley kicked her in the knee. She hit the ground groaning.

Harley growled, turning back to Terry, screaming at him, "You rotten bastard! You lied to me, you piss weak, ratbag! You used me like every other man!" She stabbed him in the chest, but he managed to step back to lessen the blow. He fell backward with a thud when she came at him again as he attempted to get up. The blade of her knife sliced across his left thigh. "I thought you were different," she sobbed. "I thought I was more to you than one of your station mates."

In the meantime, Deputy Brown was back on her feet, pistol aimed at the attacker and yelled, "Drop the knife now!"

Tommy burst through the brush followed by four deputies who grabbed Harley; one had her in a choke hold, two had her by each arm jerking the hunting knife from her hand. In an instant, the area was flooded with light, and Tommy saw blood oozing from the frayed fabric of Terry's slacks.

While the officers secured Harley with handcuffs and leg restraints, Tommy quickly spoke into his radio calling for an ambulance. He knelt beside his friend, as Terry held on to his injured leg, his face contorted then he seemed to lose consciousness.

"Terry, you okay?" he asked frantically. He wasn't moving. Had an artery been cut? Blood was pooling on the ground. "Jesus, Terry stay with me, you can't die now. We have to go fishing, and I have to be your best man." He patted Terry's face which brought him around. "Shit. Willow will kill me."

"Not before she kills me," Terry murmured, clearly in pain.

Tommy's shoulders sagged with relief, then he checked him over to make sure there were no other injuries. The vest had done its job keeping the sharp point of Harley's hunting knife from piercing Terry's chest. Tommy gently pushed him to the ground when he tried to sit up, "Stay put, help is on the way."

He did as he was told, then got his breathing under control while Tommy unbuckled Terry's belt, pulling it out of the loops in the waistband of his slacks then wrapped the belt around his thigh above the knife wound.

"If you pull my pants off everyone will know how you really feel about me," he warned his buddy, in an effort to remain alert and lighten the frightening situation.

"Yeah, you wish."

Terry needed to stay focused as he fought the nausea trying to overpower him. "Willow's definitely going to kill me. Either that or she'll tell me to get lost. She was pretty mad," he said in a sluggish voice, worried about how she'll feel hearing the siren that was now audible to everyone.

He heard the officers lead Harley into the bushes towards the patrol car. Her shouts and growls could probably be heard for a mile around, but they stopped abruptly when the car door closed. That was it.

She was out of his life.

The EMTs attended to Terry's wound then got him on the gurney and into the ambulance. Willow doesn't deserve this. I have to promise her I'll never keep secrets from her again. He yelled to Tommy, "Get Willow and bring her to the hospital."

"Will do," He radioed the deputy on watch at Willow's to take her to the hospital.

Chapter 22

*B*ack at the house, Willow reached for the whiskey bottle, but Norma grabbed it and put it back in the cupboard. "Two shots are all you get right now."

"Party pooper," but she knew her friend was right. Then, Willow covered her ears at the sound of a siren. "Oh no! Please don't let it be for Terry."

She went to the front door and yanked it open hoping she was wrong about the siren. "Maybe it just means they have Harley," her voice pleading.

Norma stepped up beside her when the deputy standing watch out on the deck said, "Sheriff Logan told me to drive you to the hospital."

"Was anybody hurt?" Norma asked.

"He didn't say."

She draped a jacket over Willow's shoulders before they got into the patrol car and headed out to the road as the ambulance sped toward town. "I'm so mad at him for doing this to us! He shouldn't have been involved."

"We don't know if Terry was hurt. The ambulance could just be for Harley," Norma said.

They pulled up in front of the emergency entrance as Terry was being unloaded at the ambulance portico. The deputy opened the back door and Willow raced into the hospital waiting room with Norma close behind.

The deputy spoke to the nurse on duty, with a jerk of his head, "They're with the stabbing vic they just brought in." He made sure they were seated and reasonably comfortable before heading to the sheriff station.

Tommy went into the waiting area to see about Willow and Norma as soon as Terry was in the hands of a doctor and a couple of nurses.

He sat next to Willow and laid his hand on her shoulder. "Terry has a knife wound, but it's not life threatening, he lost a minimum amount of blood. He's going to be okay," he reassured them, before giving details of Terry's injury.

Willow covered her mouth wanting to fight back tears. "Can I see him?"

"The doctor's stitching him up so hang on a few minutes," he said.

"But, he's okay otherwise?"

"Yeah, he's alert and asking for you."

Once they got the OK, Tommy and Willow stepped inside the privacy curtain. Terry tried to sit up, wanting to hold her, but her tear stained face hurt him worse than Harley's knife. Again she fought back tears at the sight of Terry's bandaged leg and his trousers cut away. He reached for her, "I'm okay."

She nodded and kissed him on the cheek, "I was so scared when I heard the siren."

"Are you still mad at me?"

"We'll talk later," she said wiping tears with the back of her hand. "We need to get you home."

The nurse came in with the discharge paperwork and instructions. Terry would need to use crutches for a week or two so as not to put any pressure on his wounded leg, keeping it elevated as much as possible. Driving was out of the question.

The nurse handed Willow a list of symptoms to watch for before wrapping a sheet around Terry's waist. He shook his head when she asked if he wanted what was left of his trousers before sitting in the wheelchair and heading outside.

On the ride home Norma sat up front with Tommy while Terry sat in back with his left leg resting on the seat, Willow nestling against him.

It was nearly 2 a.m. when they pulled up in front of the house, everyone offering to help Terry in any way they could.

Since no one seemed to be in a hurry to go to bed, they gathered in the kitchen where Willow pulled a chair out for Terry. "I'll get a pillow so you can prop your leg up," then reached in the fridge for three beers knowing Terry shouldn't drink with the meds he'd been given.

"Wish I could join you," Terry said sounding dead tired, groggy from painkillers, and the sheer scope of the day and evening. She knew he was grateful Harley was in the hands of the law now, thanks to Tommy and his deputies. "I appreciate you taking care of Willow," Terry said to Norma.

"Of course," she replied, glancing at Willow who'd returned with the pillow. "We girls look out for one another." Norma took a swig of beer and grinned, "Gee, y'all sure do know how to pack a day with excitement up here in Wy-o-ming!"

They chuckled, in spite of being exhausted and feeling a little slaphappy.

"Well, if you kids are okay on your own, I'm going home," Tommy announced setting his half full bottle of beer on the table. "Do you need help getting down the hall or undressing?" He added with a smirk.

"That's okay Tommy, I'll help him undress," Norma offered with a smirk of her own.

"Apparently, we've all been up too long. I *am* still in the room," Willow said feeling she'd had all the fun she could stand for one day, then yawned. "I think I can help Terry get ready for bed."

"And, I'm not completely helpless. Just a little loopy," Terry said rubbing his forehead.

Norma pushed away from the counter she'd been leaning against and said good-night. She gave Willow a hug and whispered in her ear, "Go easy on him," before heading to her room with what was left of her beer.

Tommy hoisted himself out of the chair, his eyes on Terry who was mustering the strength to stand. He fumbled with the crutches, gave his friend a bear hug and thanked him for the way the night turned out.

Hobbling to the door, he gripped Tommy's shoulder before his friend went out into the darkness.

Willow turned the lights off and followed Terry as he tottered down the hall to the bedroom. "Brand new damn pair of slacks ruined," he said while she helped him remove what remained of his clothes. A small sacrifice knowing that crazy woman was behind bars and would be heading back to Australia soon. Tommy had told them, if all went according to plan, Harley would be black-listed from ever entering the US again.

Willow folded the covers back and made sure Terry was as comfortable as possible with his leg elevated on a stack of pillows.

She took her time getting ready for bed feeling grateful Terry's injury wasn't any worse. But she couldn't shake the thought of him keeping her in the dark about Harley stalking them. Yes, she appreciated him wanting her and their friends and family to be safe. And, maybe it wouldn't have made any difference if she had known about the sting to capture Harley. But don't partners keep each other up to speed with what's going on in their life? Was there anything else he was keeping from her? Anything else happen in Australia he hadn't told her? He certainly hadn't shared much about his life there. She brushed her teeth then reminded herself not to superimpose the lack of trust she'd had in her ex-husband onto Terry, but he hadn't left her much choice.

She loved Terry with all her heart, there was no denying that. She'd been in love with Chet, though not in the deep meaningful way she loved Terry. But Willow didn't want to be looking over her shoulder wondering what else he might not be telling her.

~

Sleep came quickly for Terry, but he relived the violent confrontation over and over in his dreams, feeling almost as tired when the sun came up as when he'd laid down. He thought of his dad, pretty sure they'd already left. Maybe that's what woke him, but he was grateful they hadn't been alarmed by the siren out on the highway. He'd hoped they would stay and visit but things sometimes work out for the best. He wouldn't have wanted his dad to worry if he'd told him about Harley before the party, just like he hadn't wanted Willow to worry. Then a light flashed in his head; he and his father had both been involved with lunatic women. They hadn't been very smart but both were happy in their relationships now, although, he himself had some major fence mending to do.

He reached over to touch Willow, but she wasn't there. Probably in the bathroom he thought. After several minutes, he sat up wincing in pain, knowing it was past time for a pain pill. Must be around 5 a.m.

Where was Willow?

Terry made his way to the living room and found her on the couch one bare foot hanging over the edge. He'd have loved to stoop down and kiss her toes. Something to look forward to. The blanket looked like she'd tossed and turned the whole night.

When he tried to cover her shoulder, she sighed a little murmur then her eyes flew open. "Terry," Willow said springing from the couch, touching his arm. "What's wrong? Are you okay?"

"I'm fine. Just worried about where you were."

She yawned, "I didn't want to roll over and bump your leg. I thought you'd sleep better if you had the bed to yourself."

"Is that the only reason?"

Willow took the crutches from Terry when he flopped down on the couch feeling lightheaded.

"Stay here while I put coffee on."

But, he clumsily stood and followed her to the kitchen.

She began filling the coffee pot then said, "Let's get through the next couple of days, I don't want anything to slow down your full recovery and Norma will be leaving day after tomorrow."

~

And so they did, though Willow was quieter than usual and had little crying episodes watching Terry struggle to walk or sit comfortably. But mostly because she felt unshakable sadness that their relationship was on rocky ground.

Two days later with Terry in the back seat of Willow's SUV, his foot resting on the console between her and Norma, they headed to the airport. Willow hoped she and Terry could talk on the way home, without any distractions.

Once they were underway, Norma told them Bruce had offered to drive her to the airport, "But I said you thought Terry needed some new scenery," she turned to look at Terry.

He arched his brows, "In a way, you're right."

"Well, in reality, I couldn't have handled another disappointment since Bruce had to cancel two dinner dates because of emergencies. Besides, he's just settling in here in Elk Valley and I've got my new place in Chicago."

After hugs and good-byes at the departures terminal they drove out to the highway.

"Terry, I'm going to Jackson to see Mom and Dad before they fly home."

"I don't know if I can do that, Willow. I need to get back to work."

"Yes, I understand. That's why I'm going by myself."

"No. I don't want you to do that. I'm sure I can take a few more days off."

She shook her head, "I mean, I want to go by myself. I can't think when I'm near you. I just want to be with you, but I also need to take care of myself."

He started to speak, but she held her hand up. "Wait, before you say anything else, I need to get this out." After a deep breath she continued. "The last thing I want to do is hurt your feelings. You told me you kept Harley's intentions from me because you thought you were doing what was best for me. But it wasn't best for me. I think you should have known that."

"Willow..."

"I'm almost done." She looked out the side window for the strength to keep from crumbling. "Right now, *I* want to do what's best for *me*. I'm going to Jackson for a few days, and I plan to do some serious thinking about us. I know you love me," she reached over to put her hand on his arm. "I never thought it was possible to love anyone as much as I love you." She swallowed the catch in her throat.

"Willow, please don't do this to us...."

"*I* didn't do this to us."

"Okay, you're right. I'm totally to blame. But I'm not having an affair, and I'm not a closet drinker. I'm struggling to understand what was so wrong with my not telling you about Harley. Are you really saying I should have known better than to try and keep you safe? It makes no sense to me."

She could hear the desperation in his voice. She didn't want to lose him either, not after everything that's happened in the past couple of months.

"Let me come with you, or at least let's keep talking, because I don't understand what would have changed if I had told you Harley was stalking us." He was close to yelling. "I'm sorry, I didn't mean to raise my voice."

Her brow knitted, "I might have had time to prepare myself...."

"Which might mean you would have had more time to worry, you might not have enjoyed our engagement party. Then everyone would have worried about you and might have wondered what was going on."

"The party? We could have postponed it or had it at Buckaroo. As it was, our family and friends were in danger because you kept this secret from me."

"Willow, I know Harley. I know how she thinks, and I never believed for one moment she would hurt anyone but me." He ran a hand through his hair. "I'm sorry. I thought I was doing the right thing. Besides, Tommy said in order to have her deported and blacklisted from entering the US again, she had to be caught in the act. We couldn't just throw her off our property. She would have come back."

She lightly nodded understanding what he'd said and the logic in it. "I just want you to respect me enough to let me in on something so important. What if she'd killed you?" her eyes teared up. "I need to know I can trust you to be honest with me."

That evening, they had dinner with Tommy, and he assured Willow he'd look after Terry while she was gone. She gave him the list of symptoms to watch for along with the meds Terry was taking. He reminded her, "I'll bet I've had more first aid training than you. We'll be fine, but I'll stay at your house just in case."

Thursday morning, after promising he would take good care of Stormy and Midnight, Terry helped Willow put her suitcase in the back of the car and told her, for the third time, to drive carefully. They hugged and kissed not wanting to let go, then he closed the door after she fastened her seat belt.

She checked the rear-view mirror every few seconds to see Terry, crutches helping support him, standing in front of her house watching her drive away. He looked so alone, she wanted to hit the brake and make a U-turn. But, at the road, she opened her window and waved.

He didn't wave back.

On her drive to Jackson, Willow wondered, as she lightly shook her head, how did we get to this point where Terry doesn't think he needs to confide in me and now, after keeping me in the dark, can I trust him? Then she went over everything that had taken place after discovering the dead rabbit by the garage staircase. Harley killed it to let Terry know she was there, to create fear and punish him for leaving her.

Why would Harley go to the trouble and expense of flying halfway around the world to frighten the hell out of someone she loved. I think I know Terry pretty well and can't imagine him capable of hurting someone intentionally to the degree that would trigger Harley's actions. On the other hand, I also didn't think he'd keep something so important from me.

She felt kind of sorry for the woman though, but there may be other reasons for her hostile behavior toward Terry. He did say she was psychotic.

When she was in Santa Barbara, hearing her dad tell the story about her parents separating had been an eyeopener. She always thought they had the perfect relationship, but it nearly fell apart!

When Dad realized the most important thing to him was the three of us being together, they made a commitment, and everything worked out for them. He'd wanted her to know relationships weren't always smooth sailing. 'Building a relationship is give and take. Sometimes its 50/50 and sometimes its 60/40'.

She'd thought her life with Terry was ideal. She wanted to feel that way again. He's a wonderful man, kind and caring. He makes me feel like I'm the center of his universe. How can I give that up?

Why would I want to?

When her cell rang, she could see it was her mother calling and put the earpiece in so she could talk hands free. "Hi Mom, I was just thinking about you and dad." Willow was happy to hear her voice, even though her own quivered.

"How are you sweetheart?"

"OK. How's the condo?"

"It's lovely, perfect location. I think you'll like it," then she got right to the point.

"Honey, we have to leave. Your dad needs to be in the bank tomorrow for a surprise audit and I think I may have sold that ocean-front property on Via Marquez, so I need to get back to help my assistant with the paperwork."

"Darn. I wanted to see you before you left."

"I know, we were looking forward to it as well. You can come anyway, if you want."

"What do you mean?"

"Well, we love it here so much and since you live not far away, we bought the condo we're staying in. Escrow closes in three weeks."

"That's great Mom. I'm so glad you guys did that."

"We'd love for you to see it, so come and stay. It's paid for through Monday."

"Actually, I am on my way."

"Just you, not Terry?"

"Not this time."

Chapter 23

An hour outside of Jackson, Willow was enveloped by a heavy feeling of exhaustion. She saw a sign for a rest stop in one mile and sang with the music to keep her eyes open. After using the restroom, she bought a soda from a vending machine knowing the caffeine would help her stay alert for the next hour.

Willow thought Terry might call to hear how the drive was going, but she knew he was busy. The closer she got to Jackson, the darker the sky. Hope I get there before it rains.

Once in town, she stopped at a market and bought some cheese and a couple pieces of fruit, before continuing on to the rental office. The receptionist handed her the key and a site map with a circle drawn around the building where the condo was located.

"Wow, this place is awesome," she declared, stepping inside the entry with its fifteen-foot ceiling. But touring the rest of the house would have to wait. She was ravenous and felt a little woozy.

She pulled a protein bar from her purse and ate it out on the balcony along with one of the pears she bought and watched lightning streak through the sky, thunder quickly followed. She continued thinking about Terry and how they could dissolve the wedge between them. Willow knew how to make everything go back the way it was before Harley showed up. She only had to forgive Terry and move forward. "But it's something we need to work on together," she said as the sky continued to darken. "I want our relationship to be transparent. No secrets."

Willow hurried inside when the first raindrops hit her. She found the master suite, it was huge and nicely furnished, but she didn't want to get into that big bed by herself. She took a pillow and light blanket from the bed and laid on the couch in the living room and slept.

~

That same evening Terry's cell rang and he was surprised to hear Patrick's voice, then panicked wondering if something had happened to Willow.

"Terry, I just wanted to give you the address to the condo we stayed in, you know, in case you needed to have it. Frankie and I have high regard for you. We think you are perfect for our daughter. And by the way, we had to leave early, so Willow is there by herself."

"Thank you, sir. I appreciate you calling me. I don't want to crowd Willow while she's... well, while she's having some time to herself."

Terry ended the call and sat at the kitchen table after feeding the cats. He still thought he'd made the right decision in not telling Willow about Harley, but never imagined she would think he'd been devious. She did say her ex-husband had lied to her on many occasions. How could Willow not be furious with me? What a piece of shit her ex must have been.

"But what am I going to do to make things right with her?" he said to the kittens when they came looking for attention. "I have to convince her I was only thinking of her safety. That's right isn't it Stormy?" he asked picking her up.

Or was he just embarrassed he'd allowed such an unstable person into his and Willow's life? Why hadn't he been man enough to break up with her before he left Australia, so there was no doubt the relationship was over?

The kitten curled into his lap when he picked his phone up off the table and touched his dad's number.

"Dad," he said when Alain answered.

"Thierry, how are you?"

"Well..." and he told his father all about Harley and that he had ended up in the hospital with a knife wound and his relationship with Willow was in jeopardy. They talked for forty-five minutes, Alain reassuring his son that Willow would forgive him in time. He said, "When she's telling you something or asking a question, it's important to listen to every word. Give her your full attention. That's something I learned from your mother. She once told me, 'men often only hear half of what their wife says.' They were silent for a moment, then, "Your mother would have loved Willow and her family." Terry swallowed the lump in his throat.

"Thanks dad. I needed to hear that." He promised to call with an update in a few days.

Terry made sure the kittens had plenty of food and water before Shannon pulled up Friday afternoon to give him a lift to Jackson. The doctor had suggested he use a cane in case he needed a little support. Two hours and change later, she dropped him at the condo and said, "I want everything to work out okay with you and Willow."

With a hard set of his jaw, he nodded, and thanked her before pulling his duffle off the back seat. Terry paused at the front door and ran his hand down his pant leg before ringing the doorbell.

Willow opened the door and tears of relief spilled from her eyes. She let loose a slight moan and stepped into Terry's arms, pressing her forehead to his chest.

No woman had ever brought him to tears, but it sure felt like a tear rolling down his face. He kissed her lightly, but when she responded with a hungry kiss he let go of his duffle and held her tight, kissing her with sweet affection.

"I'm so glad to see you," she said wiping tears with the back of her hand. "I know it's only been two days, but I've missed you terribly.

"I feel the same. I'm grateful you didn't shut the door in my face."

She managed a smile and stepped back to look at him, "It was a long way for you to drive with your injured leg."

"I didn't drive. I hitched a ride with Shannon. I stopped at her store yesterday to see if she was coming this way. I suspect maybe she wasn't planning to, but when I asked, she said she'd be happy for the company."

"Shannon's a dear friend," Willow said, then led Terry to the couch where she sat curling her legs under her and patting the cushion wanting him to sit.

"I see you replaced the crutches with a cane. That's good isn't it?"

"Yeah, Tommy took me to the doctor yesterday and he said I was healing faster than expected but recommended I keep the cane close in case I need it to lean on."

"Terry," she said, her pained expression hid nothing. "I'm sorry I left. I should have stayed to take care of you, and we could have talked."

He shook his head, "No. You were right, we both needed time alone to process what happened. I should have known better than to keep my suspicions of Harley from you. I just wanted to protect you, keep you safe, but I went about it all wrong. Then when we were planning our engagement party, I didn't want you to have anything more to worry about."

"I get that. I was just afraid of being in another relationship like .... the last one."

"How can we put this behind us? I'm prepared to do whatever it takes."

"Yes, I want that too." She leaned toward him. "We

need to start by learning to make important decisions together, things that affect us both."

He nodded, "I know that now. But, I'm a fast learner. I take direction well. And besides," his voice hushed, "I love you more than I imagined possible."

"Oh Terry, you are all that matters to me." She reached over and cupped his face with her warm hand. "I love you so much."

He kissed her palm. "I called my dad, we had a long talk and I remembered my parents sitting at the kitchen table while they discussed a project they wanted to do, mom jotting down ideas on a yellow legal pad. Sometimes dad looked fidgety, probably wanting to get on with it. But he stayed put until they were finished. Maybe we can keep that tradition going," he said while stroking her palm with his thumb.

"I like that idea." She giggled, "I even have yellow pads of paper at home."

Terry released her hand then stood, hobbled to the sliding door and looked out at the darkening sky before turning to face her. "More importantly, I think the real reason I couldn't tell you about Harley stalking us is because I was disappointed in myself that I hadn't ended the relationship, so she'd understand it was over between us. I took the cowards way out." He returned to the couch and took Willow's hand again. "I won't *ever* do that again. I want to learn to be a better partner, so I'll be a good husband."

She gave his hand a light squeeze, "We come from different backgrounds but we both grew up in loving homes with parents who cared for us as much as they cared for each other. Like your dad said, we need to pay attention to each other and listen." She leaned forward and looked into those sapphire eyes she loved. "I want to be the wife you always imagined having."

"Funny you'd say that. I never saw myself getting married. After losing my mom then believing I'd also lost dad, I kept everyone here at a distance. In Australia I put up a barrier. No one there knew what I'd been through and I wanted to keep it that way. It felt too painful to get close to anyone. Then when I came back home and met you, I wanted you to know everything about me." He turned to look out the patio door when he heard rain falling. "You know, when we met, both of us had just gotten out of difficult relationships. We liked what we saw in each other, but I wonder if we were still angry with our ex's?"

"Oh," she said eyebrows arched. "You're right. I hadn't thought about it that way. Maybe we need to thank them for helping us realize we wanted something better. Something far more meaningful."

His hand caressed the back of her neck pulling her into a kiss that was sensual and possessive then became overpowering with need.

"There's a really nice bed down the hall ...."

Terry got to his feet, extended his hand to help her up. "Lead the way lady," he said in a seductive way, the deep blue of his eyes intensifying.

They walked down the hall arms around each other turning into the bedroom where Willow pulled the spread and blanket back catching a whiff of lavender. She began unbuttoning Terry's shirt while his hands slipped up the inside of her sweater.

Unhooking her bra, he gently ran his hands over her breasts taking pleasure in their silky softness. "I'd almost forgotten what this was like," he whispered nuzzling her neck before lifting the sweater over her head. They weren't in a hurry; they had all the time in the world.

She kissed him sweetly before removing his shirt, letting it fall to the floor. Then ran her palms over his hair-roughened chest, her thumbs making slow circles on his nipples as she kissed him. He let out a groan, and his knees buckled when she unfastened his belt and jeans, then remembered his boots.

She gently pushed him to sit on the bed, and tugged his boots off, then dragged his jeans and briefs to the floor.

Terry rose up on his elbows to watch as Willow slowly slid her thong over her slender hips. He was hard as steel when she positioned herself on him with a quick thrust, then began gliding up and down, slowly at first while he fondled her breasts. Their momentum quickened, Willow arched her head backward, then forward, her hair whipping Terry's face in her climax. He let loose a primal, deep throated groan, forcing air from his lungs.

Willow drew in a sharp inhale.

"I'm okay," he said, breathing hard. "You didn't hurt me." He laced his fingers through her hair, pulling her to him. "But I think you touched my soul."

Willow carefully rolled off him, resting her head on his out-stretched arm. He smoothed long strands of gold hair from her face. "Making love to you feels sweeter somehow. Maybe because I thought I might lose you."

"I'm not going anywhere. I feel so much better now that you're here." She traced his lips with the tip of her finger. "We've been through a great deal in a short time, but we've been there for each other to lean on. You're the man I've always wanted."

"Do you know I dreamt about you on lonely nights in Australia, longing to be with a woman just like you? You are precious and I want to spend the rest of my life making you happy. I love you so much." He kissed her with a tenderness that brought her to tears.

Terry turned on his right-side gathering Willow into his arms where they slept most of the night.

While spending a lazy morning in bed, Terry told Willow all about the barn and everything else he'd been doing the past day and a half knowing she would be pleased to learn the cattle he bought would be arriving soon.

"What would you like to do today?" He asked thinking she might enjoy walking around town until hearing a loud clap of thunder.

"I want to go home. To our home."

That sounded just about perfect to him.

After a leisurely shower, they put their bags in the car and dropped the key off at the rental office. As Willow pulled out of the condo complex, she turned to Terry with a grin. "I have a surprise for you."

Terry thought his heart might burst with the love he felt for her. "What do you have in mind, little girl?" he asked playfully.

"It's a surprise and you won't know until we get there."

For a brief moment, he wondered if she might be pregnant. That would be the best gift he could think of. "You seem to have given this some thought."

"Yes, and I'm very excited. Let's go."

It was easy to get caught up in her excitement. He was game for whatever she had in mind. She hadn't disappointed him yet.

They drove north on highway 191 a few miles past the edge of town, then made a series of turns until a small dirt road became visible. They turned in and Willow looked like she might bounce out of the seat in excitement. As they approached a house and big barn, four large, rambunctious dogs came running to greet them followed by a woman with a pleasant smile.

"Hello," she called as they got out of the car. "You must be Willow."

"Yes, and this is my fiancé, Terry."

Terry offered his hand and a friendly hello.

"I'm Sara," she turned to see her husband approach. "And this is Marty."

After more greetings and handshakes, the four walked toward the barn.

"Willow, what are we doing here?" Terry asked quietly, more than curious as he limped along.

Her smile was as big as the sky. "You'll see."

They walked into the barn and were drawn to a pen where three chocolate Labrador puppies were on display. Terry was almost in tears when he leaned over to have a close look at the fluffy pups, each clamoring for attention. He looked at the owner, "May I pick one up?"

"Of course." She watched him carefully hoist the pup into his arms and begin stroking his soft fur. The puppy responded with a stroke of his tongue on Terry's chin.

"He's male, the last one of the litter, and the one you have," she said to Willow, "is female."

It took mere seconds for them to bond with the dogs. When they heard the third pup whine, Willow looked at Terry with pleading eyes. "No, sweetheart, we can't take all three. I'm sure Midnight and Stormy will have their paws full with these two." Looking down at the lone puppy, he almost caved.

Once Sara and Marty assured them the remaining pup would be placed in a great home, they paid for the dogs and headed back to the car. Willow had thought ahead, of course, and had blankets for them to lie on in the car. Once everyone was settled, they turned back to the highway towards home.

"What do you think of the name Ranger for this little guy?" Terry asked.

"I think Ranger is perfect. It's very male, and he'll be with you out on the range when you're herding cattle, or whatever you do out on the range."

He smiled at her, nodding, seeing the same picture in his mind.

Willow had one hand on the little pup by her side, scratching her belly. "I think this little girl looks like a Sienna." Terry didn't seem convinced at first but then the little pup looked at him with those big brown eyes and knew that was the perfect name for her.

He wanted to climb the highest mountain and shout to the world what a lucky SOB he was. He and the love of his life were going to be married. They were building a home, and a business. They had a four-legged family, and he couldn't wait for them to have children. His whole being was vibrating with excited energy.

"While we're thinking of names", he said, "what do you think about calling our ranch, the Willow T Ranch?"

"The Willow T, I love the sound of it."